BY INVITATION

CHARLOTTE BINGHAM
BY INVITATION

Doubleday

LONDON · NEW YORK · TORONTO · SYDNEY · AUCKLAND

TRANSWORLD PUBLISHERS LTD
61–63 Uxbridge Road, London W5 5SA

TRANSWORLD PUBLISHERS (AUSTRALIA) PTY LTD
15–25 Helles Avenue, Moorebank, NSW 2170

TRANSWORLD PUBLISHERS (NZ) LTD
3 William Pickering Drive, Albany, Auckland

DOUBLEDAY CANADA LTD
105 Bond Street, Toronto, Ontario, M5B 1Y3

Published 1993 by Doubleday
a division of Transworld Publishers Ltd
Copyright © Charlotte Bingham 1993

A catalogue record for this book is available from the British Library

ISBN 0 385 40229 5

484073 Printed and bound in Great Britain by
Biddles Ltd, Guildford and King's Lynn

For
Terence, Candida and Matthew,
John and Paul,
and
Charles.
All for different reasons.

A Fourth Movement
in a
Less Than Stately Minuet

1

Everywhere across Wiltshire on that early summer evening people were staring at the green velvet of their lawns, wondering, if their lawn was of a rolling nature, whether to make themselves a glass of Pimms, or, in the case of its being a short strip, a cup of something with a spoon.

Jennifer, the wife of the seventh Marquis of Pemberton, was no exception. She too was staring at the immaculate turf of the garden belonging to the Hall, but for a very different reason.

'A raised floor, you say, to cover all of this?' she asked, picking up her tapestry and thrusting a needle through the canvas.

Fulton, acting as her amateur party organizer, smiled, because he could see that already Lady Pemberton's heart was going out of the whole idea of giving a Summer Ball, and since he had just suggested a peach silk-lined marquee with peach flowers, peach food, peach napkins and peaches for dessert, he really didn't want her enthusiasm to sink with the already setting sun.

Silently he thanked heaven that the whole thing had been her idea in the first place, and that she had called him over to the Hall to adjudicate at her decision-making.

'It's very easy,' he told her in a soothing tone, 'much

easier that you'd first think, really. What happens is a little man comes along and covers the whole lawn with a floor, and then they tent all the garden, flower beds, everything, they all become part of the decor. Sybilla Adelstrop did it for the "Brass Hearts for the Aged" last year. It was very successful. Except the pelargoniums didn't *quite* match.'

'I'm not doing anything *for* anything,' Jennifer put in, with the sudden force of someone who felt she might be taking on too much.

'No, of course not. Particularly anything in aid of the Cathedral.'

'Especially not the Cathedral. Anyway, what on earth is Sybilla Adelstrop doing giving old people brass hearts?'

'Oh, I don't know. 'Parently they're like food coupons, only they didn't want to offend the old dears, so they called them something else. Elliott thought "Brass Necks" would be more fun, but no-one took him up on it.'

'I think,' Jennifer continued, warming to her theme, 'I think the modern spectacle of charity organizers who do nothing but buy their wretched evening frocks and feed their families for the next millennium on the backs of poor starving people is, to say the least, a disgrace.'

She stopped, suddenly wondering if Fulton's stunningly cut safari jacket had been purchased on the back of the Brass Hearts Ball, but, seeing it had a rather old-fashioned half-belt at the back, decided it wasn't.

'I see you too are going for a daisy lawn.' Fulton looked down at his feet.

10

'It's for the children,' Jennifer told him absently. 'Nanny likes it. You know, daisy chains and things.'

'We ourselves, at Flint House, we too have gone for a daisy theme. Daisies in the lawn, marguerites in the beds, daisies in dahlia form, for later on. We're getting a tiny bit excited about it, as you can imagine.'

Fulton was referring to the imminent arrival of his wife, the former Lady Tisbury's, second baby.

'I heard about that from Lady Tizzy,' said Jennifer, her expression warming. 'Such a lovely idea, Daisy-Marguerita. Charming names. So much better now they can tell which sex Baby is going to be. Two girls. Couldn't be more lovely.'

She placed a hand on Fulton's. She thought it was wonderful that he had married Patti. Everyone in Wiltshire thought so. And then to let her have not one but two babies was generous in the extreme, particularly since everyone knew that the first one could not have been – Jennifer stopped, wondering suddenly if 'sired' or 'fathered' was the better word. Unable to decide, she dropped the thought and went on to another.

'You're a hero, Fulton, really you are. And Elliott. Lady Tizzy is a very lucky girl.'

She sighed slightly, as Fulton smiled slightly. Lady Tizzy *was* a very lucky girl, but then he and Elliott were very lucky boys. They were friends, he had a wife, and now they were about to have two daughters, the Misses Benedict-Montrose-Cavanagh. What could have been a disaster of a minor sort had turned into something rather different. Which all went to show that nice things could happen sometimes.

'Real heroes,' said Jennifer again, tactfully avoiding

11

the question of the paternity of Lady Tizzy's children. A question which hung, and would always hang, over the nursery at Flint House, as all Wiltshire knew. 'Do you know, Fulton, our babies see each other so much nowadays, they've even grown to look alike, Nanny says.'

Fulton gazed straight ahead of him after this last remark, and then rose from the garden bench with some alacrity. Since the seventh Marquis was the father of all the children in the nurseries of both the Hall and Flint House, his alacrity was understandable.

As he rose to his feet he could feel that the complicated pattern of the ironwork of the bench had imprinted itself upon his derrière. When he undressed that night he would doubtless be able to continue to admire the pattern of Tudor roses and scrolly ivy leaves that made up one of the many garden benches at the Hall.

'I fear I have thrown out a clout before May is out, and I'm going to pay for it,' he said, shivering a little. 'We must continue our little plans towards the end of the week. *After*.'

'Of course. After Patti's inducement.'

'So we'll take it as read it will be private, by invitation only—'

'And matching.'

'Of course.'

Jennifer quickly put her tapestry into her basket, and they trod back across the lawn to the house, during which time Jennifer thought gratefully that at least this year she didn't have to face an inducement of any kind, except to persuade Pember to pay for the ball. And Fulton reflected that their dearly beloved Marchioness had somehow managed to make the all too medical word 'inducement' sound quite charming, like a churching or a christening.

'Tallywhack and tandem all over Wiltshire,' sighed Fulton, sinking into the large feathered cushions of the kitchen sofa. 'Lady Pemberton is giving a dance and I'm ordered to design it all for her.'

He raised his eyes to the ceiling and his hand to the glass that Elliott was holding out to him.

'Well, that was just about the only thing I wanted. How did you know?'

He gazed happily first at the contents of his glass, and then at Elliott, who had gone back to making his very tiny mushroom pies for their *fête champêtre* to be held in the garden the following day.

'I knew,' said Elliott, neatly flattening his pastry with his glass rolling pin, 'I knew from the way you drove the Golf into the gate rather than through it that a serious drink was needed.'

'How's Lady Tizzy?'

Elliott sighed and raised his eyes to heaven, and then sighed again and lowered them back to the rolling pin and the pastry.

'She is,' he murmured, 'impossible. Her feet have swollen, she says. She doesn't like having babies in the summer, she says. She never wanted this one in the first place, she says. That's how she is. She won't come to the *fête champêtre* tomorrow unless you buy her a new dress to cover her tum, she says, and even then she'll only come if she's allowed to sit down under the apple

13

tree and people are brought up to her one by one, she says.'

'Did you tell her it's for the Cathedral?'

'Yes, and she said if she had to go to one more thing to do with the Cathedral she'd be sick.'

'I know how she feels,' said Fulton, stretching out one elegantly shod foot in front of him, 'we all do. But that's how it is.'

'Not with Lady Tizzy, it isn't.'

'So. It's being a naughty Patti, is it?'

'Naughty? She's like my grandmother faced with a bad kipper.'

'Fined. Fifty pence for the Cathedral. No "likes" to be used until the end of May.'

'Oh, very well. But tell me, tell me please about Lady Pemberton and her *thé dansant*, or whatever.'

'No "*thé dansant*", this is all whatever. A tremendous whatever, one enormous huge whatever. I'm to design it all, inside and out, special colour for the tenting, special tenting for the house, the house to match the flowers, the flowers to match the napkins, the napkins to match the waiters, and the waiters to match the guests, the guests to match the weather, and the weather to match the hostess, the hostess to match it all. Game set and match.'

'Sounds terribly tiring.'

'Tiring. I tell you it's going to have us all in such a spin you won't believe.'

'But so unlike Jennifer.'

Elliot raised his rolling pin and set it carefully aside. He hated people, particularly people he knew, doing things that weren't like them. It was muddling and

14

strange. Everyone knew that Jennifer, whatever her drawbacks, which were many, was not a social person, that the mere thought of going to London was enough to send her into a three-day migraine, and equally the thought of London coming to her. She never received weekend guests unless she was absolutely forced, and yet here she was preparing to tent her lawn, and ask a great many people to dance and dine and be very careful of her flower beds.

'It's all a bit strange, for Jennifer,' he said slowly. 'You must admit.'

'Now you're not going to do one of your Inspector Remorses about this, are you? Because if you are, I refuse to let you. There is nothing sinister about the Marchioness of Pemberton giving a dance. Full stop.'

'She must suspect,' said Elliott, turning from the Aga suddenly. 'She must suspect what Pember and – to what Lady Tizzy and Pember are up – to. To what they are up. Have been up. To. If you know what I mean?'

'I hope not,' said Fulton slowly. 'I sincerely and totally and absolutely hope not.'

'We can't shut our eyes to it. Every day, week in week out, before lunch and after tea. I mean he's hardly managed to get out into the garden. Apparently Jennifer complained, and only last week, to the Village Voice, that they'd never had so few bulbs at the Hall, and that Pember had put it all down to a plague of mice.'

'Very biblical.'

'So's what Lady Tizzy's been up to, but that doesn't make it holy.'

Elliott stood back to admire the last tray of pies. Very

15

tiny and very sweet. He could just imagine them sitting under the apple tree tomorrow looking festive.

'I can't take it. I can't take one more drama. Not with another baby on the way. We've got Nanny in the guest wing, the night nurse in Nanny's room, Victoria in the day nursery, the new baby when it arrives in the night nursery, and that is drama enough for six weeks for me.'

'And me,' Elliott agreed, 'but it has to be faced that if Jennifer ever finds out who the father of our children really is and they divorce, then Pember might feel forced to marry Lady Tizzy and Lady Tizzy might feel forced to take our children from us.'

'I know, I know,' sighed Fulton, pouring a great deal more vodka than was strictly necessary into his glass, and then topping it up with far too much tonic by way of a penance. 'I know only too well, but what can one do? Face it, one can only cross one's fingers and pray, because there's nothing one can do.'

'It's not crossing her fingers that Lady Tizzy needs to do—' Elliott muttered.

'Please.' Fulton held up his hand. 'Please. No, please. None of that. I'm going through a religious phase, and I can't take rude asides.'

'Aside from that we're going to have to keep an eye. One eye each, at least. Really. The future of our children depends on us keeping things terribly straight.'

'I've got a feeling that it's a little too late for that kind of talk.'

Fulton inhaled the top of his drink, and Elliott watched him with some interest.

'I was thinking of sending her away, you know, after the baby,' he said, having finished his short inhalation.

'Oh, so you have been worried?'

'Of course, of course I've been worried. Victoria's our daughter. She bears my name. Of course I've been worried. We're all worried. I keep staring at my curtains at four o'clock every morning and falling asleep saying my prayers that there will be some kind of outcome that will make everything easier for us, that will stop us worrying, but I can't think of any, except pushing Pember off a bridge.'

'Not bad, but I'm superstitious over murder. You know how it is, people's faces coming back to you in the night. Voices shouting "alack, alack" just as you're dropping off into a nice post-prandial siesta. It would be better if it could be arranged naturally for us, by God.'

'I'm not sure you can pray for someone to fall off a bridge accidentally. I think that's sort of cheating. Anyway, we like milord, don't we? We just wish he wasn't quite so randy, really.'

'Where's Lady Tizzy now?'

'In her bedroom eating tinned peaches.'

'She will eat tinned. Remember last time?'

Fulton sighed. 'Last time she ate so many tinned apricots I was quite sure that Victoria would be born with a Del Monte label round her tum.'

'I suppose I should go up?'

'You don't have to. She's quite happy eating peaches and watching re-runs of "Pogley and the Pegtops".'

'What a good idea to give her her own little recorder. That was certainly a good idea.'

'It was desperation,' said Fulton quietly. 'I was beginning to feel I *was* a pegtop.'

'Shall we go through to the sitting room cum drawing

room with its tasteful display of mixed antiques, and dine quietly in the window overlooking the lawn?'

'Why not?'

'It's only going to be very quiet dining, Chicken Kiev and funny pink lettuce.'

'As long as the lettuce doesn't match anything I shall be quite, quite happy.'

Fulton followed Elliott and his tray. The vodka was beginning to take effect. The last of the spring flowers could be seen through the French windows. They would sit in their own little window and picnic. He had been right in his earlier assumption: in between all the other bits, life, after all, could be really very nice.

Georgiana lay upon the sofa and contemplated the stucco ceiling of her drawing room. The sofa upon which she lay was, she knew, full of fleas, but at that precise moment her real concern was with a cobweb at the end of which hung a money spider. The money spider dropped upon her arm, and she let it tickle its way down to her hand before shaking it off into a crack between the floor boards. She then lifted one of her legs and looked at it. It was perfect. Slim ankle, slight tan, altogether perfect.

She lifted her other leg. It too was perfect. She had a pair of matching legs, satisfactory in some ways, indeed a pair of perfect matching legs would be enough to satisfy many girls she knew, but she herself felt demonstrably unsatisfied. In fact 'less than happy' would perfectly sum up the owner of the perfectly matching legs.

She was living with Gus, her lover, and George, their

son, at Longborough, and they all enjoyed living at Longborough, and it ought to be enough, and she was aware that it ought to be enough, but it wasn't. The truth was she wasn't happy just living. It just wasn't enough.

She had thought about dried flowers. In fact she had thought about dried flowers a great deal lately, and then become depressed. Just the phrase 'dried flowers' was so, well, dry really. And just thinking about them made her feel as if she had turned the wrong corner in her life.

Of course dried flowers made sense, of course they did, they made a great deal of sense, and that was their trouble, they were sensible, incredibly, horribly sensible. It was natural, of course, to think about dried flowers, goodness knows they grew enough of the real things at Longborough, it was only sense to dry some of them, but even so, every time she thought about putting them into artistic little bunches, and hanging them upside down, Georgiana found that something happened to her, there was a tightening of her throat muscles, her back began to ache, and she wanted to scream.

Perhaps if Gus were not away painting in Israel at the invitation of the government, perhaps if it were not beginning to be such nice warm weather, perhaps if she were preparing to take a picnic with wine down to his studio, perhaps she would not be lying on her back lifting each of her legs in the air, one by one, but as it was she was, and he was, and there was very little that she could think of doing to relieve this unremitting feeling of boredom, of being someone about whose whereabouts no-one knew, or cared.

She could make a Symingtons table cream of course. But she could only make it if Nanny and Gus's mother

19

were out of the kitchen, and had taken George for a walk, otherwise they would watch her and criticize. When she was a child she had always made a table cream when she was bored. Sometimes her mother had found her and smiled distantly from the kitchen door, and sometimes Nanny had found her and told her off for 'waste'.

She glanced at her watch and then sat up quickly. It was four o'clock. Four o'clock was one of the highlights of her day. Time to go to the post.

She retrieved her shoes from under a chair and put them on. They were made of thin gold straps. Kaminski, her first lover, had bought them for her. She still loved them with a passion, as he had loved her, and then left her because she was young and boring. Now she was nearly twenty-five, and probably still as boring to someone like him.

Last week she'd been to see Kaminski's latest film at the Cinema Club in Berridge. They had all watched the film, and then, afterwards, the Club President, wearing a collarless denim shirt and tin glasses, which meant that as far as Berridge was concerned he was dangerously intellectual and had left-wing tendencies, had promoted a discussion about it.

Most members of the Berridge Cinema Club, annual subscription two pounds, had not understood the film, and Georgiana had been among them. There had been a great deal of play with 'reality' and 'non-reality', and the actors had been used to portray actors who were really portraying themselves when they weren't actors, at least that was what the Club President had said, and since he had tin glasses and a denim shirt no-one present had been prepared to argue with him. Even so Georgiana had returned home wondering what on earth the film could be about?

It had been a lonely experience, driving home wondering how it was that at nineteen she could have been so interesting to someone like Kaminski, because she *had* been interesting to him, for those few weeks in London. But then, probably because he must have known that she would grow into the sort of person who wouldn't understand his films, he had left her and gone back to Los Angeles without a backward glance, and she had been left alone with just the memory of what it meant to be something special to a great man, a man that people wrote about constantly in newspapers and magazines, a man who was seen in the company of interesting, as well as beautiful, women.

Even now she could remember how she had cried when he told her that all great love affairs must end, and then how he had made love to her, and she had been left standing at the window of his apartment looking at him being driven off with his partner in their limousine. At nineteen she had been the dusty past, and he had seemed to be the vibrant present, and she had wanted to kill herself for being finally so deeply uninteresting to him.

Just lately she had started to wonder if she wasn't just as uninteresting to Gus as she had finally been to Kaminski. It was an unavoidable thought. Gus used to paint her, now he no longer painted her. He painted his mother and George, and landscapes and other things like water that seemed to hold a fascination for him far greater than Georgiana. And all this in between 'earning a crust', as he called doing his syndicated 'The Lady

Loves' cartoons for America, and doing 'pretty ladies' for the birthday card business that Georgiana had encouraged him to start, which was being run very successfully by his brother from a small printing works in Devon.

She sometimes found it quite funny that he had never bothered to marry her, or even asked if she might like to marry him. Sometimes she found it quite funny, and sometimes she found it quite beastly of him. After all, to someone like him, a Lady Georgiana Longborough should be quite a bargain. But Gus didn't think like that. It wasn't that he even rejected thinking of that kind, he just didn't even begin to adopt such a line of thought, it was utterly foreign to him.

Occasionally his mother, dear 'Nan', would remonstrate with him.

'You gotta marry Georgiana, Gus, because of your boy. George is gonna get teased in the playground else, if you don't, you just gotta marry his mum. It's only right.'

But Gus would only smile and pour himself another glass of wine, always forgetting anyone else in the room might want one, and light another of his strong-smelling French cigarettes, and then rub his bottom lip with his thumb, a habit of his he always observed when he had 'switched off'.

Georgiana never mentioned it, of course. She wasn't that keen on marrying someone who wasn't that keen on marrying her, and nowadays she wished that 'Nan' wouldn't bring the subject up. She was far too proud to do so herself. One marriage and divorce had been quite enough for her. Besides, men seemed to change so when they became husbands. Her first, Stranragh, had been really perfectly all right before they got married, but afterwards he had become like the monster from the lake, practically growing long fangs and sucking the last drop of blood from her veins. No, now that she knew that Gus wasn't fascinated enough by her to want to marry her, she had become convinced that she too wasn't fascinated enough by marriage to want to try it again, really. At least not for the time being, anyway.

By now Georgiana had reached the post box at the end of the long drive. The walk had done her good, not a wholesome kind of boarding school 'good', but a proper kind of enjoyable good, and she was able to slip her hand into the wire cage in which the postman left their letters without feeling a sense of dread. She would even be able to face the fact that Gus had not written to her yet again, not even a card, and for the fourth week.

Instead of a card from Gus there was a nice stiff white envelope among all the nasty buff floppy ones. It was quite childish but Georgiana felt her heart give a little leap, and she allowed it to as well. It was an odd dizzying kind of feeling, and one that she hadn't had for ages. It was an invitation. She turned her eyes quickly away from seeing the handwriting on the envelope, or the postmark which would tell her where it was from, and started the return walk back to the house.

Suppose the invitation was something exciting? Suppose it was to the kind of occasion to which she had always been used to be asked? One that would demand an evening dress with a long Winterhalter-type skirt. It would be incredible if it was. She stopped walking suddenly, and her heartbeat slowed to its normal pace.

It could just as well be an invitation to a wine-tasting. Lately vintners had grown into the habit of sending out stiff cards in stiff envelopes.

And only last month she had had an engraved invitation to a party to view Italian sheets, of all things. This could be another one of those. Well, whatever it was, she wasn't going to let Nanny or 'Nan' or anyone else, for that matter, see it. This was going to be one secret she would keep from them. She stuck it up the front of her old darned cashmere jumper as she walked back into the house, deliberately throwing all the other envelopes down on the silver salver in the hall, so that she could have the pleasure of watching Nanny, who was a great deal less deaf than she liked to pretend, leafing through them all, searching for some kind of letter from Gus, and then see her smiling when it failed to materialize.

'Nothing from Mr Gus again, I see, Lady Georgie,' she would mumble, and then go quickly down to the kitchens to tell Nan who would shake her head, laugh, and pretend to be shocked, when all the time she knew that Gus had never written a letter in his life, unless it was to enclose a bill for one of his pictures. Nan had no illusions about Gus; he was her son, and she'd made him that way, and it was something of which she was proud.

'You'll never change Gus, Georgie,' she would say when she was on her second glass of cooking sherry of an evening. 'He's the spit of his dad, is Gus, and he never wrote to me in his life, except during the war to ask for some thicker socks, and that was only for cleaning his gun. The rascal. No, there's nothing you

24

can do about it, girl, just stick it up your jumper, and get on with your life.'

Just at that moment, as she slid carefully past Nanny, Georgiana hoped that the invitation, which was by now getting quite warm down the front of her jumper, wouldn't find its way to the floor.

'No letter from Master Gus,' mumbled Nanny, but by that time Georgiana was up the stairs and down the long corridors to her own suite of rooms where she quickly closed the doors, and locked them.

It was wonderful to smuggle things past Nanny once again. When she was little she'd smuggled dog biscuits, particularly the black ones, up to the nursery to share with her toys; now – how strange – it was invitations.

Just lately Georgiana had become convinced from the way the two old dears seemed to follow her everywhere that Gus had asked them to watch her every move while he was away. For apart from being very much himself, and doing exactly as he pleased, Gus was violently possessive. He might not want to marry Georgiana, he might not paint her any more, he might not pay attention to her from one day to the next, sometimes not even speaking to her for hours on end, but nevertheless he wanted her there, permanently, for him. She was his person in waiting.

Georgiana slid her nail file under the crease of the envelope, and neatly slit it open and pulled out the stiff invitation, for invitation it was, a lovely hard en-graved invitation. She shut her eyes quickly and tried to trace the words and the name on the card with her finger, before opening them again. How heavenly, it was properly engraved, and with a name that was all too familiar.

The Marchioness of Pemberton
By Invitation Only

Georgiana gazed at her old friend's name. A name that might have been Georgiana's, if she had taken John Pemberton up on his marital offer. All too easily the invitation could have been coming from her, and not from her old friend Jennifer. It could have been Georgiana's name written on the piece of stiff engraved cardboard with the tissue paper across the top.

She daren't think how long it was since someone had been at home 'By Invitation Only' to her. Since installing herself, Nan and Nanny at Longborough, following her parents' unfortunate demise, she had only received telephone calls by way of invitation, or little bendy cards with 'Regrets only' scrawled across the bottom. This was going to be a real dance with real people of the kind to which she had been used to be used. She lay back against her large Victorian lace pillows. How wonderful, at last, after all these months, to be asked out somewhere proper. And how pathetic to feel so excited. It seemed that it wasn't so long ago when she would have turned such invitations away and accepted something more exciting than a married friend's dance, but now she was over the moon just because Jennifer had remembered her.

And then she remembered Gus. And she knew at once that she would not be allowed to go. Worse than that, she wouldn't be allowed to go for a really good reason. Gus didn't like socializing, and he didn't like Jennifer.

In fact, he was violently opposed to it. Particularly if it had anything to do with anything to do with Georgiana's past.

What was more, the mere sight of an invitation from 'the Marchioness of Pemberton' would be enough to bring on one of his diatribes in which he would go to great lengths to describe Jennifer as something really horrid, and his mother as the 'salt' of the earth.

Georgiana closed her eyes and let the invitation slip to the floor. Suddenly she felt tears, childish tears she knew, but proper tears nevertheless, welling up behind her closed eyelids. Of course. Gus would never let her go, not in a million years. She wouldn't be able to have a beautiful evening dancing and forgetting all about Nan and Nanny, and whether or not to go in for drying flowers. Instead she would have to stay shut up at Longborough, just as if she was in exile, or banned from London by an old-fashioned husband, instead of cooped up with a bolshie lover.

Indulging in her silent tears was very restful. She let them drip upon the old soft cotton of the pillowcase, sliding gracefully, first cold, then warm, into white oblivion. Then she opened her eyes and stared, as she had so often as a child stared, at 'Lady Desborough' opposite her bed. Lucky Lady D. – she had never had these awful problems. Losing a little at a game of chance, wondering if her husband was going to be late back from the club, or whether or not to reprimand the maid for bringing her the morning cup of chocolate late, those would have been matters of concern, but not, most definitely not, dried flowers.

And then too she would not have had the awful

experience of a lover, of all things, just a lover, trying to stop her going to a ball. He would have wished most heartily that she would go to a ball, and her husband would have gone too, and they would have met all sorts of exciting people there. Her husband would have met his mistress, she her lover, and they would have all enjoyed themselves in a most courtly way. But all that was foreign to Gus, insisting as he did on early-to-bed-early-to-rise routines, and a life about as exciting as that of a chartered accountant.

Until she had come back to live at Longborough with Gus it had always seemed to Georgiana that painters were very exciting, colourful people, and anything but normal, for that was how Gus had seemed to her when they were crouching in their little semi-detached house in South Sheen, London.

But once at Longborough Georgiana had discovered to her great concern that Gus and his way of life were dull to the point of boredom. Just painting, and all day long, too. No wild moods, no slashing of canvases, nor orgies in hellfire caves. He never wanted to throw a party for other Bohemians. Or even dress up as one.

Sometimes, particularly during endless winter, Georgiana had found herself hoping that Gus would suddenly discover that he was Spanish, and start painting all night, like Picasso, or would cut off his ear in a fit of pique and send it to someone in the post, and cause the kind of scandal that excited 'In Focus' interviews purveyed by In Depth journalists, and she could be photographed in a harsh light wearing somewhat out-rageous clothes. But nothing of that sort ever happened at Longborough, where the most exciting event of last winter was the Aga going out just when Nanny was making tea.

If only she hadn't had George she could leave Gus. It would all be quite simple, but as it was she loved George, and he loved her, in his sticky way, and although he did look horribly like Gus he was nevertheless her son, and you just didn't leave your sons because you'd grown bored with their fathers. Georgiana knew this. She knew it the way she knew how to sing 'I Vow To Thee My Country', and to always be kind to animals, and to keep your voice down in restaurants. No-one left their children, not ever. They sent them away to school, of course, but they didn't leave them.

Georgiana leaned down to the floor, and picked up the invitation again. The ball looked twice as nice now that she knew Gus would never consider letting her go to it.

Any day now dreaded Gus would be back from Israel, filling the house with his demands for black coffee and smelling out the rooms with his strong French cigarettes, and lecturing his houseful of women about everything he had seen and done. There was no doubt at all that he would have become embroiled in kibbutzes and things, things that would make his mother yawn with boredom and drink even more cooking sherry. Things that only Georgiana would attempt to pretend to be interested in.

And as everyone else slipped off to watch their tellies, she would be left leaning on her hand and smiling as best she could while Gus banged on, crossing and re-crossing her legs under the table until they looked like nothing so much as the parcel into which the rats had tied Tom Kitten. It was such a pity about the things that interested Gus, because he could really be quite nice when he wanted to, and quite a lot of people liked him, even country people, but he was, and she had to face it, just a bit boring.

Georgiana jumped off the bed and flung open one of her wardrobes. All her old dresses from yesteryear hung there covered in plastic bags. Just seeing them made her sad.

Dear sad dresses, what lovely evenings she had enjoyed in them, and now they stood stiffly on their hangers guarding their memories, their petticoats erect beneath them, their diamanté embroideries still glowing.

There was the dress that Kaminski had given her to wear for the film ball at Longborough, and there was the long evening coat to match. How marvellous they had been together, that dress and coat, and yet it seemed that that was the night when he had decided to part from her, so she couldn't, after all, have looked quite good enough, and that was all there was to it.

Georgiana buried her head among her old dresses and prayed. The God to whom she prayed was quite a nice God. He wore an expensive suit, of course, and at this time of year it would be made in a lighter cloth, probably in a pale grey with a slight pattern running through it. He wore a finely striped shirt made of nice soft cotton, His tie was silk, naturally, and His socks were thin and silky, His shoes discreetly black with possibly a small tassel on the front if He was feeling just a little festive.

Georgiana prayed to her God quite often. He was a kind of heavenly godfather who had sent her some nice things, and some disappointing things too, as godfathers nearly always did, but on the whole meant quite well, even if He had made some slip-ups. She prayed to Him now. Please, please, please, help her to find a way to go to Jennifer's ball.

She settled herself in front of her dressing-table mirror, and stared long and hard at herself as if she was lunching with a friend. She had no friends who lived near, so she had to advise herself, be her own best friend, bang on to herself.

The problem was that her lover would not let her go to the ball. Worse than that, if he knew she even wanted to go there would be a horrid row, and he would go on and on about the things that meant a great deal to him, but not much to her.

He had such respect for things like socialism, and so little respect for the things that meant a lot to her. Even so, physical beauty and luxury of a certain kind were very important to him, while they didn't matter quite so much to Georgiana. Things being nice meant a great deal to Georgiana. She had always rather someone was kind first and beautiful next. And she didn't care for luxury nearly so much as she cared for the past, and what that meant. That's why she cared for Longborough, because it was both kind and the past, and although it was cold and dreary and cost a fortune to heat most of the time, it stood for something that you couldn't write down, something that was very difficult to explain to someone like Gus who thought his garden studio a great deal too small, and the light wrong in his winter studio, and had never once been allowed to see a central heating bill, because if he did he would probably burn the whole place down, or sell it to a foreigner who would put in double glazing and wall to wall carpeting.

31

If only those were the only things that Gus went on about. He also went on and on about George and what he should be doing, and what he shouldn't be doing. He wasn't going to be allowed to go to private school, on principle, although whose principle Georgiana couldn't discover. He wasn't going to be allowed to ride, in case he was tempted to hunt. It was pathetic. The poor little chap was only just getting his first pair of wellies and Gus was insisting on them being red rather than green.

By now she had banged on so much, Georgiana was beginning to bore even herself. And yet she still hadn't formulated a great plan. A plan to deceive Gus, who after all, she reasoned, not unreasonably, deserved to be deceived, especially since he wasn't going to allow George to have a pony, only a donkey.

There was another reason that Gus deserved to be planned against. He would never allow Georgiana to read either *Vogue* or *Harpers & Queen*.

Georgiana of course could not do without either of them. But, purely on account of Gus's ridiculous attitude, she had been reduced to reading them in the back of her car, while parked in the municipal car park in Berridge. Many a long winter afternoon had passed away in secret dreamings and yearnings, and then she had been forced to drop the magazines into the litter bin before driving home feeling vaguely discontented, as one always did after a 'binge' of any kind.

Although she had no copies of *Vogue* to which she could refer, Georgiana knew what she should look like for Jennifer's ball. Her dress would have to be long and romantic. She sighed. Nothing, but nothing, romantic had happened around Longborough since Kaminski had

32

filmed there. Romantic. Even the word had a scent to it, not suffocating like jasmine, but deliciously delicate. It was crushed silk, celandine, tiny wild orchids, and spun sugar.

Georgiana stopped by the door of her bedroom, and before inserting the key back into the lock she thought how exciting life had suddenly become in the last two hours. Terribly, terribly exciting, and full of promise once more, not all stagnant and stale, or worst of all dried.

She knew why it was. It wasn't just that she had been invited to a ball, a real ball, by invitation only, it was because she was going to be 'Lady Georgiana Long-borough' again. She was fed up to her little soft elbows with being 'Gus Hackett's live-in love'. 'Gus Hackett's bit of posh.' 'Gus Hackett's girl.'

That was it. She was going to be able to be herself once more, and she would make sure she would stay that way. She would buy a wonderful dress, and every-one connected with it would be sworn to secrecy. She would buy marvellous shoes, and they too would be bought in the highest secrecy, and finally she would go to the ball, even if it meant wearing a mask if necessary, but go she would, and she would look beautiful, and after the ball she would hide the dress and the shoes and everything else, and she would sit smiling nicely at Gus across the kitchen table with the Aga at her back, but her legs would no longer be crossing and double-crossing themselves, because she would have double-crossed him for once.

As Georgiana turned the key of her bedroom door, she shuddered slightly. It was really very exciting, just a tiny bit like being unfaithful, and just a tiny bit like leaving someone too. She hadn't felt so exhilarated in months. Thank heavens Gus hadn't bothered to write to her, not even a card with an ex and his name on it. It made everything so much easier.

2

There was no doubt about it, the Countess sighed, there was very little left of England now, just the monarchy and the National Trust.

She was gazing from the train on to the green strips of countryside that were flashing past the window. It was nice to see there was still the odd scarecrow, although why it was nice to see a scarecrow she really couldn't imagine, especially since so many people nowadays so closely resembled them. Still, it was nice; nice also to see that there were still villages and church towers, and horses grazing beside the railway track – that was all very nice, but it was not enough.

She knew, everyone knew, that life behind the green façade was changing, and not always for the better. Why, only last week her housekeeper had told her that she found it embarrassing referring to the Countess as 'Lady' in front of her friends, and that she called her 'Mrs' instead because otherwise her friends made fun of her, poor creature. Time was when people had been only too happy to say they worked for a Countess, but nowadays it seemed it was a decided drawback, and something of which they were ashamed, something to hide from the neighbours as in the worst excesses of the Russian Revolution.

It was no good blaming any one person for the way

things had gone, but one thing could be blamed, of that there was no doubt. One thing alone had made the civilized world crumble, and that was communications.

She had written a letter to the local paper on the subject. If communications had not become what they were everything would have stayed as it had been, which was undoubtedly much better than it was now. If people couldn't fly, or drive, or whatever, to wherever they wished at a moment's notice, then the rape of Old England would never have happened. For rape it was, with houses made of paper growing up beside and on top of the old façades of every town and village, and solely because people had driven to see them, and then decided to settle there. Whereas in the past, before the advent of 'better' communications, they wouldn't even have known about them.

And what good had it done anyone, she asked herself. Just how little was plain to anyone with ears who had the misfortune to have to go to a post office to collect their just dues. No-one was happy, despite having pensions, despite having health insurances, and entitlements to everything from elastic bandages to new tin legs; all they did was stand in a line and grumble.

In the old days none of them would have had a pension. Quite a lot of them wouldn't even have had a post office, and as for spare legs, country people had made their own. That's how absurd everything had become. And not only that, but nowadays a letter took as long to be flown by an aeroplane as it had to be taken by post-chaise with six changes of horses between York and London, so that's how far ruining the countryside and building tatty roads had got us.

It wasn't as if you could send a telegram any more. Not even if you were dying. Which was absurd. Particularly since so many people were quite obviously addicted to killing themselves on their motorbikes that there must be a crying need to find some of them a career in telegrams. But no, the Post Office was happy to let them go on killing themselves without purpose, instead of with a telegram. So – the Countess suddenly kicked the underneath of Andrew Gillott's foot – so much for communications.

'You're snoring,' she told Andrew as he awoke with a kind of 'what' noise, and then slid back down his seat again with his eyes shut.

Sleep and drink, sleep and drink, that's all the poor chap did on the train. No-one would have believed, looking at him now, what a handsome man he had once been. Why even Freddie, her husband, had been a little jealous of Andrew Gillott's looks. And every woman in London had made a play for him, with the sole exception of herself, of course, because she had, after Freddie, always been a one-man woman. Freddie had been all in all to her, and she to him, and the one thing she could honestly admit to was that, although she never did, of course. Sometimes she tried to remember how they used to laugh and gossip together, and sometimes she tried to forget, because it really wasn't very constructive, and she just had to get on with life and stay on its moving staircase until she finally got off at her floor, which she only hoped wasn't going to be haberdashery.

So there it was, and there was Andrew slowly sinking down again beneath the frightful plastic table so thoughtfully provided to make utterly certain of train passengers' discomfort. He hadn't even finished his first class breakfast, probably because he knew she would pick up the bill for it.

The Countess's gaze returned to the countryside, like the past flashing by comfortably fast. She was going to meet her friend Lavinia for lunch. This was the reason she was wearing a hat. The last time Lavinia had worn a hat, and she hadn't, it had made her, the Countess, feel underdressed, and she had gone away wondering if living in the country permanently as she did now (having let her London house for a fortune to some perfectly horrible foreigners) hadn't perhaps affected her fashion sense.

Life was too good for Lavinia, that was her problem, of course. Too much had gone her way. A wonderful lover late in life, holidays abroad on a yacht whenever she wanted, a vast dress allowance, an account for flowers at Pulbrook and Gould that must sometimes make even her lover's straight hair curl. And she still had everything sent round from Fortnum and Mason's. It was incredible. Of all the people she knew, Lavinia still seemed to live in a way that no-one else did, just as if nothing had happened, as if London was still the London they had all known and loved. And she still spoke of everything in the same way too, as if nothing had changed.

'Lovely, lovely flowers,' said Lavinia, not looking at them, and leant her chin on her hand. 'Lovely, lovely flowers, what will you have?'

They both stared at the menu. It was quite obviously going to be bits and pieces food, as the Countess always thought of it. An egg with a little sauce over it, one bean

38

arranged decoratively, a stiffish sort of bean, a mousse with sauce round the bottom that tasted like very pleasant green blancmange.

'I don't want any prawns that you have to pull to pieces because they make such an untidy mess,' said Lavinia firmly in reply to the waiter's suggestions. 'And don't read us out Today's Specialities; we all know they're Yesterday's Flops.'

'I shall have a little cold soup,' said the Countess. 'And you?' she asked Lavinia pointedly, because it was her way of making Lavinia understand that they would each be paying for themselves.

No sooner had Lavinia finished deciding than the Countess made a resolution. If Lavinia began by asking after her early tomatoes, she would leave. It was a put-down, and they both knew it. The moment Lavinia sat down she would ask the Countess about either her cabbages or her tomatoes, as if to ask after anything else would confuse the now country-based countess.

'I'm opening up the house this month,' she said, treading safely away from vegetables and perhaps sensing the Countess's resolution. 'You must come and stay with Ozzie and me in late June when Lady O's famous borders are at their height.'

'I'd love to,' agreed the Countess as they both tackled their fish mousses, served with tiny pieces of dried toast. 'But—' she paused, 'I am, for my sins, being coerced into helping with a private ball.'

Lavinia's eyes narrowed, and it wasn't because of a fish bone. Private ball. Two words that Lavinia had not heard in many a long while. They rang around the Countess's head too, whirling round and round, dancing in and out of her imagination as prettily as a waltz tune when one strolled home from a dance.

'Oh, what a pity. The borders are really at their best in June.'

'I know,' said the Countess, 'you told me.'

Lavinia's purchase of someone else's famous house had become the bore of the century. You would honestly think from hearing her banging on about Lady Muzzeline Ottell's house and garden that she had built and planned the whole thing herself, instead of just having a lengthy affair with the man who had bought it for her.

'But I am called upon, alas, to help out. There are to be three marquees, a small orchestra before dinner and a band afterwards, and we shall sit down to a dinner for two hundred before being joined by another two hundred. But the work, oh, the work. I mean nowadays, really, with the shortage of proper staff, it calls for a committee, but there is none.'

'I suppose it's an old friend giving the ball?'

'No, quite a new one, as a matter of fact, a new, young one. I like having younger friends nowadays, they do you good.'

'Yes, it is good for one,' Lavinia agreed, and then she stopped suddenly, hesitating before she said any more, and the Countess could see that she was wondering whether she should be saying 'one', or whether it wasn't a little passé for 'one' to be saying? And whether the fact that the Countess was not saying 'one' meant that 'one' was not being said by anyone?

'Has one stopped saying "one"?' asked Lavinia suddenly, and quite bravely.

'I'm afraid so,' said the Countess, giving her a gentle but patronizing smile that held more than a hint of 'correction' in it. 'One is not being said, although "you" and "me" are. "I" should still be avoided, of course, as much as possible. Especially in letters.'

Lavinia frowned, but only lightly.

'It's very difficult. Do you mean to say I have to write "me is very well", if I'm to keep up to date now?'

'No, just "we" or "everyone" will do.'

'But supposing you're not a "we". "We are very well" sounds a little grand for one person.'

'It's the principle of the thing, Lavinia. There's been far too much talking about "oneself" going on. Far too many people talking about "one" when they mean "I", and covering up their wretched manners by so doing. We are all, in Wiltshire, we are all working very hard to reverse the trend of modern egotism, and small beginnings can turn into large movements. Just look at the Keep English Simple for the Simple Society. It's booming, despite initial difficulties.'

'Are you trying to say I talk too much about myself?'

'No, you talk too much about oneself, and that's not good for any of us. Believe me. We must make an effort to stamp out "one" and smother "I" in conversations, and stick to you. "You look very well." "You look very pretty." "You look very good in green." Much more pleasant, don't you think?'

Lavinia smiled suddenly.

'Oh – do you really like me in green? I was a bit worried when we chose it. You are, aren't you? I mean, we stand in fitting rooms with no-one to help – er – us; you worry and worry what you look like, until someone tells us. Now, in future, we shall be quite happy knowing we look good in green.'

Lavinia smoothed down her skirt, a look of relief spreading over her face as she realized that she had successfully manoeuvred the labyrinthine twists and turns of conversation required by not using the first number in relation to herself.

The Countess sighed and turned to her handbag for the comfort of a Russian cigarette with her coffee. Lavinia hated her smoking, but just at that moment what Lavinia liked or disliked was neither here nor there. Poor thing talked such tosh.

'So. There's to be a private ball and you are going to organize it?' Lavinia returned abruptly to the subject in hand.

'Certainly there is to be a private ball, and I am helping. There is no social secretary to hand, alas, but nowadays they get everything so wrong, I don't suppose it matters. So often the wrong type. Women who never quite made it ending up organizing other people's lives when they couldn't organize their own. How's your secretary?'

'Sacked. Found her reading Ozzie's love letters.'

'Oh yes, I remember now. But why sack her?'

'Because they were private.'

'Private perhaps, but they weren't to you.'

'That's what made them more private. If they'd been to me, it wouldn't have mattered. No, if we split up, I shall need those.'

'Have you read them?'

'Of course. How else should I have known to sack the secretary?'

'Well, no, I don't suppose you would.'

'They're – how can I say?'

'Hot?'

'No, no, not hot, sizzling. And I'm keeping every single one of them, the little dears – very useful. In case he leaves me for someone else.'

'That's usually the reason someone leaves you.'

'No, it's not. You know it's not. Especially since we all got older, a great many people are being left for no-one at all. Personally I think that's worse. I mean it's so blatant. It looks as if someone would rather be with no-one rather than one, well – you. If Ozzie were to leave me for no-one that would be the end. The laughter. The mockery. One's friends. Our friends. I'd rather he left me for you.'

The Countess breathed two matching curls of smoke through two perfectly matching sculpted nostrils, and decided to continue the story of her ball rather than take up the issue of boring Ozzie.

'Anyway, we're not having a social secretary, even though the numbers can't be kept under five hundred. At least not as far as I can see, although we're telling her husband, poor dear Pemberton, that it is four hundred. Actually it doesn't matter because he won't notice, we won't let him. On the night we'll fill him up with champagne so he won't be able to count how many, or how much – and anyway men don't ever really notice those things, not at all, any more than they notice the flowers.'

'But you haven't told me . . . you still haven't said which of your young friends is giving the dance.'

'Ball. No, I haven't, have I? How ridiculous. I wonder

43

whether they're going to bring us coffee, or whether we'll have to scream for it? Waiter?'

'It must be a very dear young friend, or you wouldn't be helping her. You gave up all that sort of thing when you left London, remember? Or so you said.'

'Temporarily left London—'

'When you temporarily left London.'

'It's Jennifer.'

Lavinia's eyes narrowed once more.

'Jennifer. Not that plain fat girl who used to get on your nerves when Georgiana was doing her little Season thing?'

'No, not that Jennifer,' said the Countess hastily.

'Not the one that married the – er – who was it? Yes. The Marchioness of Pemberton. Not Jennifer Pemberton, who wears those dreadful home-made skirts and has no style at all, and you could never understand how she landed Pemberton and Georgiana your niece didn't? Not that one?'

The Countess drew on her cigarette holder, and then puffed out again.

'Yes, that Jennifer,' she finally agreed. 'But she's changed a lot – a great deal, in fact. That's one of the reasons why she wants to give a ball, so that she can enlarge her social activities, show everyone how she's changed. A good thing, I'm sure. She feels she's fallen into a rut since having all her babies and she wants to stop being in a rut and get out more, out and about. This is a start, at least.'

'I never thought you'd be friendly with her. She doesn't sound your type at all. She doesn't sound the sort of ''young'' that you like.' Lavinia snapped the clip

44

on her crocodile handbag so suddenly that the gold initials on it appeared to wobble uncertainly with the impact.

'She's not my type, but in Wiltshire one – we learn to get on with each other, as indeed we must; it's either that or spend the whole week in church doing the flowers. Anyway, the poor girl needs help. Doesn't get on with her mother at all – Ah, the coffee – at last. Anyway, her poor mother is a thorn in her side, a tasteless woman, a woman on whom no-one can rely, which is almost worse than being one on whom everyone relies. Oh. By the way, did I tell you? I've been helping Jennifer with her hall at the Hall? We have been trying hard to introduce the more natural element. We have banished the African masks, and the reproduction suits of armour, done away with the medieval look and returned to natural eighteenth-century simplicity. She's very pleased. We're both pleased.'

'I know the sort of thing – Colefax and Fowler curtains, and I don't know what everywhere.'

'Oh no, not in a hall. Far too drawing roomy. No, simplicity is the key note. Polished flags, a chest, of course, flowers in a casual display, fire burning, logs piled up, a club fender, you know the sort of thing.'

'I've got Colefax and Fowler in my hall,' Lavinia interrupted, 'and even Ozzie likes it.'

'I know, but your hall is not the hall of a Hall, yours is the hall of a small country house.'

'I know a great many halls that are smaller.'

'Yes, but I don't suppose the halls in the Halls are as small as your hall. There's a need for dressing up small halls. You were quite right to fuss it up with curtains.'

45

'I didn't fuss it up with curtains, you did. It was you who suggested them.'

'Well, I would. I knew that the fussy look would be most welcoming, but not as it happens in the hall of the Hall.'

'I think I had rather you had advised simplicity for me too. I think that sounds much more the thing. I think I must come down and have a look at the hall of the Hall and see what simplicity looks like, even if my hall is smaller than the hall of the Hall.'

'But you can't come down, Lavinia dear, I've just told you, we're preparing for the dance, busy, busy, busy.'

'I thought you said it was going to be a ball?'

'It is a ball.'

'I'm sure your young friend wouldn't mind in the slightest if I came down to her hall. She can't be that rushed off her feet, if you're helping her,' Lavinia reasoned.

'Oh, but she is. Babies and Nanny, and all those things, it takes it out of you.'

'Give me her telephone number, and I'll telephone her and ask her myself.'

'I haven't got it on me, I'm afraid.'

'Well then, I'll ring you for it when you get back to Wiltshire. You'll have it in Wiltshire, surely?'

'I don't think – well, of course I'll have it in Wiltshire,' said the Countess, and she stubbed out her Sobranie Russian cigarette a little too savagely.

She suddenly knew exactly what Lavinia was up to, to what she was up. She was up to being asked down to the summer dance by Jennifer. The Countess knew how she'd do it, too. First a call to say how much

46

she'd heard about her hall, that the hall of the Hall was such a success, and she was trying to re-model her own, and could she come and see it? And then once she was down, she'd make sure to befriend Jennifer in her most oleaginous way, and then she'd ask her across to see Lady O's wretched borders, and before you knew where you were she'd probably be helping with everything, imposing her taste for dark colours and finger food, and Ozzie and she would be standing just behind Jennifer helping to receive the guests.

That's how Lavinia worked. And she was brilliant at it. You had to admire her technique, because the moment Lavinia apprised herself of a situation she took it over, and in no uncertain manner. She would take over Jennifer, totally and completely, and before Jennifer could turn round everything would be dark blue and silver instead of cream and green as the Countess wanted it.

The Countess shuddered inwardly. There seemed so little between her and Lavinia, and Jennifer Pemberton's telephone number. Even now as Lavinia snapped her powder compact shut the Countess could see her working out how to get the Pembertons' telephone number from someone else, probably before the Countess even arrived back in Wiltshire.

She gave Lavinia a sudden and piercing look which contained the proper amount of sudden, forgotten panic.

'Oh dear, how naughty, I'm going to be late for the chiropodist. You know how it is, toe people are always so terribly demanding, must rush, so much to do before one – we totter back on to the evening train. Lovely to see you once more. We'll do this again, and very soon.'

She waved vaguely to the waiter for the bill. She couldn't wait to leave the restaurant and hurry out to a telephone box.

Once she was well out of sight of the restaurant, she would ring round everyone she knew and tell them not, whatever happened, not to give Lavinia Jennifer's telephone number, not until she had caught the evening train back to Wiltshire, and could sort things out the way she wanted.

The telephone box was quite disgusting. It smelt dreadful, of old cigarettes and new foreigners, and the floor was so covered – no, not covered, *littered* – with newspapers, that it was impossible not to spear a piece on the end of one's shoes.

She dialled her daughter Mary's number with difficulty, and with the end of her diary pencil, and as she did so the diary pencil's tip broke, so that as she heard Mary's maid answering, and as she tried to push the correct money into the coin box with a gloved hand, everything slipped out of her glove at once, and she was left dropping coins on the floor, abandoning her pencil to the filthy clutter of newspapers into which it had fallen, and falling back out of the booth as a robed person carrying one of those funny little sticks with wisps on it banged on the glass so impatiently that the Countess wondered briefly if the poor man might have mistaken the telephone box for the gentlemen's cloakroom.

She backed uncertainly down the road, eager to be away from the telephone box, because the smell of it was so overpowering, and tottered off towards a cab rank. She would have to go round to her daughter's house, and make a series of telephone calls. Mary wouldn't like it, but it just couldn't be helped, particularly since it was Mary's idea that the Countess should rent out her London house in the first place, and live off the income, instead of trying to organize people's debutantes into some sort of ludicrous little Season.

Mary was not in. The Countess could tell from the way Juanita, her Portuguese maid-thing, was looking sideways all the time, as if she was afraid of admitting her without permission from her mistress.

'Never mind, Juanita. I only wish to use the telephone, and to leave Lady Mary a message, that is all. Nothing complicated, but you may bring me a cup of afternoon tea with lemon, to the study, please.'

It was with some satisfaction, and not a little sense of comfort, that the Countess sank into her daughter's study chair. Wherever Mary was, maybe even hiding from her round the house somewhere, it really didn't matter. Here she was in a newly scented study – stephanotis on the lamps – sinking into a chair covered in a nice muted blue, and lifting a hand to a nice clean receiver that didn't smell of cigarettes, and putting her feet on a large Persian rug and not on fifteen old editions of torn up *Sun* newspaper.

She looked around her daughter's study in the lull that followed her seating herself. Not a great deal had changed since Mary had become Lady Stranragh following Lord Stranragh's divorce from her cousin Lady Georgiana Longborough. Not a great deal, but something.

There was a new severity about the house, whereas when her former lover Lucius had been about the place, there had been a certain fey casualness, ordered disorder.

Now that Stranragh occupied the house instead – for they had sold his house for a nice profit – it was not quite the same. Fewer flowers, and stricter lines, everything much stricter. Fewer books left carelessly about, fewer messages placed at angles in the corners of things, no invitations stuck into the corners of the looking glass, everything much more sparse and tidy. It was probably better in some ways, but for a second, as the Countess started to press the numbers on her daughter's telephone, she thought with fleeting affection of Andrew and his tiresome ways, of the *Sporting Life* always spread about the morning room floor, of things carelessly set down: old race cards, stud catalogues, membership badges. He might be many things, Andrew, but he was certainly not an old maid, which, let's face it, married or not, Mary and her spouse were fast in danger of becoming.

The Countess's lipsticked mouth had just begun to form the word 'Hallo' to the telephone receiver when her eyes caught sight of a letter written in a vaguely familiar hand.

The Countess leant forward and tugged at it. It was halfway out of its envelope anyway, so it wasn't really private.

'Dear Mary,' it started, in a not too sensational manner.

But then the writing formed itself in front of her eyes as being quite certainly familiar, and the writing paper, with its rather over-blue colour and its picture of the Hall and its locations firmly engraved, even more familiar.

The Countess re-read from the top. A letter from Jennifer to Mary. It had to be read, and quickly.

'I wonder if you could help us out a little? Your

mother, the dear old darling, has offered her services to us for our forthcoming ball. Of course we are terribly grateful, of course we are; but the only trouble is that we already have an organizer, and whoops – two organizers is going to be mayhem. As you can imagine! Of course it was my fault, I should have discouraged her, but I didn't because I'm very naughty, and I never thought it all out properly. I wonder if you could "deflect" her attentions. Perhaps encourage her to visit some of those Italian gardens she likes so much?'

The letter fell from the Countess's hand on to the desk in front of her. She couldn't believe it, she just couldn't believe it. They had had a long conversation yesterday, only yesterday, on the very subject of everything to do with the ball. Jennifer must have written to Mary directly after that tea they'd had together where they had agreed to everything including the colour theme of cream and green. And now here was Jennifer banging on to Mary of all people, on her horrid writing paper, all about the peach colours that she and Fulton had agreed upon, and too many cooks spoiling the famous broth.

The Countess finished the brief but personally insulting letter, and then, having abandoned the idea of a telephone call to anyone, even the Pope, she dropped the letter back into the envelope. It seemed really rather pointless now, leaving Mary a message not to pass on Jennifer's telephone number to Lavinia, since she personally wanted nothing more to do with the silly little Marchioness who had the impertinence to refer to herself as 'the dear old darling', or whatever she had put.

She couldn't help but admit to a deep disappointment in Jennifer. What could she mean? Why on earth should she pursue her own path in this when they had already agreed to agree on everything? She might have changed her mind about the colour scheme, as she hinted in a lengthy PS at the bottom of the letter, but even so, wholesale treachery was simply not on. In the past she had always thought of Jennifer as being the kind of person who might make a social gaffe, or be a little embarrassing in her earnestness, but not a person capable, as the letter showed, of connivance.

She would face it all the moment she arrived back in Wiltshire. For the time being she would hide Mary's address book, and with it the Pembertons' telephone number.

She looked round the study for a hiding place. Not that easy now that the wretched place was so tidy. Her eyes finally came to rest on the Chi Chi china dog in the corner of the room. She happened to know that the head was removable, since once upon a time it had belonged to her husband Freddie. It had been given to Freddie on his marriage by an eccentric aunt who had never married, but had ended up being an expert on that kind of thing, to everyone's intense surprise, because before that the family had always imagined her to be just a bit of a bore.

It must have been nerves, after all that business in the public telephone box, but just as she began to lift the head off the Chi Chi dog, it slipped from her hands and fell, breaking into two halves so its curved mouth that had once seemed to put a tremendous grin on its face was now a decided grimace. The Countess stared at it. She had never liked the thing, or she wouldn't have let Freddie give it to Mary, but now she'd dropped it she nevertheless wished that she hadn't. Besides, it would really look most odd when Mary returned. It would raise all manner of questions that might remain just a little difficult to answer.

She thought quickly, for there was no time to think slowly. She would hide the Chi Chi dog behind a particularly luxuriant ficus, and leave by the back way. Luckily Juanita still couldn't understand a word of English, let alone speak it, so Mary need never know her mother had been in the house at all.

The Countess let herself out through the garden door, and then, hastily making her way down the path and past the little studio room at the back, she emerged eventually into the street, where, most uncharacteristically, she leant herself up against a friendly wall, and sighed with a sort of exhausted relief.

Her mission was accomplished. Mary would never find her address book now, at least not for years, and when she did Lavinia would have missed the chance to obtain the Pembertons' number from her. It had been a terrible adventure, but she had, after all, achieved something of what she had set out to do.

She started to walk in the direction of the King's Road. It had been a little like something in the war. In fact by the time she reached Sandini's bookshop she felt quite like Odette Churchill and other wartime heroines, and it would hardly surprise her if she had a letter mentioning that she was up for the Royal Victorian Order once she arrived home.

Certainly the whole day had been torture. The telephone box, the Third World person banging on the window, and all this while knowing all the time how quickly Lavinia must have hastened back to her house to call everyone to try to obtain Jennifer's ex-directory telephone number. No, it had been a perilous adventure, and she would reward herself with a first class ticket and a nice pot of tea and a teacake on the train journey home to Wiltshire.

It wasn't until the four twenty-four had pulled out of the station and was heading towards the beginning of a tiny bit of green, although not quite enough to quite make a belt, that the Countess remembered what it was that she had forgotten.

Andrew.

3

'The Honourable Mrs Andrew Gillott'. In spite of her impending divorce from Andrew, the former Mrs Parker-Jones, mother of the Marchioness of Pemberton, still loved to see her 'handle' written across the top of an invitation.

It was just such a pity that Jennifer had such appalling writing. Quite appalling. Her poor dear late, late father Aidan had used to describe it as 'barbed wire entanglements', and one could honestly see why. It really quite ruined the invitation, and she was only too glad it had a piece of tissue paper to cover over the top of it in the proper way. It wasn't as if Jennifer even bothered to join up her letters. All that money they had spent on sending her to Grantley Abbey, all down the drain. Still, she had at least bothered to ask her own mother to her dance. That, for nowadays, was at least something.

Sometimes Clarissa still wondered if she should really have stayed on in the country, in Wiltshire; whether, with a divorce from Andrew pending, and he back living with the Countess as her lodger, whether it would not have been better after all to have moved back to Kensington.

On the other hand Kensington had changed so much, developed in so many strange ways, with more than a touch of the Eastern bazaar about it.

And she was at least someone in Wiltshire, rather than just anyone, which she would doubtless be in Kensington. After all, in only the last three months she had been made honorary President of the Mixed Fruit and Veg Society in the village, and Secretary of the annual dance held at the Forthington Hotel in aid of the Cats and Dogs Local Relief Society. A small concern which was nevertheless very vigorous, providing holiday homes for luckless animals that might otherwise have been forced to fend for themselves while their owners were away.

She also provided an annual village cup for the largest gourd. Something that everyone appreciated very much, and which was great fun to present as it meant wearing a hat, and making a little speech. Last year she had even succeeded in getting her picture in the local advertising magazine under the heading 'The Hon Mrs Gillott and A Big Un', which though just a little bit rural in humour, nevertheless was gratifying, because after all it did show her willingness to allow her name to be 'used' for local events.

Now that Andrew had gone to live with the Countess thirty miles away, the house had become much tidier too. And the garden. She had been able to open the garden to the public on two days in June the previous year, and although her house was really too far out of anyone's way to merit anyone coming, nevertheless it had been more than gratifying to know that although no-one actually came round to see it, even had they come, which they didn't, there would have been none of Andrew's cigarette butts tossed into the middle of the Albertine, or curling round the edges of the borders, or peeping out of the tops of the stone walls.

In short she missed Andrew not at all. He may have seemed like the way out of widowhood at one time, but after only a few months he had proved himself to be merely a way into madness. No, she had done just the right thing in encouraging his trip to China, and then changing the locks on all the doors while he was away.

Of course Jennifer had been no help, but then Jennifer never was. Her butler Bloss had been an angel, quite willing to give advice day or night, and not only that, it was he who had informed her that the Countess had volunteered to take Andrew on as a sort of lodger, when he returned from his journey.

Not that he was allowed to live in the main house with her. No, he was allowed in, apparently, only during the day, then made to return to his 'dog kennel' at the top of her drive, as her lodge was referred to by the Countess. Nightly he was allowed back again, to dine with her, and then on Saturdays and Sundays he was allowed in again for telly and racing and Sunday lunch.

'He's become her walker,' Jennifer's butler had told Clarissa. 'But he's really more of a staggerer.'

They'd had a good laugh about that. Clarissa often thought she couldn't do without Bloss. Even so, it was just a little galling to have sent Andrew off, and gone to all the expense of setting divorce proceedings in motion, only to find that the Countess had found a new use for him. If she'd only thought about it at the time, she could have followed the same kind of routine. Perhaps even put him in a caravan to sleep at night, since she lacked a lodge. The Countess finding a new use for Andrew was really rather like giving a girlfriend

57

a dress that one had hardly worn and never liked, only to see her re-appearing in it and making it look quite different. Or giving away a painting and finding out too late it was a minor Master of some kind. It was most definitely along those lines. After all, she could have used Andrew as a walker just as well as the Countess.

Just lately, and she didn't know why, Clarissa had had the feeling that it was all Jennifer's fault that she had found Andrew so irritating. After all, if Jennifer had been more of a good daughter to her, if she had been more the cosy kind of girl that other mothers seemed to have for daughters, then she would have thought of it for Clarissa, instead of just sitting around in her dreadful old skirt covered in dog hairs doing tapestry and letting Pemberton have his own way in the garden. But there was nothing to be done now. Andrew was gone, and she was left with having to divorce him on the usual grounds of gross incompatibility.

She picked up the invitation again from her mantelpiece, and stared at the name at the top. 'The Honourable Mrs Andrew Gillott'. It did look so nice, she would definitely have to keep 'The Honourable' bit on after the divorce. She would insist on custody of her handle. She turned back to her coffee table, and the latest edition of *Vogue*, in particular the sections for the older more sophisticated woman. It was some months before the ball. Plenty of time to choose herself a dress, something alluring. Perhaps a tangerine *peau de soie* with a bustle effect at the back? Or an Alma Tadage evening gown with the new rising front? She was a little too mature for the Kleinstein Erstwhile collection with hand-embroidered shelling around the navel, but nevertheless there was infinite scope within the pages of the magazine.

She sat back and rang the little bell she kept on her marble coffee table for her 'housekeeper' Mrs Divine, who wasn't, but who came in to clean for her three times a week. Clarissa liked her to bring in a cup of coffee on a tray set with a cloth and a bowl of sugar with tongs, even though Clarissa didn't take sugar.

Mrs Divine always changed into bedroom slippers to do the cleaning, which was unfortunate for Clarissa, because if someone called, it hardly looked very 'staff' to have someone opening the door in a pair of bedroom slippers. Clarissa had actually bought her a pair of indoor shoes for a Christmas present, and as a large hint as to what she should be wearing when she was in the house, but Mrs Divine having made the right sort of noises about them, then announced that she was keeping them for church on Sunday because they pinched, and went straight back to bedroom slippers with dirty fur round the edges.

'Oh, Mrs Divine, if you wouldn't mind bringing in the coffee tray now?' asked Clarissa as Mrs Divine entered, making her customary soft-shoe shuffle sound.

'Right. Want it now, do yer?'

Mrs Divine nodded and shuffled out very, very slowly. She wasn't much, thought Clarissa, but not much was all you could hope for in the country. She would now take hours going down the corridor to the kitchen and fetching the coffee tray, which Clarissa herself had carefully laid shortly before Mrs Divine had arrived. She would then re-appear with it minutes later looking as if she had done it all herself, and having usually succeeded in spilling coffee on the hand-worked tray cloth that Jennifer had given her for Christmas, pretending she'd embroidered it herself, when everyone knew Elliott had had to finish it for her.

Idly Clarissa picked up the newest and latest edition of *Country Life*. Life in the country was becoming almost alarmingly fashionable, as a consequence of which she was delaying her return to deepest Kensington. Ideally of course she would like to move nearer her daughter, to cash in on the cachet of her being a Marchioness, and the owner of the Hall and a thousand acres and a butler.

Bloss was the greatest blessing of all, even more than the Hall and the acres, of that there was no doubt. He had promised to notify her the moment a property came up which was near the Hall and suitable. Bloss was on the dinner party circuit, and that was where you heard of such things, long before they reached the wretched estate agents, it seemed. He and his friends waiting at table, listening at hatches, apparently were responsible for more house sales than Paine and Windrush, the Knightsbridge Estate Agents that everyone in the country used.

Clarissa sighed thankfully as she heard Mrs Divine soft-shoe shuffling her way back down the corridor. God bless Bloss. At that moment he was the one star in a rather dark sky.

Bloss examined the end of his silver cloth. He had been seduced into buying a new polish that promised to do many things to the silver at the Hall, but appeared not to have done any more than any other polish. This was irritating, but hardly surprising since the bottles had arrived from 'No 8 Westmancott Buildings, New Blading Estate, Ilsie, Nr Badley, Brackely, Yorks.'

Bloss sighed. He seemed to be inextricably attracted to trading estates for acquiring polishes that promised more than they could fulfil, and consequently, since they were as over-priced as they were ineffectual, was always being forced into being more imaginative with the household accounts than he would ideally have wished to be. Not that his lordship paid the slightest heed to his household accounts, but her ladyship was most persistent. Nanny and he had to be able to eke out their household items as long as possible. Nanny even had to measure out the soap powder into a large glass jar in front of her ladyship, because Nanny was not allowed to do more than one wash a day for the nursery floor, and if she had any personal items that needed to be washed poor Nanny had to borrow Bloss's personal packet of soap flakes for very fine things. Not that he minded, really; he always put them down under 'Staff Tea Bags' anyway. That was one thing which her ladyship found very difficult to calculate, how many cups of tea a week they were all in need of consuming, particularly if there were men working on the fabric of the building.

Thank heavens for the fabric of the building, thought Bloss, for the hundredth time that month. It was a boon, it was a lifesaver. A stone that needed re-pointing, a chimney that needed sweeping, a fireplace with a tile loose, hurray for it all, because it all meant cups of tea, and cups of tea meant more soap flakes for himself and Nanny. Not that the new silver polish could come under 'Tetley for the men'; but, and here he paused as he put away his silver duster and took out his account books, the polish could certainly feature as 'Cooking Sherry' or there again 'Plant and Grow' mats, or as string and brown paper for parcelling up items that guests had left behind. That too was something of which her ladyship could never keep track. Bloss had only to clear his throat and gaze out over the garden for her ladyship to colour and cease to enquire further as to what had been left behind and by whom.

Happily his lordship was as generous as her ladyship was mean. He was profligate by comparison. His little nightcaps with the butler were, at his insistence, more than generous, they were positively toe-curling.

'Come on, Bloss, what's wrong with your pouring arm?' he'd mutter. 'We're not at one of her ladyship's social teas just now, you know.'

Her ladyship, just lately, had started to give social teas. His lordship naturally found them appalling. Standing around having to listen to a whole lot of hens' talk was not his lordship's idea of how to spend the afternoon. Tea to him, he was always telling Bloss, was a meal that a man had either in the stable with the lads pulling his riding boots off after hunting, or when he was in the bath, or when he was behind *The Times* at his club. The very idea of asking in a whole lot of people to eat bridge rolls and sip sherry and cups of china tea was horrendous. No, it was worse, it was horrible.

Bloss disagreed. The fact that her ladyship wanted to entertain at all was to him a miracle, and one to be encouraged. It not only helped with the imaginative side of his accounts, but it also helped with other things. It helped him to keep track of all that was happening in the village. It helped to distract her ladyship from the fact that his lordship was not only having what was called nowadays a 'raging affair' with Lady Tizzy, but had spawned not only one but soon to be two children with her, which while admittedly fertile and manly, might be said to be overdoing things.

Bloss had to keep control of every event. It was one of the duties of a butler. The principle event of which he had to keep control was that her ladyship must not find out, or even vaguely suspect, that the child, soon to be children, at Flint House were anything to do with his lordship's aristocratic predisposition to beget offspring born on the wrong side of the blanket. There must, after all, be no divorce. Bloss was a strict Anglican, and even if the rest of the Church might be giving way at every turn, he was not about to do the same. He did not believe in divorce, and never would, not even for gain.

He started to pull off his silver-cleaning gloves, and then changed his mind. There was still the muffin dish to do, the all-important muffin dish. He picked it up, and started to rub the new polish into it. What fun it all was. He wouldn't swop places with the King of Mesopotamia, if he still existed, or it still existed. He sometimes thought they changed the names of places in Africa just to catch out the BBC. There was something about a name, whatever anyone said. There had to be. There was after all a lot less trouble on the African continent when Pogopogoland was still going strong under its own name, but get a bunch of intellectuals at work on names and you could only expect to get the muffin dishes thrown out with the crumpets.

The wall telephone rang in the snug where Bloss

reigned as King Emperor. Bloss stared at it. He had mastered Mr Bell's invention years ago. If the telephone rang shortly it was trade, if it rang long and insistently it was Something of Interest. It rang and rang.

Bloss picked it up. It was her ladyship's mother. She had a soft spot for Bloss, which was just as well considering Bloss was in sole charge of so much. If Mrs Parker-Jones was not encouraged to think that soon, very soon, there would be a small Georgian gem of a house for sale very near her daughter at the Hall, she would return to Kensington, cease to annoy her ladyship, and her ladyship might start to notice that his lordship was not always where he had told her he was going to be. No, the mother, the teas, the dance (Bloss's idea, of course), they were all essentials to the peace of life in rural Wiltshire. Everyone could go on bee-ing and bird-ing as much as they wanted, so long as certain rules were observed – and the number one rule with wives with straying husbands was distraction-at-all-costs. Then everything in the garden would remain lovely, and the goose would hang high, instead of being cooked.

Really, when Bloss thought about it, and he did a great deal, particularly when Mrs Parker-Jones was on the blower, really the Church of England owed him a greal deal. Persons such as he should be styled Butler-Bishops, because they, in their way, helped to keep everyone married, and if not moral, at least channelled somewhere near the paths of righteousness. It was important, and let's face it, it was due entirely to persons such as him that the *Daily Telegraph* still had sales, and a little part of England was still England and not Los Angeles or Hong Kong.

Mrs Parker-Jones was still on about her little house.

Bloss made soothing noises while sipping his pre-lunchtime sherry. He'd heard of a friend who, while serving at a dinner party, had overheard that Moss House, Little Kingbury, had a quite unnaturally old owner, who might be booking her passage to Florida in the near future. He would pursue it, he told Mrs P-J. No promises, of course. He replaced the receiver. The jolly thing was, for once what he'd said was true.

A 'jobbing' butler he knew had passed on this knowledge in exchange for a tip for the Epsom Derby. Bloss smiled to himself. He had managed to get wonderful odds. If he also managed to move Mrs P-J as near as Little Kingbury, her ladyship would be driven up the wall and down again, and there wouldn't be a second in the day when she would have the time to turn round and wonder where his lordship was, or to what he was up. He must pursue the matter with all speed. Meanwhile the dance, the ball, the whatever, was all that was being discussed behind the drawing room doors. He must pop in with the lunchtime drinks and catch a bit of the drift.

Jennifer was seated in the window with her embroidery. She liked embroidery in the drawing room, and tapestry for outside. Opposite her was Fulton, and next to him was the Countess. Bloss stiffened. He had let neither of them in. They must have come up the drive and round the back to the garden without his knowing it. It was all too aggravating, particularly since from the ominous silence it was obvious something must be in the balance, something that he would have to strain to catch up with.

'There's no need to ask anyone if they want anything,

65

Bloss,' said Jennifer sharply when she saw Bloss hovering. 'We've got lemonade.'

'There's every need,' said the Countess. 'Bring me a gin and tonic with two pieces of ice and one piece of lemon, please, Bloss.'

Bloss went back to the drinks. The Countess could always be relied upon in every exigency. He would take his time over the making of the drinks, and that way, as soon as conversation was resumed, all, as some would say, would be revealed.

'Well,' said the Countess, relieved to see Bloss already busy slicing lemon with a very dangerous-looking little knife. 'There seems to be a somewhat unfortunate misunderstanding. And personally speaking I think I can solve it. Thank you, Bloss.'

She took a large sip of the exquisitely satisfying drink handed to her, before she allowed her eyes to whip Fulton and Jennifer together in one glance, lash them to the mast, and then leave them gasping with the speed at which she worked.

'I think I should leave you two to cope with all the details, and generally now get on with it.'

Jennifer didn't like the way the Countess had just said 'get on with it'. It had a slightly spiteful ring, as if the ball had suddenly turned into a hole-and-corner affair instead of being that rarity of all rarities, a perfectly private dance in aid of nothing more than pleasure.

'Then of course, if there is a problem,' again her glance included herself out, and tied Fulton to Jennifer's party strings in no uncertain way, '*if* anything goes wrong, which I am quite sure it won't, I shall always be on hand. Personally I think Fulton's idea to go for the peach tones is charming, really charming. It will give a wonderfully passé feel to everything, very Proustian.'

Jennifer didn't know what 'Proustian' meant, but she thought it couldn't be anything nice from the way that Fulton stiffened, and having removed a very, very small piece of cotton from his very, very clean trousers, walked over to the papier mâché Victorian wastepaper basket and dropped it very carefully in, with such intense interest on his face. It was an interest which Jennifer knew had nothing to do with his having supplied her with the wastepaper basket from his antiques and restoration business, but had everything to do with real anger. She knew also that she must be right about 'Proustian'. It must not be at all nice, otherwise Fulton wouldn't still be tensing his rather charming backside in that way, so that it looked less like a backside and more like two very new tennis balls.

'Perhaps not peach,' she said in a low voice suddenly, 'perhaps people would prefer the cream and green, more fresh and more country, perhaps?'

She dropped her head quickly to her embroidery. Little tiny leaves and flowers, so small she had to put on special glasses to see them. She wished she'd never started the wretched tray cloth for the Lord Roberts Workshop guest tray in the mauve and blue bedroom. She would have preferred to do it in drawn thread work, but Elliott had put her off. That was another thing that was someone else's fault. So much was.

'I have just had Twinks prepare three peach boards in varying shades, but if you prefer cream and green, I'll leave straight away before she gets too far in.'

Jennifer looked hopelessly across at the Countess.

67

Fulton was practically by the door, and still she had not spoken.

'We'll have to talk about which cream and which green, though,' he called from the door. 'Or will you leave that to me?'

'Yes, yes,' Jennifer agreed. 'All to you, Fulton, and no more to be said.'

'Well, I suppose that's *something*,' said Fulton to the vast arrangement of cabbage flowers mixed with stuffed percherons, weeds and hosta heads that was dominating the hall, as he closed the library door and stalked out into the fine May morning. 'Twinks will be furious,' he told his bronzed Golf as he started her up. 'Simply furious. But then, that is always the way with the Hall. We at Flint House rescue them time and again, and they pour scorn on our least idea.'

Elliott was ready and waiting by the door as soon as Fulton pushed his way into their own dear hall, hanging his keys on the specially antiqued hook that hung under the stairs.

'Well?' he asked.

'Well,' Fulton answered, having calmed himself by watching his keys swinging to a standstill for a few seconds. 'She's leaving it all to us.'

'Well, that's something, then.'

'But—'

'But?'

'But she no longer favours the peach. She wants to go for cream and green.'

There was a tremendously long silence during which Elliott's jaw, which wasn't very large, dropped, and then righted itself once more.

68

'I don't believe it.'

'Neither did I.'

'But the food? Does she realize what this means? Molly and I have already gone through fruit dyes for the cèpes. Molly had just reached a really perceptible peach tone, which is quite something on a cèpe, I can tell you.'

'Quite.'

'Did you swear when she told you?'

'No.'

'Did you curse?'

'No.'

'In that case better have a coffee and do it now.'

'I think I will.'

'You do that.' Elliott nodded, and quickly disappeared to the kitchen to make coffee.

'I'll have to go and break it to Twinks. She's even now out in the stable staining the boards with three entirely differing and very subtle pêche variations,' Fulton called.

'Poor, poor Fulton,' Elliott told the coffee machine. 'The work. And what shall I tell Molly? She's done at least a dozen cèpes, and we all know what they cost.'

A hideous thought occurred to him. He hadn't told Jennifer anything about the cèpes, in which case the cost would all be down to him. He wouldn't tell Fulton about it. He'd just have to make sure he saved from the housekeeping somehow, and make it up that way. Although trying to save from the house-keeping money had become somewhat of a joke, what with Lady Tizzy eating more than a horse in train-ing, and Nanny and Victoria having good healthy appetites, and likewise himself and Fulton, not to mention Twinks.

Poor Twinks. Fulton had scooped her up out of a nowhere place on the Great West Road where she'd been recovering from a terribly broken heart, and a man who had left her in favour of a woman who would marry him, which Twinks could never possibly afford to do, having only a very small income from an equally small great aunt who had died just in time to leave her enough to be going on with, but not quite enough to be able to afford to keep a husband who might go off with half of it. Now she was living over the stables at Flint House, and busy making papier mâché trays and wastepaper baskets in the Victorian manner, as well as helping the men out with reproductions of lightly painted early nineteenth-century Scandinavian furniture.

Elliott laid the coffee out on one of Twinks's trays that had not been a big seller. It was one of her less good ideas, being of a classical nature and involving nudity, which made putting cups and saucers on it seem rather odd, which was probably why it had not sold, even as a magazine offer.

He was just going into the hall, past the old bronze bust, and into the drawing room when he heard a scream from upstairs. He paid not the slightest attention, but continued on his way to their own special window where they liked to sit.

Lady Tizzy screaming had become just another sound of the countryside. No more worrying than the cry of a small animal in the night as the owl swooped, or the sudden lurch of the hay lorries against their old wall which ran, most unfortunately, by a small road which led to the main highway. Elliott continued to pour the coffee as yet another scream floated downstairs to force itself to his attention. He went to the door.

'What now?' he called up. 'What now?'

Last week just such a scream had heralded the dreaded news that the ITV had announced its final re-run of 'Pogley and the Pegtops'. Now, doubtless, Bede, her favourite character in 'The Inside Outers', had contracted something beastly.

Elliott looked up. High above him at the top of the stairs, draped dramatically over the banisters, was Lady Tizzy, and she was upset all right. Her long hair tumbling in its vast array of coiffured and tortured curls, her large poitrine shaking with emotion, she was, Elliott had to admit, a magnificent sight, if you liked that kind of thing.

'Elliott, Elliott, Elliott—'

'Yes.'

'Something terrible has been happening—'

'Don't tell me.'

'I've got to—'

Elliott thought for a second.

'Not Bede been taken hostage *again*?'

'No, Bede's fine. As a matter of fact, he's just got out of hospital – you know, after having had his thingy reversed.'

'Poor Bede—'

'But, Elliott—'

'Yes?'

'I'm afraid you'll have to borrow Mr Burrow's four wheel drive and get across the fields on that blooming short cut to the hospital what you worked out – I've only started!'

'That you worked out,' said Elliott, only too anxious as always to correct and help. 'Fine.'

He turned as Fulton came back into the house.

'She's just started,' he said calmly. 'Lady Tizzy has just started.'

'What?' asked Fulton.

He continued on into the drawing room, Elliott following.

'Oh, coffee, coffee, coffee.'

'There's something about this morning. Everyone keeps saying everything three times.'

'Must be something about the merry month of May,' Fulton agreed as yet another scream rent the air and floated down from upstairs.

'Lady Tizzy's screaming so loud,' said Fulton sipping his coffee thankfully, 'anyone would think she'd started.'

'She has.'

Fulton carefully replaced his coffee cup. 'How do you mean?'

'She's started, I told you, she's started.'

'You don't mean to say she's started?'

'Oh, but I do,' said Elliott still hanging on to his calm, 'I do, I do, I do. See, now *I've* done it.'

'You do realize that if she's started,' said Fulton, breathing in suddenly, and pointing up through the ceiling in the vague direction of his wife, 'you do realize that that means that she's started all over the very carefully chosen nineteenth-century extremely rare kelim that Twinks gave us as a stable-warming present? I mean, you realize what that means?'

'I'm determined on calm,' said Elliott, finishing his coffee. 'It's ridiculous. We've worked out the route, we know the form, all we have to do is cut through the three bridleways that we have spent all winter opening up, and *eh voilà*, we'll be there. We've been through all this before. Birth is perfectly – natural. The suitcase is packed, there is nothing to do but get on with the show, and see to the kelim when we get back.'

They nodded to each other, breathed in deeply, and headed towards the staircase, Lady Tizzy, the terribly well worked out route through the fields in Mr Burrows's borrowed four wheel drive, and Nanny and Twinks left in charge. Nothing to it.

Always and for ever afterwards Elliott could never see a pregnant woman without hearing Lady Tizzy's screams as they encountered the first bedstead thrown across their carefully worked out cross-country route which Fulton had insisted upon.

'Now what!' She kept screaming that. 'Now what!' Just as if they had thrown the wretched bedsteads across the bridleway that was meant to be kept accessible to everyone, especially those cutting across country to the hospital.

And then again. 'Now what!' as they all peered over a gate with a huge enormous bull and five randy-looking cows in it.

'Now what!' as they climbed over barbed wire fencing and through hawthorn, and Lady Tizzy's bump seemed to be sliding further and further down to her knees until not even Fulton could look at her without getting a contraction of his own. She would keep leaning against the gate posts and panting. In the end, seeing that the parcel was just about to be delivered, they both seized her by the elbows and ran with her, her legs sort of paddling over the ground, until they reached the hospital grounds, where they forgot all decorum and went in the entrance marked 'Strictly Private', at which point they all three screamed.

'Being so near you seem to have left it a little late,' said the gynaecologist, when he at last deigned to arrive.

Fulton glanced out of the window at the gynaecologist's Rolls Royce. He did hope he would get going and go in to Lady Tizzy, really earn his fee. More than he did last time, when he stayed behind to deliver one of his prize pigs instead.

'Shouldn't be long now,' he beamed at Fulton. 'If last time is anything to go by, you'll have a nice little bundle to cuddle in just a few secs.'

Fulton shuddered.

'A nice little bundle is what he costs,' he said, going to the tea machine and pouring himself a small cup of nasty water, because he could never hold tea in a paper cup without burning himself.

Fulton and Elliott walked up and down. It was just like last time, only a tiny bit less so. Elliott was right. They were calmer, despite having to leave the four wheel drive in a very nasty farmer's field, just beside a mattress that had not only seen better days, but worse ones too.

'Cooee!'

They stood to attention in a way they normally only did after the Queen's speech on Christmas Day. The gynaecologist beckoned them to the door of the delivery room.

'I'm afraid there's a little bit of a hitch.'

74

Fulton's eyes narrowed. She might be his wife, but he loved Lady Tizzy, and so did Elliott.

'What kind of a hitch?' asked Fulton coldly, his backside contracting in much the same manner as when he had lost the battle over the peach tones earlier that morning.

'*Well*,' said the gynaecologist, 'you've got a beautiful baby.'

Fulton and Elliott looked at each other delightedly.

'And it's a boy.'

They both stepped towards the masked figure, who had hastily pulled his mask up again when he saw their faces.

'What!'

'Yes,' the gynaecologist went on, speaking through his mask. 'A fine baby boy.'

'What!'

'A fine big, bouncing baby boy born at three minutes after twelve.'

'A fine big bouncing baby booboo, you mean!'

'You said,' Elliott breathed out, his nostrils flaring as they always did when he was most especially indignant, 'you said,' he said, 'that it was a girl. A girl. A girl. A girl.'

'Well, it's a boy, a boy, a boy.'

'But it can't be,' said Fulton.

'No, it can't be.'

'We've re-done the Duc de Berry in very fine – peach.'

'Oh, I don't suppose he'll mind,' said the gynae-cologist, dashing back into the delivery room. 'People put boys in anything nowadays.'

'We'll sue him,' hissed Fulton to Elliott as they

75

walked up and down the corridor. 'How many scans did we pay for? Tests, tests, and more tests. The man should stick to prize pigs, he's a fraud with a buttonhole. Carnations indeed. He wouldn't know a baby girl from a baby boy.'

'I wonder what one sues under?' Elliott mused. 'Certainly not palimony.'

'The daisy garden, the marguerites. We can't call a boy Daisy-Marguerita. Dozy. We could change it to Dozy? Or Desi, like Desi Arnez?'

'He was Mexican, they don't mind what they're called. Besides, the daisies will still be there, won't they? What will Nanny say? Oh, what will Nanny say?'

Elliott sat down suddenly, and put his head in his hands. Fulton sat down beside him.

'I don't like boys. I never have done.'

They both stared at the floor.

'Cooee!'

They both looked up again.

'Cooee!'

The masked figure stood once more outside the delivery room.

'I do wish he'd stop saying that,' sighed Fulton.

'Mr Benedict-Montrose-Cavanagh?'

'Pretty near.'

'More good news.' He lowered his mask and beamed. 'A little girl.'

'Oh—'

'Thank heavens—'

'You got it wrong—'

'No, I mean Lady Tizpots has surprised us. One of each, one of each, one of each.'

'One of each of what?' Fulton faltered.

'One of each sex, both beautiful. Here's nursey. You can hold one, and you can hold the other.'

But Elliott couldn't. He'd fainted.

4

In the ladies' rest room, now with a newly painted sign declaring it to be a Persons' Waiting Room, Georgiana was pretending to read a very old book about Molière. She had found, given that she had really rather fascinatingly long legs, and was not yet of an age when she could be called upon to knit or sew on a train journey, she had found that reading a really rather old book with a nice marbled cover, particularly on the return journey, discouraged old sillies in first class from playing footsie with her all the way to Penbury.

Every time the waiting room door opened, which was all too frequently, Georgiana found herself looking up from her very old book on Molière, and a part of her sinking right to the bottom of her heart, if not to her feet, as she imagined that any minute now Gus would appear and hoick her out of the waiting room, tear up her first class return ticket, and frog-march her all the way back to Longborough. She dare not even yet congratulate herself on escaping from Longborough, not until the train really did draw out of the station with her on board.

In a way it was amazing that she had got so far. Her excuse had been that she had been called up to see the old family lawyer, and that she must go and see him, because it was all to do with making Longborough over to George. Naturally no-one at the house had discouraged her in this idea. In the event of her premature and quite untimely death, Gus would be only too happy for their bastard son to inherit, and so would Nan and Nanny. So they had let her pack her suitcase and go without a murmur, and Georgiana had taken care to hide all the relevant papers from them in her absence. Even so, up and down went her head as each new arrival burst noisily through the waiting room door. Each person seeming, for just one ghastly second, to be going to be Gus.

The train arrived with the usual sense of drama that a train arrival brings, umbrellas attached to their owners, owners attached to over-labelled suitcases, suitcases being removed over heads, heads ducking out of the way of umbrellas, all activity, Penbury being a country station, being accompanied by the usual chorus of 'Wait, wait' as bicycle owners tried to load their precious old basketed jalopies into the luggage van in the short three minutes that the station master had deemed was time enough for the train to stop. His flag waved menacingly as the last wheel disappeared on board, and the last train door slammed uncertainly behind a latecomer, and the train drew out.

Georgiana almost threw her old crocodile dressing case down on the seat in front of her. Freedom at last. Soon the countryside would imperceptibly start to recede and slowly creeping towards the train would come first stockbroker villages, emptying their tired but perfectly suited occupants into the first class carriages, then suburbia where the waiting platform occupants fronting their stations would display a sartorial preoccupation with anoraks and rainwear; and finally, gloriously, at last would arrive the blackened city buildings and the vulgar billboards, not creeping on all fours but strutting, crouching, and pouncing towards the train, telling Georgiana that very soon her feet would be touching proper pavements, and her life would once again be that of a girl rather than a retired person.

It was wonderful, even standing in the taxi queue, to be able to see real people again. Executive women in smart suits, and men with properly furled umbrellas, not like Berridge where all the men hurried along smoking and staring at the ground, and all the women ambled by clutching small telescopic umbrellas in dingy colours, and staring at nothing at all, as if there was nothing to look at, as if they were alone, not passing anyone or anything.

Georgiana climbed gracefully into a taxi, knowing that at least half a dozen pairs of male eyes were eyeing her long slender legs in their stiff high-heeled shoes, shoes that had had to be dusted when they were removed from their shelf. She sat back and held the passenger strap, and stared with fascination at the neat parks, and the late spring flowers all planted out so evenly, and in such wonderfully bright vulgar colours, and at the horses and ponies walking smartly out with their uncertain but perfectly attired riders, and at the horse guards sit-trotting through the sandy rides, and at the busy occupants of other taxis, and she gave one enormous intake of breath and let it out. Taxi fumes, and leather seating, and real city dust, how much she had missed it all.

She shopped as someone hungry would shop, incessantly producing her cheque book and her credit cards, and she accumulated bags and boxes in such a short space of time she might have been a food addict cramming her mouth with so much that an onlooker could have been forgiven for believing her intake was so fast it would choke her.

And yet still she shopped on, always for clothes, or shoes, or little items that people in the country didn't even know were necessary to pretty girls, the exactly right shade of stockings, the exactly new scent. It was delicious, and lunching in glorious solitude, not having to listen to Nan and Nanny admiring the way George was dropping bits out of his mouth, or throwing his mug on the floor, was such a luxury it might have been a celestial gift. Even so she could hardly wait to eat her small plate of delicately arranged pasta, or drink her small glass of rough-tasting red wine, before she hurried on, to yet more shops.

Finally, not because she was tired or satiated, she stopped. She had to because the shops were shutting, the sales ladies throwing cotton drapes over the counters, or multi-locking the small doors that fronted the fashionable streets, leaving only curiously wigged models in their narrow windows to tell of their trade through the evening and the midnight hours, until dawn came and with it the milkmen, and the cats, and the early morning taxis returning home from night shifts.

Georgiana walked slowly to the hotel in which she had chosen to stay. It was small, and newly fashionable, and she had read about it in Berridge car park in one of her glossy magazines. She walked in, her arms full, her head filled with the champagne of extravagance, that lightweight devil-may-care feeling that only spending money on yourself can bring. With each purchase came

81

no agonies of uncertainty as to whether the recipient might like it, no self-doubts about taste, for she knew she had bad taste because Gus so often remarked that she had. So what if she had displayed her inimitable conservative but vulgar preferences? Only she was aware of it, and only she would know of it when she opened the boxes and the chicly named shopping bags. There would be no-one to mock her, no-one to hold her up to ridicule.

And she still hadn't even approached the problem of buying herself a dress for the ball. She laid out the parcels on the bed, over-tipped the bell boy, because he looked her up and down so appreciatively, and then looked round her room.

The hotel, right from its entrance, had been everything she had hoped, and now so too were her bedroom and bathroom. The hotel as she had stepped into it from the fading sunlight outside had straight away shouted 'affair'. This was not a place to which married folk would come. It was just a little too dark, just a little too over-decorated, too expensive, too un-proper, too filled with the newly rich, to be designed for anything other than business or love, or quite probably both. None of the other clientele were anything except underdressed, and none of the men wore suits, they wore jackets, but not sports coats, they wore leather and suede, and showed pure brown unreddened tans beneath the open necks of their shirts. At the small, discreet desk where she carefully wrote her name in the visitors' book as 'Mrs G. Hackett' rather than 'Lady Georgiana Longborough' and her place of residence as 'Wiltshire', there were no old school ties, no pinstriped suits to remind her of the country, and of the people who plunged down to their estates to bray at each other at point-to-point meetings or shooting weekends. In short, the moment Georgiana had walked into the hotel she absolutely knew that she had booked herself to stay in her personal idea of heaven.

Once she had unpacked she lay across her small double bed in a silken peignoir, and gazed at the erotic prints around her with sensuous satisfaction. The walls were so dark they might have been lined with blackout material, the curtains wonderfully overlaid with gold, and her bed a riot of swirls and loops and yet more gold braid. She sighed with satisfaction.

The day with its extravagances had brought so much to think about, not horrid things like menus, or Nanny not liking turnips, or Nan wanting a different sort of tea from everyone else, but nice things. The precise placing of a silk scarf, the angle of a hat, the right jewellery to wear with a suit that had braiding and buttons in gold, the seam of a stocking, the fun of a black silk slip that would make Nan raise her eyebrows when she ironed it, because the slits at the side quite obviously went a little too far up to the top of Georgiana's legs.

Eventually Georgiana chose a new dress to wear. Very little of it, all straps, black, and desperately expensive, it shouted to her to wear it first. She just hoped that the bar, to which she had every intention of repairing, did not have as dark walls as her bedroom, for if it did she would not show up at all against it, and she couldn't have that. She would either have to change bars, or change dresses. She smiled at herself in the mirror, for it was certainly not a looking glass, and leant her head forward a little, and then backwards too, to make sure her long dark hair was swinging as it should, and then she let herself out of her room and into the arena of the world outside her suite.

The room was a deep red, so she was quite able to stay in it. She sat up at one of the stools set around the bar, her long slender legs draped in perfect arrangement. She would try to trick the barman, she thought mischievously. She would order a cocktail which he wouldn't know how to make.

'California Dreaming, please.'

He looked at her, dark and hispanic, his large black eyes remaining implacably unfazed.

'Certainly.'

Kirsch, pineapple, topped up with champagne; he knew it exactly, and without hesitation. Georgiana smiled. In the pale rose mirror around the room she could see reflected couple after couple, staring at each other, into each other's eyes, letting their imaginations roam ahead to intimacies already perhaps known, or yet to be discovered. Aloud they wondered whether to dine in at the restaurant next to the hotel, or out; or merely to send for room service while they occupied each other with things other than eating.

There were business people too. But they did not stare up at each other, but down at their glasses or fractionally across at the rest of the room while they paused, and hesitated, and wound their way round what they really wanted to say which was 'how much?', not like the rest of the room's 'when?'.

The business people, not as in the country, were

mixed: men, women, sometimes just men, sometimes just women, sharper, more wary, less carefree in dress, all except one pair of males. They unlike the rest of the couples stared at each other, and talked and gestured, and didn't look round the room but in some emotion at each other, until one of them, his face still in the shadows, stood up, and still gesticulating somewhat emotionally for such a place of quiet enjoyment, came over to the bar, saw Georgiana's legs, looked up at her, and almost instantaneously allowed his face to break into a thousand pieces, as a plate might if thrown to the floor with terrific force.

'Dear God in all his throned glory, I just don't believe this.'

Georgiana turned. In the country, around Long-borough, someone you had known all your life and who might even have some affection for you would only slide out a squeezed sound when they saw you. This over-extravagant greeting could only come from one kind of person, an American.

'E.F.,' she said, factually and with understated certainty, because this writing partner of Kaminski's whom she had known so well and so briefly when she had had her first affair was unchanged, except for a little white around the red of his hair, as if cotton wool had been left there inadvertently.

'Let me look at you. You little minx, you've dared to stay the same, you've dared to remain unchanged. How could you!'

'E.F.,' Georgiana repeated, even more certainly, for she suddenly realized, and it filled her with a dreadful panic-stricken excitement, that he was not alone, and that the other man with him, the man whose long elegant legs were stretched across the carpet in front of his table, was Kaminski.

Eyes meet, hands touch, and what is being said is 'How are you?' 'Can you believe this?' but what is really being said is 'I remember every inch of you.' 'I really loved your body.' 'You excited me like no other.' 'How could you have left me as you did?'

Kaminski, the sometime master of 'le rouge regarde', the look that says, 'now or if not now, soon', paused before reseating himself, and sitting with his hands in a suddenly all too familiar praying position with the tips of his fingers touching his nose didn't smile at Georgiana, he stared.

He always stared. Kaminski had always stared, and Georgiana had always ignored him. And in ignoring him she had unwittingly encouraged him to stare some more. They had no need to say anything, and they both knew that E.F. was watching them because he was talking for all of them, while staring at both of them.

'This I don't believe.'

E.F. had always said that, particularly when he was pleased to know that he believed it very much.

'I just don't believe this.'

Georgiana looked at him, and she smiled with her eyes at him.

'I'd forgotten that you always say that,' she murmured.

'What are you drinking?'

E.F. seized her glass, and looked down at her. With his tall frame, his red hair, his freckles, he suddenly seemed like an old acquaintance, and yet it had only been such a very few weeks.

'You're very kind,' she murmured, 'but really, two Californias Dreaming and I'll be anyone's.'

'Don't be anyone's, darling,' E.F. called back to her as he returned to the bar, 'be somebody's.'

And then Georgiana did something which she knew was unmistakably terrible. She blushed, and was immediately helpless, avoiding Kaminski's eyes, while he very definitely wasn't even attempting to avoid hers.

'So,' said Georgiana, at last, and she raised her eyes to his. Kaminski didn't smile, because he never did. Even Georgiana had remarked on this. But at that moment, which was somehow unfair, she suddenly felt as if her underpinnings (silken, and deeply lacy at the right moments) had shrunk and that it would be very nice, after all, to be staying at Browns, where Kaminski would not be staying, and neither would E.F., and she would by now be dining alone, not saying 'So' to Kaminski in a way that made him put his hands in that praying position.

Over by the bar E.F. was enjoying watching them both in the pinkened mirror. Neither he nor Kaminski had forgotten Lady Georgiana Longborough. After all, why should they? They had made a very successful picture around a character like hers; and to make it even better, the picture had cost very little money and made a great deal for the studio, which was why they were both back in town right now to research yet another picture, but not so cheap and not so little.

Because he was eager to watch the minuscule, but perhaps emotional events that might be unfolding behind him, E.F. made a great play of forgetting his room number, and of trying to find some change to tip the barman, just so he could go on watching. He hadn't seen that look on Kaminski's face in a very long time. It was most definitely not the look that he had when he was with Sofia, his present rather disturbingly beautiful mistress who was even now probably changing into something as exotic and disturbing as herself in Kaminski's suite, and would most likely knife him if she came into the bar and found him talking to Lady Georgiana. Normally Kaminski only put his hands into the praying position when he was thinking out his next move at chess, or writing a script with E.F., or listening to E.F. explaining a plot point.

Eventually, having made his point, E.F. was able to accompany the drinks back to their table, but by that time, as he discovered when he looked up and caught the look that was not a look but a whole past being held between this fifty-year-old White Russian and the young beautiful aristocrat, he realized he had overdone the delaying tactics, and that things had progressed beyond the drinks stage. Although he was surprised that within half a minute they both got up and without a word left the cocktail lounge, leaving him with three drinks, at least two of which were not to his taste, he was not, after all, that surprised, and he was not at all shocked, for, he thought enviously, as he watched Kaminski following that slender figure and dark hair out of the room, Kaminski was famous, and this was fame! Women would do anything to be with fame, and so would a great many men. But most of all women. He knew of a famous Italian tenor, of great voice and even greater weight, for whom women of all kinds would crowd the bar in hotels all around the world, waiting patiently for him to finish

88

with his little coterie of opera fans and critics, until, with some indication known only to him and the girl of his choice, he would rise to his feet, and leave with her for his suite, and a night which he would forget as soon as he stood in front of his shaving mirror the next morning, but of which the girl in question would boast for the rest of her life. Now *that* was fame.

Kaminski had said as he left, 'Go to Sofia, and tell her I have been called away.'

'Thanks, but no thanks.'

Even as he was left alone staring into Georgiana's cocktail, E.F. started to write the scene that would now take place between himself and Sofia.

First he would knock on the door, and then he would wait interminably for Sofia to open it. Finally Sofia would appear, probably with a 'Yes?' thinking it was room service, but because she was brought up partly in L.A. she would make sure to open the door with the chain on, and then seeing it was E.F., whom she hated and despised for taking up too much of Kaminski's time with work and more work, she would shut the door again, and make a great play of re-opening it to him.

'May I come in?'

Sofia nodded. Her hair was still piled up high into a large white fluffy towel, and her body was completely enclosed by a large white fluffy towelling robe with the name of an American hotel written across the pocket.

'Yes?'

Sofia had a husky Italianate voice, which if you didn't know about some of her passionate Italianate scenes was really attractive.

'Yes?' she said again, still husky, still Italianate.

'May I say, first of all, how beautiful you are looking, Sofia?'

Sofia walked away from him. It was a heavy-footed walk, and it gave E.F. time to notice that her toes were surprisingly stubby as she trod across the thick carpet.

'Yes?' she said again. It was obviously heavy dialogue for Sofia.

'Yes, Sofia, you are looking really beautiful. Your dark skin against that white towelling. I wish I had some ace photographer with me, it would be sensational, really.'

Sofia turned her dark eyes on E.F. Normally she despised him, normally he mocked her. He had never attempted flattery before, and now he realized how stupid that had been. She looked instantly sensual at just the mention of herself.

'You think so?'

'White towelling is – how can I say? – amazing against that incredible skin. I tell you, that's how we must photograph you.'

Already he and Kaminski had had to agree, or rather E.F. had had to agree, to write a small, showy, very unwordy – with luck about two words – part to be written for Sofia in the new movie, to justify Kaminski's knocking her off, and also to allow him to get rid of her at the end of the picture, or whenever he became bored by her, whichever was the earlier.

'E.F., do you think that my part should be maybe written around this towelling robe, around my looking like this?'

'Sofia, I think this is the greatest idea, and now that

90

I see you in that against the crimson of that bed, even more so.'

'You really think so? Fix us both a drink, will you, E.F.? Scotch on the rocks.'

E.F. went to the bar and obediently did as he was told, all the while wondering that he still had not had to mention Kaminski or his whereabouts. Normally Sofia would badger him on this point, always suspicious that he was with some other girl, but now that he was with some other girl she seemed less than interested. More than that, she had parted the opening of her dressing gown and was now swinging a leg over the side of the bed, the rest of her magnificent and very ample body stretched out beneath the towelling.

'Do you think this would be a nice angle, E.F.?'

'Magnificent,' she was told, as he handed her a drink.

'Where is Kaminski?' she asked, after a thoughtful pause, and E.F. felt his heart sink. Now would surely be the start of a scene.

'He's been called away urgently, to see someone. You know some of the locations are going to be here in London . . . anyway, he won't be back until later tonight. He said you were to go on right ahead with the evening, and he'd be back in about one, maybe two.'

'Sure, I understand, sure.'

Sofia turned her magnificent amber-flecked brown eyes on E.F.

'Perhaps we could work out something together?' she murmured. 'Are you free right now?'

E.F. nodded. 'Sure, Sofia, I'm free.'

'Good, so am I.'

She smiled, and picking up his free hand she placed

it under her robe where the rise and fall of her amplitude was hidden, but not still.

'Lock the door, and let's rehearse,' she told him.

E.F. was only too glad to obey. He had rarely been so quick on his feet.

'Draw the blinds,' she commanded.

He did so, and as he did so he realized with a jolt that he too must be famous, for after all, would she be doing this if he wasn't?

As Sofia's white towelling robe fell open it seemed to E.F. that he maybe might allow her four words in the picture, not just two. A little later he adjusted that to a dozen.

Georgiana had forgotten just how dextrous Kaminski was at undressing not just himself, but her too. When they had first made love she had always thought it was something to do with his abilities as a director. But now it seemed to her that it had more to do with his abilities as a lover.

He kissed her in a way she had forgotten men could kiss, with a sort of deeply felt concentration, but not so long that it was tiring. Her dark hair swung around her body, and her arms went up around his neck and her face to his neat dark beard. She laughed up at him.

It was his turn to say 'So?' but not how Georgiana said it, how a very impatient man might say it. More meaning 'What of it?' or 'What now?'

'You are still so beautiful. No, worse, you are more beautiful, and I see you have had a child. That has given you a fuller figure.' He turned her round in front of him, back and forth. 'That is quite beautiful, the fuller breasts with the narrow waist.'

Still in her black silk, lace inset, newly bought slip, Georgiana felt her last command of the situation falling away from her. She was as helpless as she had ever been with this tall, dark, bearded man with his intellectualism and his strange films of which she understood not a word. She wondered briefly what it was that fascinated him, or her, about each other.

But it was only briefly, in the time that it takes for a thought to present itself, or an image, for from the second that Kaminski touched her they were caught in a complexity of sighs and sensations, rushing through however long it was to the other side of reality, to where only love counts the minutes.

Kaminski allowed himself to be astonished. Not for a second could he, even if he had wanted to, not for one second as he made love to her could he remain outside himself, a detached observer of his own sensual activities, as he was used to doing with his many other mistresses.

Georgiana's personality, not just her body, required his whole concentration. Perhaps it was her oddness, or her way of laughing at him, or her own seeming detachment, but when he finally lay back against the dark hangings of the bed, Kaminski was reminded of those weeks he had spent with her when he was filming all that time ago, when he had found it so difficult to be ruthless with her, to leave the flat, not shut the door, but lock it and throw away the key, as he always did with women.

Now as he looked at her beautiful face lying in his

arms, her eyes shut, a slender white hand under one pale cheek, he wondered to himself something he had never allowed himself to wonder before: perhaps she was, she might be, after all, everything he had ever wanted?

Fulton and Elliott stared at Lady Tizzy. They had waited until she had returned from the very expensive room at the very expensive private clinic that had only recently been built so conveniently near to Flint House, to approach the subject of Lady Tizzy's private life. But now that a decent interval had passed, they had both agreed that the nettle must be grasped.

'Although I'm not quite sure that is quite the right phrase or saying,' Fulton had murmured, as they proceeded up to her bedroom.

The way in which they had themselves passed through the really terrifying crisis that had faced them, was, they had also both agreed, magnificent. There was no other word for it. It was magnificent, it was stupendous, and it was undoubtedly the stuff of heroes. They had immediately hired another nurse to help Nanny, and now there was a tribe of starchly aproned people in the wing, the blue bird of happiness seemed once more to have settled on the roof of Flint House.

Nanny had been an angel, and, as it happened, without effort, for while Fulton and Elliott had longed for two daughters, Nanny had been yearning for a boy – 'So much more affectionate, Mr Fulton, really. Nanny's really pleased with her present.'

And so she was, humming happily as she changed nappies at what seemed half-hourly intervals, and leaving Daisy-Marguerita to the monthly nurses, and Victoria too.

'Of course she's quite abandoned Victoria now that we have a son. It's a shame, really. Not that Victoria seems to mind – she's besotted with the new monthly Irish nurse, and learning how to say "cheers", in Irish with her Ribena, which, after all, is fairly cosmopolitan.'

'I must say I still can't believe it, you know, not really,' said Elliott, sighing slightly, as if each time the realization made him just a little tireder than he had been before. 'You are going to tell her, of course? I mean you are going to be really, really strict about it?'

'Of course.'

'She won't like it.'

'Well, isn't that just too bad?'

'Mmm, suppose it is really.'

Neither of them ever entered Patti's room without first either putting on dark glasses, or totally suspending their sensitivities, positively posting them off to a far country, just in case they happened upon something they might not like, or saw something which might make Elliott feel a tiny bit faint.

This morning it seemed Lady Tizzy had awoken early, and then having executed her usual glamour over the room, festooning it with dropped diaphanous garments, retired back to bed in an enormous sleeved peignoir that puffed up round her ears in a way that was sensational, given that her hair was also piled up in extravagant mounds several inches above the sleeves, her mouth not just lipsticked, but glossed, and every one of her eyelashes carefully spiked with mascara. She had acquired a very large diamond ring from someone who

95

would doubtless prefer to remain nameless, but who Fulton and Elliott happened to know lived not very far from Flint House at the Hall. Quite obviously the arrival of the ring had coincided with the news of the twins' arrival, for it – the ring – had arrived at the hospital 'anonymously' – except that the package was postmarked Stanton, and very few people in Stanton, especially not anonymous people, could afford to send Lady Tizzy a ring the size of an ostrich egg made up entirely of very old, very expensive diamonds. Trade might be good, but not that good.

'Good morning, boys.' Lady Tizzy smiled at them.

'Good morning, darling,' said Fulton, and he leaned forward and kissed her affectionately, because he was after all her husband. Elliott just blew her a kiss from his fingertips, because he wasn't.

Ever since he entered the room he had stared right ahead at Lady Tizzy in the bed. Now he dared to look just slightly sideways, and around. These days the daily person who did for them came and did for Lady Tizzy's room too, because what with helping Twinks in the stable with papier mâché reproduction trays, and the Cathedral fund, Elliott had found that he just hadn't the time to spend retrieving old Del Monte tins from under her ladyship's bed.

The daily who came and went, Elliott quickly noticed, had done quite well, but she had fallen, as everyone did, by the wayside, and abandoned all hope, as even the bravest might, when it came to Lady Tizzy's dressing table.

It was an altar to the art of salesmanship. In the centre was a bowl of lipsticks, filled to the brim in a kind of plasti-clad confusion, a pot pourri of the old and the new in lip coatings. Then there were the innumerable plastic cases full of face blushers and powders, the small puffs, the big puffs, the half-filled bottles of scent, and even of perfume, clustered together in groups, small and large, old-fashioned and new. Like members of the chorus, they seemed to be staring around them wondering if they would be the chosen one when Lady Tizzy next visited the scene of her face before her dressing glass. And over everything lay not dust but a thin coating of face powder, because she dearly loved her largest puff, a lengthy affair on a stick with a ribbon on the bottom, and would wave it in a mad fairy gesture over her face before departing for whatever she had never in mind. It was a gesture that always mesmerized Elliott whenever he saw it, and he felt he would be quite unsurprised, if, as she finally finished, he had vanished.

'So how are we feeling?'

Patti looked momentarily saddened by this question.

'You sound just like that silly gynaecologist,' she sighed. 'Next thing you'll be asking me if I'm thrilled with my pigeon pair, and whether I've—'

'Oh no we won't,' Fulton and Elliott chorused.

'No,' said Fulton firmly, sitting down on her bed, and leaving Elliott to sit in the buttoned Colefax and Fowler bedroom chair. 'No, we have something else to talk to you about, which the doctor certainly won't talk about.'

'Oh.' Patti looked from one to the other surprised. 'You're not leaving me 'cos I had twins, are you? I didn't mean to,' she added, bursting into tears, but only a very little, not enough to make her mascara run.

'I certainly am not leaving you, and nor is Elliott, but

we certainly are going to talk to you, quite strongly, about your position, our position, the whole family's position, and most especially the bank manager.'

'This is a deportation—'

'No, but it could be if you don't listen.'

'Deposition is what you meant,' Elliott told her helpfully. 'And you're right, it is.'

Patti looked away from them both, and her eyes, large and suddenly conveniently blank, stared at a little bird pecking on her window sill.

'I know what you're going to say, you're going to say I've got to take a job to help support the kids, that's what you're going to say.'

'No, nothing quite as bad as that,' Fulton comforted her, but his voice remained grave. 'But two things have got to happen. First, you have to tell certain people that there are grave responsibilities attached to fatherhood, and our bank manager would appreciate some assistance towards these crippling responsibilities, and secondly—' Fulton paused, 'secondly, someone around here is going to have to have an operation of – shall we say – curtailment? Because three is quite enough, if not two too many.'

'You were quite happy about Daisy-Marguerita.'

'Of course I was, but being a father to a son is quite different.'

'I don't see why?'

Fulton got up and walked to the window.

'I shall have to sell the gold Golf, and wear quite different trousers,' he told her after a pause. 'And that's just the start. I shall have to start thinking about prep schools, and visiting headmasters in nasty three piece tweed suits and sporting some infernal public school tie.'

'But you went to a public school—'

'Bad enough.'

'You went to—'

'I know where I went, thank you.'

'You were there with Pember.'

'I know. I just never thought I'd have to go back there, especially not to put the little wretch down.'

'You can't put him down, I shan't let you!' Patti wailed.

'That's what you do for schools,' Elliott explained gently. 'It's not like going to the vet. You just put them down, so they can go up, or be sent down, or whatever it is they do to the next school, or to that school, and it's fine.'

'Well, and what happens after that?'

'Oh, they just grow up as stupid as everyone else, and get to wear a rather silly tie, and keep quiet about it, except in front of headmasters or people who work in ICI. You mustn't worry.'

'Were you put down, Elliott?' Patti asked him, sniffing.

'Yes, but not for long. I had very frail health so I was sent to Switzerland, where all I learned to be was a pastry chef, the fees they charged were vast, but so long as I was away and at school my parents were quite happy. Besides, it was much nicer. But we don't want Beau to have frail health, so he must be put down, and then we can see, see?'

'Yes,' said Patti doubtfully, because she quite obviously didn't. 'And then what?'

99

'Well, then Beau has to go away to another school when he's about eight, to a really horrid prep school where the headmaster and mistress will be married and pretending to be terribly nice, but actually waiting until all the parents have driven off so they can rush upstairs and produce canes and whips and beat the poor little devils into such a heap that when their parents come and fetch them after the first month, all they ever dare tell them is how much fun they're having.'

'Fulton!'

'Elliott's being very naughty,' said Fulton. 'We shan't let that happen to Beau.'

'No, of course not,' Elliott agreed, 'but it usually does, if you're not very careful and give fearfully large donations to the school rebuilding fund, or pay for the whole staff to go on skiing holidays.'

'But when we had Victoria none of this had to happen.'

'No, it's different for girls,' Fulton agreed. 'You can send them to very pretty places where very gentle things happen, and no-one minds at all.'

'Well, why can't Beau be sent to a very gentle place where pretty things happen?'

'I don't know, darling, but he can't.'

'Oh, Fulton, you're right, you're both right. None of this should have happened. I mean, we'll have to get a second nanny, won't we?'

'Don't worry. Fulton has already booked a young person from the village with suitable credentials.'

'Oh, what are they?'

'She used to keep pigs. No, she's fine, the daughter of the district nurse, Twinks knows her, very suitable.

She's quite ugly, and Nanny will scare her rigid and make her do lots of crochet when she's watching telly.'

'Oh, the poor babies—' Patti wailed again.

'Of course you could look after them,' said Elliott doubtfully. 'You could help Nanny on her day off.'

Patti immediately stopped wailing which they both knew she would.

'Last time I did that she said she never wanted to see me in the nursery again,' Patti told them bravely.

'She was right. Now about the curtailment.'

'No, don't worry, I'll see to it. After all, something's got to be done, hasn't it?'

'That's one way of putting it. Of course you could just give up seeing each other,' Fulton added hopefully.

'Oh, we could,' Patti agreed, 'but you know what happened last time. We didn't see each other, and then we did, and all of a sudden it was like one of those Saturday afternoon movies. We have no need to speak, we just look at each other, and that's it. Quite mindless it is.'

'Wordless,' said Elliott automatically, avoiding Fulton's eyes, while Fulton did his best to find something very cold to look at, and failed.

'Well, long as that's all right, that's all right,' said Fulton at last. 'Now we're off to the nursery. Want to come?'

'Not really,' Patti sighed, 'Nanny only really likes you two.'

'I'm not surprised,' Elliott murmured as he shut the door.

Fulton and Elliott walked along to the nursery wing

in the usual stunned silence that always followed a visit to Lady Tizzy's boudoir.

'You've got to admit there's no-one else quite like her,' said Elliott.

'I'll admit anything as long as she calls a halt to the production line,' sighed Fulton. He paused as he reached out to the beautifully decorated nursery door handle, all hand done by Elliott, little tiny bears and things with a matching finger plate with 'V' for Victoria entwined within more little tiny bears. 'I mean, Nanny told me last night that we've had so many babies so quickly the village is beginning to suspect I'm a left-footer.'

'I'm going to have to re-do those finger plates to add "D" and "B",' murmured Elliott as they passed through into the nursery rooms.

Inside everything was a riot of activity. Two monthly nurses laying down the twins in cradles, only one of which was the reproduction of the Duc de Berry, Beau's having had to be hastily borrowed and draped with blue ribbons. Victoria was running from one cradle to the other wearing a beautifully starched dress that Elliott had had made for her, and it certainly suited her lovely blonde hair.

'Daisy-Marguerita looks exactly like Victoria did at the same age, Mr Fulton, the spit of yourself.'

Fulton gazed down at his newest daughter.

'Miracles happen every day,' murmured Elliott.

Fulton gazed at the babies, but only briefly, before sitting down in the wicker nursing chair and looking round him in fascination. Flint House was not a vast house, but it was big enough, and now it had somehow even managed to accommodate not one new baby but two, and not mind. Everywhere there was a nice clean smell of freshly laundered linen. Elliott and Nanny had fallen into one of their deep discussions about drawn thread work and smocking. Things, after all, might be worse.

When Pemberton got a message from Bloss it was always in code. The only trouble was the code was sometimes somewhat difficult to read. For instance before Lady Tizzy got banged up for the second time, when they were meeting in the pool house at regular and very sublime moments, Bloss would leave out a bag of oats in the snug. If on the other hand she was unable to meet, and had rung Bloss on the staff telephone, then at the usual hour Pemberton had only to pop his head round the snug door to see no bag of oats to know the score. It was a simple sort of code, and it worked.

This particular afternoon Pemberton had been feeling just a little ishish. Jennifer was in one of her preoccupied moods, all tatting and chatting about this infernal party-thing she was insisting on giving. He had been happily gardening when she came out and started to pace the lawn, for all the world like a water diviner without a stick, muttering and murmuring about the size of the suspended floor and heaven knew what, with the result that Pemberton had had to go into the house just to get away from the irritation of the sight of her in her gardening shoes saying 'No, that's wrong' every fifteen seconds, and going back to the apple tree to start again.

It was while he was walking by the snug that Pemberton had popped his head round the door, for no other reason than habit, and had seen the glorious sight of the bag of oats. The dearest sight in the world to him, quite honestly, and so he'd hurried off to the pool house to meet his inamorata, newly restored to her divinely curvaceous shape.

'What a wonderful surprise,' he whispered. 'You little darling.'

'I've missed you, Pember,' Lady Tizzy told him. 'I love Fulton and Elliott but frankly we just don't share the same interests.'

'Well, you wouldn't.'

'No, we don't. And I mean babies is fine, but after you've had them, and I mean they're all right and everything, who wants to talk about them all day long? They love it, but you know, there is a limit. And anyway Nanny only really loves them, she doesn't much like mummies, she always says they interfere with her work, so there's not much for me to do right now.'

'No, well, there wouldn't be,' Pember agreed, pausing in his act of kissing her deliciously soft white neck. 'Goodness, I have missed you. Your poitrine is like no other.'

'This is not a poitrine, Pember darling,' said Lady Tizzy, teasing him. 'You are funny. It's called a "bustier".'

'By "poitrine" I meant that which is within the bustier—' Pemberton began, but then seeing Lady Tizzy's expression of innocent enquiry, he dropped the subject and turned to the item in question.

Patti stopped him. Not that she wanted to, because she loved her Pember so much, and it was already beginning to be quite like the old days, but she knew her duty, and she must be loyal to Fulton. Whatever happened she owed something to Fulton, most of all not to have any more babies.

'The thing is, Pember,' she began, still whispering. 'I've not come here just to talk to you and all that. No, I've come to tell you about the twins and Victoria and everything.'

'Oh.' Pemberton's face fell. 'I see.'

He didn't, of course, but he always said 'I see' when he needed time. He looked up helplessly at Lady Tizzy's beautiful face. He did hope she wasn't going to talk babies like Jennifer. It would make him want to end it all if she did. Normally the magnificent thing about Lady Tizzy was that she just wanted to make love, she never talked babies. Sometimes being with her was just like being with a real friend, a person, not just a woman.

'I've promised Fulton, no more babies, see? So one of us, if we're going to go on seeing each other, one of us is going to have to do something, you know.'

'You don't mean not see each other?' asked Pemberton, shocked and panicked.

'No, silly, do something, you know, go for a very little cheap little – curtailment Fulton called it. They do them everywhere now, apparently, Fulton says. Specially for men. There's even an advertisement in the *Parishioner* for it. You just ring up, and that's it, ever after plenty of oats and no more babies.'

'Jennifer reads the *Parishioner* from cover to cover,' said Pemberton doubtfully.

'Yes, well she would. So does Elliott, that's how come he read me out the ad. Here it is.'

Patti opened a handbag bulging with old love letters

105

and handed Pemberton a tiny scrap of cheap magazine paper. Pemberton took out his half-moon spectacles, and placed them on his nose. He read 'Men! You want it? Come and get it! Just ten minutes and the wife's best friend can really be that! Call *Real Man* for a carefree lovelife!'

'Sounds good,' Pemberton told Lady Tizzy.

'Yah, and it really works,' Patti told him. 'Really. So will you be a good man and go?'

Pemberton looked across at Lady Tizzy. The bustier was doing everything except contain her magnificent prow. He knew what she meant. To be really carefree there could be no more babies for either of them. Altogether he now had six within two miles of each other, and on both sides of the blankets. His title was secure, his wife was virtuous, his mistress was divine, and he was rich. Considering everything, he had to face it: it was his duty to make sure that Fulton and Elliott should no longer suffer from his insane passion for Lady Tizpots.

'Very well,' he said. 'Very well, I will be a man, and go to *Real Man*.'

'I knew you would,' said Patti happily.

She got up to go.

'Not yet, please,' Pemberton whispered desperately. 'Please, not yet.'

'Once you're a real man Bloss can leave out the oats every day,' Lady Tizzy whispered back, before moving out of his reach, and referring to yet another piece of paper from her handbag.

'Oh yes. Next is putting Beau down for the usual schools, and endowments. Apparently Fulton just

106

doesn't make enough from reproduction antiques, even though the trays have really taken off.'

Pemberton sighed. It really was going to be like being with Jennifer. Humbly he took this second piece of paper from Lady Tizzy. He'd do anything for her. It was no use pretending he wouldn't. Anything. Even go to *Real Man*.

5

As Georgiana awoke in her hotel room, without Kaminski by her side thank heavens, she wondered a little. Not just at herself, but at everything. She wondered at life, which seemed to be a continual set of either clashes, or engagements, or devolvements or, as in this case, re-involvements.

She sat up, letting her long shining dark hair tickle the sides of her shoulders, and then very quickly she glanced at herself in the hand mirror that she always placed to the side of her bed, together with a small handbag-sized bottle of scent, and a comb. Sometimes she wished that she wasn't so vain, and sometimes, as now, she was very glad that she was. After all if she had not been a little vain she would not now be staring at herself with such satisfaction in the hand mirror, and she would not be remembering yesterday evening with quite the same sense of delicate, if sensual, delight.

She lay back against the pillows and sighed happily. It was terrible, it was awful, what she had done was quite out of line, but it was real, and it had happened, and she had let it, and she didn't mind one bit that she had. Then, having thought of all that, which because she was in a lovely mood was some effort, she wondered idly what it was that she had done.

It could not be called a 'one night stand', because it

had only been early evening. It could not be called the start of an affair, because she'd already had one with Kaminski, and anyway it had ended. It could not be called adultery, because she wasn't married. It might be called fornication, but then to be called fornication surely you had to do it a lot, and she had only done it once. Once was simply not enough to be such a long and serious word. She stared at the ceiling rose, a rather ghastly affair, mock plaster, really plastic, picked out carefully in pink. She would have to find the word for what she had done with Kaminski before she stepped out of bed and into the shower.

'Partied' was too American, and anyway seemed to imply that other people had been involved. She continued to stare at her reflection. It had certainly not been an orgy, and she could not, ever, copulate, that wouldn't be her at all. Nor could she have done any of the things that Gus sometimes referred to, such as 'had it off', ghastly things that made you think of alleyways and dustbins. At last the proper phrase to describe what she had done with Kaminski entered her mind, and like all proper phrases that were exactly right it was entirely simple. She had made love.

As soon as she realized what she had done Georgiana put her feet on the thick pile carpet and pattered over to the shower. She knew she could not have got on with the day until she had found out what she had done the evening before, so quietly and so passionately, with Kaminski. It would have preyed on her conscience all day if she had not been able to think of the right word or phrase. People who did not know what they had done were always a terrific bore. They got drunk and they

109

made life difficult for other people, which was not the way to be. As long as you knew what you had done you could quite safely get on with the day and not feel guilty, or as if everyone was looking at you and knew what you had done, even if you didn't. To have made love was a beautiful thing, to have been made love to beautifully was a wondrous thing; Georgiana could now float through the day feeling wondrous, and beautiful.

She dressed carefully, putting on a monstrously simple new dress that had cost a great deal of money, but which she could pay for, since she had been saving up for what felt like years, and now it seemed to her it had been all worthwhile, not just because she loved new dresses, particularly when they were monstrously simple and completely new, but also because she thought she quite deserved them. Her body after all was still fairly lovely, and so was her face. Not to be nice to them would be silly, like neglecting a building, or not polishing a piece of silver, and quite as wasteful. She stood in front of the dressing table and bent her knees. The dress was of a lovely rich blue. The colour reflected in her eyes. Georgiana leaned forward to the mirror and gazed into them. They too were monstrously simple and lovely.

The train journey home was full of delightful expectation. She had lunched alone, wearing dark glasses, and thinking to herself how lucky it was that a lonely and unhappy childhood had made her appreciate her own company; no, not just appreciate it – relish it. As she lunched she did not long for the company of other girls, with their silly observations about their boyfriends or husbands, and their prying ways as to her own good or bad fortunes.

'Is Gus still selling those funny little card things of his? Oh, he is, good. He must get awfully tired of them. You certainly look tired. Terribly tired. You don't feel tired? Well, you certainly look it. I don't suppose you've had a holiday in years, have you? You certainly look as if you haven't had a holiday in years. You should put on some weight. It would suit you. Really.'

No, she didn't miss lunching with girlfriends. Nothing nice was ever said over lunch, certainly not at any she had ever been at, anyway. The only thing a person should hear at lunch was 'Are you ready to order, please?'

And Georgiana had been. She had been very ready to order *oeufs mollets* – soft-boiled eggs gone cold with a sort of pale green mayonnaise coating. Very good. Then a tiny little chicken breast carved into a fan on another sauce of a pale lemon colour with one or two beans to the side. Utterly pleasant, she thought, remembering how good it had all tasted, and how with a glass of cold champagne and white wine she had been able to sit back and savour her meeting with Kaminski, its subtlety and nuance, and its superb passion. In the far distance, from the train window, she saw from the approaching water tower that Penbury station, her station, was about to appear. Georgiana sighed happily. That was the whole point of going to London, wasn't it? So that she could appreciate, or re-appreciate, Longborough and Gus, and even Nan and Nanny. By the time she had driven herself slowly home through the winding lanes they would all have changed for the better. And that too was what had to be said in favour of making love, about making love: it changed everything for the better, made you feel quite able to cope with things like dried flowers and Gus and

111

his eternal quest for something that everyone knew didn't exist.

Georgiana sang a light snatch of Mozart, something she didn't even remember she knew, and in Italian too.

Kaminski stared at E.F.

'I don't believe what I'm hearing,' he said slowly.

'No, really,' E.F. stated. 'I read her last night, when you were otherwise occupied, when you needed me to keep her quiet, and she was really quite excellent.'

At that moment, as Kaminski turned and stared at him, E.F. was only too glad that he was a scriptwriter. Not a terribly brilliant scriptwriter perhaps, but not a terribly terrible one either, which was just as well in the circumstances. The circumstances were that Kaminski was now giving E.F. his number one deep director's look and not believing a word he was trying to say, and E.F. was remembering to look furtive, and to not look Kaminski in the eye, which would double bluff Kaminski, a quite considerable chess player, into thinking that E.F. was looking so underhand he must be telling the truth.

'Sofia read well? You have to be picking peppered pickles, as my old nurse would say. You're lying to me, aren't you?'

'No, really. She read really well, and – and she read long, I mean we read along together quite a bit, and she was – terrific. Really.'

'So what are we talking about? You want to put her forward for the part of whom?'

'The part she really impressed me with was the girl

who comes out of the sea and seduces the marine biologist.'

Kaminski put down his coffee cup, and turning to the chimneypiece in his suite, he carefully lit a cigar, something he normally never did in the morning unless he had just been to a breakfast meeting.

'The girl who seduces Harris has at least seventy lines, and I don't think Sofia is capable of saying more than seven words on celluloid, and then only on a week by week basis, one word a week for seven weeks, leaving plenty of room either side for dubbing. E.F., tell me, please, what happens to you the moment I let you out of my sight? I was only gone a few hours – two hours.'

'It was only an idea,' E.F. said, feebly, while all his insides trembled with the thought of what Kaminski might do to him if he found out that he had tasted of his, Kaminski's, private store of fruit. Never mind that he had been preoccupied with some other far more fatale femme, that he had been cheating on Sofia. Kaminski was an aristocrat, a White Russian, anyway in his own mind, and every slave girl within a hundred miles of his set was his by droit de director, and heaven help some overweight randy scriptwriter like E.F. who might come between him and his divine, utterly divine right. Directors. They got all the fun. E.F. sighed mightily. He had to get Sofia something or else, or else indeed. 'How was our heroine?' he asked after a short pause.

Kaminski took a long draw on his cigar. They both knew who 'our heroine' was, she around whom they had written a very cheap, very successful film.

'She's changed. She's different.'

'Lost her innocence, huh?'

'No, not lost her innocence, gained even more.'

E.F. stared at Kaminski. For once he was interested in what he was going to say next. Being the egoist E.F. most surely was, he found he only really became interested in something when he was extremely interested in it. The rest of the time he was merely pretending to be where his body was, his mind being elsewhere, usually at some scene from the night before, preferably a good one. Because he was so interested, he said nothing, and merely waited until Kaminski chose to continue, which he knew Kaminski liked, and which he knew was very effective because he sometimes, not often, but sometimes, liked to use such pauses and phrasing in his scripts.

'What has happened,' Kaminski went on slowly, 'is that she's had a baby, and she's matured because of it, not because she wants to, of course – our heroine would never consciously mature – but the experience, quite naturally and simply, has changed her, given her more confidence, and made her aware, not of her charms, but of her own desires.'

E.F. frowned. Certainly to him Georgiana had looked, if that was possible, even more beautiful, but still very much a class act. He certainly hadn't noticed any overt self-consciousness.

'It was that good?' he asked Kaminski, giving him a wry look, and pouring them both some more coffee.

'Oh, it was more than that good,' Kaminski told him. 'It was perfection.'

E.F. stared. It was unfair. Here was a man who could have anything, and usually did. Who could have the world's most beautiful women, for whom women lined

114

up to be noticed. Yet it was not enough that he travelled with the kind of mistress that would keep most men in nights, he had also to take a couple of hours out to go and find 'perfection' with a young British aristocrat.

'You don't really want to make this picture, do you?' he asked Kaminski, because he wanted to throw him, and because he felt insatiably jealous that this man was able to enjoy his life in such a way that he never even paused to think about someone else who might not be enjoying theirs at the same level, i.e. his best friend and scriptwriter E.F. 'I always know with you when you don't want to make a picture; your eyes go glazed when I mention it. They glazed over when I just mentioned Harris or Jumby Island, they become what the French call *en gelée*, they become set in an aspic boredom. I-must- write-that-down.'

'It's not that good,' Kaminski told him as E.F. immediately obeyed himself.

'Not to you,' E.F. agreed, 'but to me it could be liquid gold one soggy, foggy morning in London Town when I'm in a white heat facing the white sheet, and not the kind I like, but the one that goes in the typewriter.'

Kaminski didn't even bother to shrug his shoulders, or to disagree with E.F. He knew, they both knew, that it was true. He was bored with making a picture about a marine biologist, but as Henry Fonda had said, and wisely, it was the 'Sex and the Single Girl' pictures that paid for the 'Twelve Angry Men' pictures, and he spoke for all of them. Making pictures was a business. It might be a business that needed and used great art, and sometimes even great artists, but nevertheless it was a business, and if he had to make a picture about a marine biologist he would, and then next time round, as always happened, he would be allowed to make a picture about whatever he wished, and just so long as both were successful he would be all right, and that fat chump, the red-headed freckled face E.F., would be too.

'Come on, to work,' he told E.F.

'No thanks for keeping Sofia quiet?'

'No. Because you didn't. She woke me this morning with nothing but your promise, your damn promise, to give her lines. So, thanks to you, she will have to be written a part, by you, and then she will be given it, and I will have to shoot it, and then we will have to cut it. So your method of keeping actresses quiet is very expensive. It will now cost thousands of dollars to keep Sofia quiet.'

'But from the look of you, it will be worth every penny, huh? You are wearing your number one ''OK, give the kid some lines look'', Kaminski. I know that look. You won't regret it.'

Kaminski said nothing. He knew how he looked. Tall, dark-bearded, slim, elegant, perfectly shod and perfectly clothed, yes, he knew all that, but he didn't know how he actually looked, whether he looked different, even if he looked different. He couldn't deny he felt different, as if every moment of his life now had added significance. That cup, the taste of the coffee mingling with the rich taste of the cigar, the way the sunlight was falling on the floor, just in front of the book-filled table, they were all being seen by him as if for both the last time and the first. He didn't believe in love, of course he didn't, probably because with the women at his disposal he didn't need to believe in love. That was what power did for you, it made it possible to avoid love as you would avoid the measles. Yet last evening, as Georgiana lay in his arms, something had happened to him, something he had never wanted to have happen to him: he held something, someone, in his arms whom he didn't want to leave (he always wanted to leave everyone) and that he didn't understand. He knew himself too well not to know that the panic he had felt as he dressed and left the room was the fear that he might have just made love to someone who was capable of understanding him. It therefore followed that he must avoid that person. Tonight, he resolved, he would make terrifyingly passionate love to Sofia. They would have a scene, not the kind that she loved to make, but the kind that Kaminski liked her to create. Only that way could he perhaps drown the memory of that dark-haired girl who had smiled at him as he let himself out of her suite, a smile that told him he was free, absolutely free, to go, and what was better, so was she.

'Back to Harris,' said Kaminski, 'scene a hundred and eighty. He is just about to set up a marine biology station on Jumby when he discovers that the Republican candidate has vetoed—'

'Scene a hundred and fifty now, on the re-write,' E.F. reminded him. 'But maybe that is beside the point.'

What the point was going to be he didn't quite know, nor did E.F. quite care. He had won Sofia her little part and by so doing he had concealed from Kaminski that he had made a successful pass at his, Kaminski's, presumably prized mistress. Really, all in all, E.F. thought to himself, he had done more than well, he had been very successful, and what's more, judging from the

117

way that the esteemed director of the picture was humming 'Violets for her Fur', E.F. could only imagine that he might have a chance of making another equally successful pass at the same lady some fine afternoon soon, if not soonest.

The end of the afternoon was always the Countess's favourite time of day, and now in late spring, looking at the lovely soft colours all around from the safe haven of her newly structured conservatory, it was proving even more satisfactory, and that despite the smell of Andrew's nasty cigarette which was drifting over the box hedge from the wild garden. Moving to Wiltshire from Sussex had, the Countess reflected, proved immensely success-ful for her personally. (People nowadays were always saying 'personally' as if they were forever in doubt about who they actually were. Perhaps it was some sort of backlash from everyone dropping 'one'.)

Of course, she thought, watching a cat stalking something through a small patch of grass under the old apple tree, she was well aware to what the success of Wiltshire was due, and that was her quite astounding ability to hold on to those nearest to her, and attract their continuing irritation. After all, there was very little point in living to a moderately early old age if you couldn't enjoy the fruits of your own mischief, just no point at all. It would make not having a second gin and tonic at lunchtime, and not having a second glass of cham-pagne at dinner, quite pointless, all that sacrifice for nothing.

She sighed a little with the satisfaction of everything. She had won a battle over Andrew, not just finding a use for him – walker to the aristocracy – but also insisting on his smoking out of the house. She had won a victory over life at the Hall, by backing out of the private ball arrangements, and so early that both Fulton and Jennifer had been left gasping. That was something she knew from military history. Strike when the enemy least expects it, early, and preferably after a short ceasefire. It was always most successful.

It had been a terrible scene, of course, of the kind that the Countess really enjoyed. First there had been the 'call' to Jennifer on the Countess's return from her horrid day in London. A short stilted conversation during which Jennifer had become perfectly aware that there was something wrong, that the Countess was mightily displeased, or she would not be requesting an urgent and important meeting of the ball committee. (Not that a private ball had a committee as such, but it certainly had to have steerage, and the Countess for one was determined that her hand was to come off the tiller.)

Then there had been the now famous, to the Countess and Bloss at least, meeting, during the course of which the Countess triumphantly gave everyone, that is Fulton and Jennifer, to understand that she would not be continuing with any help with the ball, she was bowing, or rather curtsying, out and leaving them to get on with it, as they wished, on their own, and never mind her, because it would be a far, far better thing that she did.

'But we've just changed everything from peach to cream and green,' Fulton had protested.

'Change it back, Fulton dear,' the Countess had told him, her eyes glittering with enjoyment, 'let peach tones commence, what you will. I am far too taken up with my little charity for distressed field mice.'

'Distressed field mice?'

They had both looked unbelieving, astonished, and vaguely insulted at that, as if the Countess was mocking them quite openly, which she was, because she was actually still smarting from the 'dear old thing' reference in Jennifer's letter to Mary.

'Field mice are becoming increasingly and distressingly rare. Myself and Colonel Bentley in the village have started a charity to conserve them. Hedgehogs have been well catered for, badgers are being assiduously guarded by those in the know, but field mice are suffering an alarming decrease in numbers. It's most important that we do something, and the Colonel and I are. We are establishing ideal habitats for the little creatures, protesting to farmers who spray and cut and maim our fields and set fire to everything. It is a very strong movement, a rural movement, a movement such as you would never find on the continent. Oh no.'

At that she had risen, snapped her perfectly worn handbag to, and stalked from the room, a friend of field mice, a foe of the ball. The effect had been alarmingly good, apparently. It had left everyone gasping, the Countess learned from dear Bloss, who had telephoned her a few days later to tell her that the early asparagus that he always 'let her have' was ready to be picked up by her help.

'Her ladyship is so concerned, she has come out in a nasty rash at the back of her neck,' Bloss had told her after the usual exchanges to do with tips and stalks, and hot butter sauce versus vinaigrette. 'No, Lady Pemberton is not at all herself at the moment. She is something other, I'm afraid, your ladyship, she is – how can I say it? – put out. Yes, that would be the word, put out by so many decisions. You see, Mr Fulton, as she explained to me only yesterday, Mr Fulton has his own worries and cares, the reproductions, the papier mâché trays and matching wastepaper baskets, they take up quite a little of his time, with the consequence that he really is not always available in the way that you, your ladyship, has always been available at all times. It's a quandary, if I may say so, your ladyship, and Lady Pemberton is not good with quandaries, they get her in a muddle. I've noticed it before. When the rose garden was altered she became so agitated, the doctor had to be sent for to prescribe a nice dose of herbal remedies. He's half and half, you know, Doctor Stillworthy, half herbal half lethal is what his lordship says. Still, they did the trick, the herbals, they got her on her feet and back out into the garden in no time.'

The Countess sipped her gin and tonic minutely. They were having the asparagus tonight. Very good it would be too, judging from the tiny tips of it that she had seen peeping through the top of the double boiler as Maria, quite rightly, fussed around them as if she had grown them herself. After the asparagus and tiny thin pieces of brown bread and butter they would have a little fish. Little pieces of fish that would go with the earliest of the Hall's tiny new carrots. Bloss was indeed a culinary godfather.

She must think of some way to help him in return for all his little back door gifts to Maria. Something she could do which would make him very happy, something that he lacked and she could bring about. The idea dawned halfway down her gin and tonic. Of course! If dear Pember cancelled the whole idea of the ball, refused to come up trumps with the wherewithal, and it could be seen to have been due to Bloss and only Bloss's invaluable manoeuvrings, if he could be credited with such a coup, then there was no doubt at all that Bloss would be in a position to indicate that so great a saving must be of benefit, and Pember would immediately order him up the new 'Pewgot' Starduster to which Bloss had, it seemed, referred quite longingly to Maria only yesterday.

'He does love the newest registration does Mr Bloss,' Maria had murmured affectionately. 'He says it puts him up with the rest if he's driving the newest reg, and they wouldn't be able to look down on him in the King's Arms when he parked there, not the way they do now with a two-year-old Vauxhall Astra manual.'

As the Countess savoured the new young asparagus, while resolutely blocking out the sound of Andrew savouring his, she resolved that Bloss would get his Pewgot Starduster, come what may. And Pember would get his saving.

Having backed out of any responsibility for it, the Countess was resolved, perfectly resolved, that the ball must not go on. It would quite wrong, for so many reasons, some of which were even now being given their bottles at Flint House. Pemberton, although his dear wife couldn't know it, must not give a ball, if only for the sake of his children. Six in all, at least four of whom were mistakes. (There was no doubt about it, he had no trouble in reproducing, but then the Melburys never had, not since the Conquest, when as far as anyone could gather they seemed to have fairly flooded Dorset and Wiltshire, and even been involved in the Cathedral when it first needed a fund in 1102.) No, the ball had to be cancelled, and soon, before the peach pleating for the inside of the hired tents had been done, and well before Elliott had decided on the finger food.

The Countess dabbed her lips with her napkin. The second course, after the delicious asparagus, was just a little disappointing, as entrées so often were after really good hors d'oeuvres. Still, Andrew had chosen a good claret, the kind of claret that made you gaze on the future with a great deal more certainty than you had in the past, the future being not just the challenge of the field mice, but the challenge of bringing about the demise of the ball. Mary would be of help, she felt sure, in little things anyway, persuading people who might like the idea, well beforehand of course, that the ball was going to be dull, that no-one great or grand was going to go to it, that it was not going to be a gold plate affair, that it would be little more than a hop, and a lot less than a ball. She would ring her in the morning. What would they all do without the telephone?

'Any more asparagus, Bloss?' Pemberton enquired of his butler.

Jennifer looked up. She wouldn't have minded some more either. The butter sauce had been really rather perfect, better than vinaigrette, and she and Pember had rather enjoyed dabbing their little pieces of French bread from the delicatessen in Stanton in it.

'I'm afraid there has been a small failure in that

department,' Bloss told his lordship, in his best 'deeply regret' voice, 'but Cook tells me there will be another grand supply tomorrow.'

'I should say there should be, Bloss, another great grand one. Those asparagus beds were laid out by my grandfather and used to supply enough asparagus for a fortnight's guests, a whole house full. I should say there should be a great, grand supply!'

Jennifer nodded vigorously as he spoke. Pember and she were as one on this, absolutely. After all, the asparagus season was only short, and if Pember couldn't have more when he wanted, then she too would want to know why tomorrow.

'Do you think he's been selling it off?' she hissed to Pember, after Bloss had withdrawn, taking with him his heated trolley.

'I don't know,' muttered Pemberton, reluctant to think less of his esteemed butler. 'No, I don't think so. Just didn't get Chapple to dig enough, probably.'

Nevertheless, he did wonder. It wasn't as if there weren't asparagus beds aplenty. But even as he wondered Pemberton was uneasily aware that he was not exactly in a position to quiz Bloss on the subject. If Bloss had had only a limited supply of asparagus, he also had in his possession a little bag of oats. That little bag of oats had quite a tale to tell, and it wasn't the sort of tale that Jennifer would enjoy if she heard it.

'Yes,' he repeated quickly. 'Just didn't get enough dug, I should think.'

Jennifer stared across the table at her husband. He was looking really rather beautiful and handsome tonight. Blue shirt, blue tie, blue suit. She liked him in blue. He was, had been, considered one of the most handsome men of his generation, it had said in a small inset in *Harpers & Queen* only last month. Very handsome, very elegant in his way. A little wayward, which after all was only to be expected from a man of his wealth, power and lineage. His only problem, as far as she was concerned, was his reluctance to write a cheque to put into her allowance account, so that she could really get the Ball rolling. Without the wherewithal, now becoming rather blatantly and badly needed, as dear Fulton had pointed out this morning, they could not even order up the peach pleating for the tents, or retain a jazz group for the late night disco in the dungeons.

'Pember?'

'Yes, my sweet?' answered Pemberton, feeling inordinately fond of Jennifer as he always did, once he thought of Lady Tizzy and her bag of oats.

'Pember, would you like to come for a walk in the grounds?'

'Oh, very well,' answered Pemberton, looking down at his lamb cutlet and then across at his wife. 'Might I finish my dinner first?'

'Of course, Pember,' said Jennifer graciously, 'but hurry. There's a full moon, and I want you to see the lovely dog fox coming down to the fish pond.'

'Lovely dog fox!' Pemberton's lamb cutlet turned to ashes in his mouth. 'You can't expect me to admire a dog fox, not with the amount of ducks and chickens we keep.'

'Oh, but I can,' Jennifer told him seriously. 'I have planted herbs around the fish pond, and he comes down to eat them. Mrs Chapple told Chapple that if there are herbs around the fish pond, Mr Fox will simply snip, snip, snip his herb dinner, and leave the chickens alone. It works. They do it in Australia.'

'They do a lot of things in Australia,' growled Pemberton, 'that I wouldn't want done here.'

'Why, what do they do in Australia that you wouldn't want done here, Pember?'

'They drink tea.'

'So do we.'

'They drink beer.'

'So do we.'

'They have kangaroos.'

'So could we. They've got them at Woburn, or Longleat, somewhere like that.'

'All right. But even so, I don't want herbs here feeding foxes. I don't want to watch foxes either, they make me think of dead chickens, can't help it.'

'Very well, come for a walk anyway. New moon, lovely new moon to look at.'

Pemberton pushed his cutlet away. He might as well face it, it was a great deal easier to do what Jennifer wanted than not to do what Jennifer wanted.

Out in the garden Jennifer wandered ahead of Pember, looking and looking in the moonlight for somewhere quite private, somewhere very private.

'Pember?'

'Mmm?'

'How about here?'

'What about here?' asked Pemberton, staring at a lush piece of well grown long grass that set off some really rather mighty pampas grass he had planted, to his mind anyway, to perfection.

126

'How about succumbing to wild urges here?'

Jennifer dropped her gaze from the moon down to Pember's really rather well lit face.

'I don't think I want herbs here, Jennifer—' said Pemberton, looking puzzled.

'Not herbs here, us here, Pember darling,' Jennifer replied, giggling, but determinedly advancing towards him.

Pemberton's mind, at times lightning quick, at times quite the opposite, speeded up to its optimum. Good God! Bother the moonlight. He couldn't, more babies, Heathfield, Eton, heaven only knew what, he couldn't.

'My sweet, I can't, not here, we can't, not here.'

'Why ever not?' Jennifer wanted to know. 'Why ever not?' she repeated, still giggling, but now undoing the buckle on his belt.

'Because . . . because it's illegal, we would get arrested if found.'

'We shan't be found.'

'No, but we could be, we could easily be found, and by anyone. Chapple on a moonlit dig, Bloss, anyone.' Pemberton's voice suddenly reached to a higher pitch as he remembered just how much three babies, let alone six, was going to cost him. 'Anyway, I've drunk too much, much too much.'

'You hardly drunk anything – *drank* anything.'

'Before dinner I had three martinis, and it's given me whatever it's called – I can't, really.'

Jennifer let go of his belt. Thank heavens. And then she stood back and stamped her foot.

'Well really! When just for once I'm in a romantic

mood you have to go and have three martinis. Well really!'

Pemberton watched her disappear up the lawn with a feeling of resignation, and of sudden passion. It would have been lovely. If only he had had the courage to go to *Real Man*, but the truth of it was, he hadn't. He'd made an appointment three times, under the name of Bert Ackroyd. He'd done it himself, leaving no telephone number or contact of any kind, of course, but each time the day and the hour had approached, he had found himself approaching the telephone and cancelling. Oh, dear. Moonlight, love-making, even with Jennifer, it would have been what his nanny used to call 'yumpty'.

6

On the train journey home to Longborough Georgiana
had felt very beautiful. She had felt beautiful, and what's
more wanted, something that she had not felt for a very
long time, wanted and desirable. Even so, she was
looking forward to seeing her little boy, and hearing from
Nanny how he had played with his new friend and things
like that which mothers were inclined to want to hear
about, but which in reality were awfully boring, and
made you want to scream.

George was the spitting image of Gus. There was no
doubt at all as to who had been his father, which
was just as well really, considering his dear father had
never married his dear mother. He kissed Georgiana with
great affection, his really rather permanently runny
nose leaking lightly over Georgiana's perfect petal-like
English skin. How she loved him, she thought, putting
him down, and out loud she said, 'Something in my
handbag for you?' and gave him a parcel to unwrap.

'You spoil him, Lady Georgie,' said Nan, and looked
on jealously as the little boy unwrapped his present from
London, and Georgiana showed him how to play with
it. It was a toy-thing that you pushed down, and then
you flipped a little notch at the side and all the pieces
flew off round the room. Simple stuff, as her father would
have said, but she had always longed for one as a child

and had only ever been able to play with one in the nurseries of other children. As soon as she had seen it in the toy shop she knew she had to take it home, and now that the pieces were flying around the room, and George and she flying after them unable to resist having yet another go, she was very glad she had.

'How's Gus?' she remembered to ask after the first twenty minutes of her return had passed in play.

'I don't know, love, he's been in his studio all day,' said Nan, shrugging, and then she added as if Georgiana had been away for years and forgotten where the studio was, 'down the garden.'

'Very well then, down the garden I must go,' said Georgiana, smiling, and standing up. Happily she had remembered to bring Gus back not one but two 'from London' presents, not forgetting Nan and Nanny.

'It's just like Christmas,' said Nanny in an accusatory tone, because she didn't approve of Christmas either, but she allowed Georgiana to open her present and herself tasted one of the chocolates straight away.

She was pretty blind, poor Nanny, Georgiana thought, as she strolled down the garden to Gus's summer studio. Pretty blind, but doing much better than she had been. It was all the green on the estate, one of the doctors had told her, if you stared at green a great deal your eyesight improved. Georgiana pushed open the studio door without knocking, but as she did so she wished suddenly that her own eyesight wasn't quite as good as it undoubtedly was, because in front of her, without a stitch on, stood Gus, and lying on the studio bed was a girl with long dark hair also without her clothes.

'Oh, hallo, Gus,' said Georgiana, just able to manage

130

a conventional voice. 'I didn't realize you were busy, sorry.'

She felt as if she had been kicked in the tum, but even so she managed a smile.

'See you later, when you're finished,' she added, before she turned on her heel and went down the little green path back to the garden once more.

'Probably just painting,' she told herself as she walked up to the house. 'Of course, just painting.' And – 'He had his clothes off too because it's such a hot day,' she thought, by way of comfort. 'Must be going to be quite a painting,' she went on pleasantly, to herself, and then she went into the house and straight up to her room where she locked the door and lay down on her bed quite unable to move or think.

Not much time elapsed before she heard her door handle being turned and Gus's urgent voice outside.

'Let me in, love.'

She did wish he wouldn't call her that. It was so dated and so out-moded and so peculiarly northern when all things northern had long ago passed from vogue.

'Just resting, Gus. Won't be long.'

'Open – the – door.'

Ghastly when men said things like that to you, and through closed doors. Quite ghastly, and quite frightening, so full of implied threat and impending violence. The implied threat was that if you didn't open the door, you would be for it, and if you continued to not open the door, they would break the wretched thing down. Since the door was Georgian and very expensive to mend, Georgiana got off the bed and opened it.

'What the hell do you mean by doing that?'

'Doing what?'

'Locking the door.'

'I often lock my door, I like to. It's something I've always done, mostly to keep Nanny out, if you really want to know.'

'You lock your door, and yet you walk into my studio without knocking. Getting things a bit wrong, aren't you? I've told you time and time again, knock when an artist's at work. You disturbed my model, and you disturbed me. Do you realize that image may never come back now?'

Gus was raging, so Georgiana walked over to her dressing table and quite deliberately picked up her heavy silver-backed hand mirror, and her heavy silver-backed hairbrush, before turning to face him in her black lace inset petticoat and suspenders and black topped stockings. (The same petticoat and stockings she had faced Kaminski with, but they weren't exactly having the same effect.)

Gus didn't realize it, but she knew that particular tone in a man. Stranragh had used it once to her, just before he had raped her and beaten her up so badly it had taken her months to recover. She would never let a man do that to her again, not ever. It was ridiculous to have put herself in such a position twice, but it seemed that she may well have.

'I am sorry I forgot to knock on your studio door.'

'That picture may never be the same again, because of you!'

'I am sorry, really, that your picture may never be the same again. On the other hand, just think, Gus, it could be going to be better for the interruption. Neither of us can tell, and after all, even you won't ever know.'

Gus walked over to her, but Georgiana backed off down the room, still firmly holding her hairbrush and her hand mirror.

'What are you backing away for?' Gus wanted to know. 'What d'you think I'm going to do?'

'Nothing. I'm not backing away from you, it's just that I wanted to find your present,' said Georgiana quickly, and thanked God that Harrods still did presents up in nice big boxes so that she could bang the box in front of her and really shove it at Gus.

Gus had not been so spoilt that a large box, unopened, wasn't exciting to him. His eyes, still angry, dropped to the box, and he turned and started to cut the string with some nail scissors from Georgiana's dressing table.

'Cashmere. You extravagant hussy,' he said, in a very changed voice.

'Something else too.'

Quickly Georgiana presented him with another, smaller box.

'But this is beautiful,' Gus said, this time in a broken voice.

Georgiana had had an enamelled box made of one of his paintings, not from his hated, by him, but incredibly successful 'The Lady Loves' series, but from one of his private paintings that he sold from his studio, such as the one he and his model had been 'working' on.

He leaned forward and kissed Georgiana on the lips, his eyes full of tears, and Georgiana found herself gazing back at him, happy to no longer feel frightened of him. She knew that the moment had passed, the awful moment when he could have beaten her, or violated her, done something that men did to women, it seemed, so easily. No, that moment had passed, and she was safe once more, thanks to her sentimentality, thanks to her extravagance. What a good thing she had chosen today to surprise him with the box. Today when she had also surprised him with a model. She just wished that he didn't seem suddenly like a stranger to her, and that she couldn't see herself moving around their bedroom smiling and being coquettish in a way that was slightly disgusting her, and at the same time intriguing her. After all, if she was honest, and she might as well be, she herself had deceived him the evening before. Long before Gus had even started to 'paint' his model Kaminski had been making love to her, which was why, of course, she had thought it only fair to make it up to Gus with his box and his sweater.

The worst of it was, she realized, still smiling at Gus and telling him some story from her journey, the worst of it was – it had worked. The presents, the deception, everything, it had really worked, and one part of her was glad, and one part of her was sorry. Which part of her was which she had not yet decided, but decide she must, later. For the moment she was too busy avoiding a situation that Gus was obviously intent upon, but she didn't want, not now, perhaps not ever again with him, but that too she must decide later.

'Dinner – I hear Nan ringing the bell.'

Gus hesitated as he was pulling Georgiana into his arms, and seeing the hesitation in his eyes Georgiana quickly added, 'Salmon en croûte, just the way you like it, with that nice white wine sauce.'

Greed quickly overcame desire, as she had hoped it

might, and Gus let go of her. As he released her
Georgiana felt an overwhelming relief that surprised her.
No, it didn't just surprise her, it shook her, and yet she
couldn't have said whether it was due more to how easy
she found it to manipulate Gus, or to how powerful was
the impact that Kaminski had had upon her, and in truth
she was too busy taking advantage of the moment,
quickly dressing and talking Gus's head off, to really
care.

Jennifer gazed at Fulton. She hadn't realized just how
handsome he was until now. He was looking particularly
nice because he was wearing the same kind of blue that
she favoured for Pember, but on Fulton, she realized
with a rush, the colour was even better, really making
his lovely blue eyes stand out.

'It must be terribly difficult for you now, now that
you have had to take on two nannies,' she said in her
most sympathetic voice.

'Not so much two nannies, not as such, because one
is top nanny, old nanny is top nanny, and the new one,
now the monthly nurses have gone, is under-nanny. Very
young and very sweet, and quick to pick up things. You
know, smocking and that kind of thing. Smocks like mad
even once lights are out.'

'I dearly love smocking. Another Pimms?'

'*Mais certainement*. Quite strong, aren't they?'

'Lovely and strong,' Jennifer corrected him. 'I made
them myself,' she went on proudly. 'Added things, but
not mint. They should never be served with mint, kills
the recipe.'

'One more of these in this heat and they'll kill me!'

135

Fulton looked at Jennifer a little woozily. He looked terribly sweet woozy, Jennifer decided.

'Fulton?'

'Mmm?'

'Guess what?'

'What?'

'I've got the cheque out of Pember!'

She had deliberately kept the secret until they were settled in the shade of her favourite tree, a glass of something lovely in their hands, and the sun beating down quite beautifully.

'This is good news.'

'I know. It's taken long enough,' Jennifer agreed. 'Not at all like my Pember, usually so generous. Must be awful tax and things that have held him back from signing. But now at any rate we can safely say the ball will commence!'

Jennifer took a deep draught of her fresh drink as Fulton sighed with relief. He was beginning to feel quite guilty about the cheque for the ball, what with overtures having had to be made to Pemberton so recently about Beau and Daisy-Marguerita's school fees, and endowment policies and all those sorts of things. It was as if they at Flint House were more in the nature of poor relations, instead of real relations, albeit on the wrong side of the duvet cover.

But it had to be. That's how things were. If Melburys were to be brought up Melburys and everything in both their gardens was to be lovely, then Pemberton had to pay for his little indiscretions, come what mayhem, as it already undeniably had, but which they all hoped, thanks to *Real Man*'s arriving in the neighbourhood, it would now cease to do. Even so, despite all this, he and Elliott were actually very fond of Jennifer and they dearly wished the ball to proceed, if only because everyone was so fed up with the Cathedral and its fund, but more because they were looking forward to making everything beautiful for Jennifer, who, it had to be said, was good-hearted, and by and large did not wish anyone that ill, even Lady Tizzy, who she must sometimes suspect, however dimly, had something to do with Pember's little absences.

'Fulton.' Jennifer picked up her tapestry, and eyed it a little dizzily. 'You know, we've been friends for quite a long time now, haven't we?'

'Certainly,' Fulton agreed, gazing ahead of him and seeing roses in the garden where there were none.

'Well, you don't mind, therefore, you don't mind if I'm a little honest with you, do you?'

'Yes,' said Fulton, really quite promptly, considering he had just realized that he was seeing the panoply of the Hall set against its lovely gardens as even the architect in his wildest dreams couldn't have seen it, namely double. 'I make a practice of never being honest to other people, and I like people to be the same to me, please, nice and dishonest.'

'No, but really, a close friend can surely say some things, some things that might not be said even by one's mother.'

Jennifer paused, momentarily, because she suddenly couldn't think of one thing that would not be said by her mother to her, not one.

'You know what I mean,' she went on hastily. 'There are some things, said in kindness, with only you in mind,

that have to be said, and I honestly think, well – I'm
sure you do, Fulton, if you think about it – I honestly
think that perhaps, lovely though they are, and you know
we all love them, lovely and beautiful though they are,
and fond as we undoubtedly all are and can be of them,
I honestly think – you and Lady Tizzy have had enough
children, don't you?'

Fulton turned and stared at Jennifer, and tears came
into his eyes. She was so sweet, so innocent. She knew
so little. She was lovely beyond even his imaginings.

'How sweet you are, Jennifer.'

Jennifer looked at him, her head on one side, her
tapestry on the other.

'I love children too, you know, Fulton, we have
that in common, but nowadays, two or three, Eton,
Heathfield, the expense, the endowments, even rich men
like Pember are feeling it, as he remarked to me only
last week. Really. We must think of the best, how much
it costs, and then double it, and that's, apparently, how
much our children will cost us.'

'You're so sweet, Jennifer.'

'I don't know whether you read the *Parishioner*?'
Jennifer straightened her head, dropped her tapestry, and
lifting her backside produced a copy from under the
cushion she had been sitting on. 'I find it riveting,
personally. Anyway. In here is a little advertisement to
which I think we should all pay attention. An advertisement that is for the good of the world, for the good of
each other, for the good of us. I have ringed it for you,
Fulton, because we don't want to speak further about
anything, or be indiscreet, and I know how much you
and Lady Tizzy love each other, and what a dear friend

138

Elliott is to you both, and to Nanny – all that smocking together – so I won't, you know, bang on and embarrass us both. You will see however what I mean when you read it. Page a hundred and ten eff. Such funny numbering always, all to do with the Motoring and Farm Machinery section. Anyway, you will see, as I say, not to bang on too much, you will see what I mean. When you get home. Time enough. I have ringed it.'

Of course Fulton couldn't wait until he got home to turn to page a hundred and ten eff. He waited only until he had climbed into his soon-to-be exchanged Volkswagen Golf.

Sure enough Jennifer had generously ringed the item which she thought would be so helpful to himself and Lady Tizzy. It had an all too familiar wording.

'Men! You want it? Come and get it! Just ten minutes and the wife's best friend can really be that! Call the *Real Man* Curtailment Agency for a carefree lovelife in home from home conditions.'

From the library window Jennifer watched Fulton's car disappearing, and felt that strange overwhelming sense of fondness for him once more. She knew that he would read the *Real Man* advertisement and that he would ponder deeply on her words. (She felt sure that Fulton would ponder and not brood.) After all it was only sensible. Poor chap, he must be overwhelmed by now by his own and Lady Tizzy's ability to produce, and ad nauseam, babies. *Real Man* would be the answer to their troubles. Wonderful to be able to have a carefree love.

Jennifer paused in her thoughts. Now that would be something about which to think. Perhaps that was why

139

Pember had been so timid in the garden by the pampas grass? Perhaps he too would benefit from *Real Man*? Jennifer turned away from the library window. She really had to think about it, just for a little, but it dawned on her that really, really she should take her own advice to Fulton, she should advise Pember to go to this *Real Man* Curtailment Agency, and then perhaps he would cease to be so shy in moonlit conditions?

Elliott paused by the door of the nurseries. They were the sweetest sight, their babies, no two minds about it, or three minds would be a better way of putting it.

Every one of the babies was so busy, wriggling and gurgling, or crawling across the floor. Once in the nursery with Nanny and Bessie there was no telling which way to turn, but turn he must, for he had heard Fulton's car, and he couldn't wait to hear about the ball – heaven only knew there had been enough drama already to last them a summertime, what with the Countess backing out in a huff, and Lord P not yet coughing up the wherewithal, and Fulton worrying and worrying that it was because Lady Tizzy had had twins and not even he could afford the expense of six children.

'Well?'

Fulton paused by the door his key outstretched, but Elliott had already opened to him.

'I hate that, I hate it when people open the door and I have my key stretched out.'

'I know, so do I, but I can't wait to hear all about it.'

Elliott let his eyes roll towards Fulton. He was swaying. He would deny it, of course, but he was very definitely swaying.

140

'Should you have driven home?' he asked gently.

'No,' Fulton stated, 'no, I should not have driven home, but I did. Like the Vicar. Very, very slowly.'

'Go into the drawing room and sit in the window while I make us both some very, very strong coffee, and then you can tell me everything, concealing nothing. But nothing.'

Fulton nodded. Elliott sounded and looked a little impatient, as people always did when it was not they that had been plied with too strong a Pimms. He walked towards the drawing room. It was true. He did need some coffee. He needed it very, very badly.

He sat down in the window, their window, and gazed out on to their lawn. It was a very pretty lawn, and he loved Flint House, but there was no doubt about it; ever since they'd moved into the house from the apartment in Bath they did seem to have the most dreadful ability to attract trouble. And it really had all started when they moved in, really. He had married Lady Tizzy to save her name, and given a name to Victoria, and that had seemed to set the ball rolling somewhat, so here they were, and there was everyone else, but no-one would stop doing whatever they were doing before he and Elliott had arrived, with the consequence that more and more was happening, and all of it, it sometimes seemed to him, to them.

'One good thing,' Fulton stated, sipping his coffee. 'The cheque has not bounced, the ball is now rolling.'

'Mmm, and that's what you need to be to give one – rolling. Still, Twinks will be pleased. The Village Voice told her that she had it on the best authority that Lord Pemberton was cancelling.'

141

'Twinks should stop listening to Mrs Dupont.'

'She can't, she has it over her dreadfully. Twinks says it's because she always arrives with a collecting tin, and people with collecting tins always do. I know what she means, as a matter of fact. They make you feel that you should be collecting instead of them, and that however much you put in, or don't put in, it's always the wrong amount. That's why they smile so kindly at you. They pity you, you know, for getting it wrong. 'Specially if you put in too much. No, you can't blame Twinks. Hers is a sensitive nature.'

'Not too sensitive judging from that last tray she did.'

They lapsed into silence, but Elliott knew Fulton too well and it wasn't long before he had out-silenced him, which he, in his turn, knew was something that Fulton couldn't tolerate for a single minute.

'Well. There was something. Actually.'

This time it was Fulton who lifted his backside and gave Elliott Jennifer's copy of the *Parishioner*.

'Page a hundred and ten eff. Lady Pemberton's suggestion for a quiet life at Flint House.'

Elliott riffled through the pages, passing by the advertisements for people needing to exchange a Baby Belling for a nearly-new nylon fur and four cockerels, and stared at the ringed advertisement.

'Oh, my life and tinned peaches, I don't believe it!'

'Yes, you do.'

'Yes, I do.'

There was a tiny silence.

'I suppose, I suppose when you think about it, she means it as rather a compliment.'

The silence continued, until they looked at each other

142

and they both started to laugh, and then of course they couldn't stop.

Mrs Parker-Jones picked her way up the Countess's drive. She had parked her car at the bottom, just in case there was nowhere at the top where it would be safe, or so she was prepared to tell anyone she met. In actuality her sole purpose for making her way so daintily up the drive was to see if it was as weed-free as her own short path, and now she was treading along its gravelled surface she could see that it was. Not a dandelion or a daisy in sight. For some reason this disappointed her. It was exactly like when she heard that Andrew had been behaving himself very well ever since she had decided to divorce him. Put out, that's how she felt about the Countess's drive. Even so the Countess had at least, and at last, invited her to tea. Heaven only knew it had taken long enough, and heaven also only knew what the purpose of her visit was going to turn out to be, because Clarissa knew, as only a mother, a widow, a wife (twice) could know, there would have to be a purpose. The Countess would not have asked her for nothing. Oh no, as she lived and breathed there would be a sole and single purpose to the tea.

They had collaborated before, of course, over 'the girls', as Jennifer and Georgiana were still known to both of them. They had made small plans to cover potential scandals and divert happenings that they thought might be about to happen, but never once had the Countess asked her to tea. Mrs Parker-Jones pulled down her Jason Jonet lightweight two-piece non-matching capped sleeved top, and checked its self-matching belt.

143

She judged herself dressed quite right. Not too smart, and not too country either, about right, a proper touch of class without being showy.

The Countess frowned down at the sight of Mrs Parker-Jones making her way along her drive. Even from the landing window, even from this distance, she looked quite frightful. And why was the wretched woman walking up the drive for heaven's sake? What had happened to her motor car? Had she broken down? Was she walking for some charitable purpose? And why was she early? It all looked so eager and new.

She made her way quickly down to the drawing room and settled herself in front of the fire that she always had Maria light summer and winter.

'Show her in,' she told her maid, as they both checked the room with their eyes, letting them swivel dextrously from flowers to fire and back again. The Countess sighed happily. What a boon Maria was! She always knew exactly, but exactly, what was wanted when it was wanted. They nodded briefly to each other.

'Ready, go,' the Countess murmured, as the front door bell rang.

Maria announced, 'Mrs Parker-Jones,' from the door. It was still nice to have people announced, even though no-one did any more. The Countess still did, but really only because Maria enjoyed it.

'How do you manage with such a large house all to yourself, and Andrew in the Lodge?'

'Like everyone else, so-so,' said the Countess, pouring tea. She had no intention of elaborating on that most boring of country conversational topics, staff.

'Yes, but how many do you employ here?'

Oh, the conscious vulgarity of it!

'I employ two in the house, and three in the garden,' said the Countess, handing Mrs Parker-Jones a cup of tea, and the sugar bowl, and not bothering to ask her whether she preferred lemon or milk, because she was irritating her straight away.

'Yes, I see the drive is weed-free, I suppose that does take three.'

The Countess closed her eyes and counted quickly to two, and then opened them again and counted to ten, until all in all it made a calming twelve, just enough, but only enough, to stop her coming over strange and having to ask Mrs Parker-Jones to leave. As it was she had to hold on to herself not to do so anyway. If it wasn't for the memory of that frightful letter of Jennifer's to her daughter Lady Mary indeed she would have done, but just the memory of being called a 'dear old thing' was enough to make her determined to carry on.

'Have some wartime spirit,' she told herself, and then smiled and held out a plate of strawberry shortcake to the wretched woman.

'No thank you, I never eat tea,' said Mrs Parker-Jones.

'Pity, it's very good. Maria makes it, it melts in the mouth.'

The Countess picked up a little pearl-handled fork and ate her shortcake delicately, so delicately that after two or three of her mouthfuls Mrs Parker-Jones deeply regretted that she didn't eat tea.

'At our age,' the Countess began, unfairly, Clarissa Parker-Jones thought, since the Countess was at least ten years older than herself, 'at our age,' she repeated, ruthlessly, 'we must, I think, we must stick together. We

are usually, all of us, at our age, completely in agreement
with what is wrong with the world, and what is right
with the world, are we not? We have outgrown all the
hideous idealism of youth and can sit back and see what
there is to be done and, very often, do it. Or,' she paused,
sipping her tea and then carefully replacing her cup, 'we
can see what is being done, and undo it. Would you not
agree?'

Mrs Parker-Jones nodded. She knew very well that
what the Countess was saying was true, they did both
feel the same, and why shouldn't they? Although they
might not be the same age, as the Countess had so
unkindly insinuated, at least they had other things in
common. They lived in Wiltshire, they looked after
Andrew, and they both took the *Daily Telegraph*. None
of those things were nothing, least of all Andrew.

'Is something wrong with Andrew?' asked Clarissa,
essaying to come quickly to the point, because she knew
that since he was still her husband, even in name only,
anything he had done would undoubtedly have to be
undone.

'As a matter of fact there is nothing wrong with
Andrew bar his eating asparagus a little too noisily. No,
nothing, for once. He's happy enough in the Lodge, and
I let him out at night, as you know. Although China has
fallen through, but let's face it nowadays where hasn't?
Although China has fallen through he is hoping to take
a small party of people on a trekking expedition in
Western Australia. It's a new travel agency a friend of
his has started, "Nihilistic Tours". Nothing to see,
nothing to do, it's for people who live in inner cities.
Apparently it makes the poor dears able to embrace the

146

crowded life once they return. It seems once they have tramped across the scorched earth for days on end seeing nothing but the corks on their own hats, they kiss every one of their telephones the moment they get in the door, and stop complaining about conditions on the underground, and litter and things. Really makes them appreciate civilization. They're booked out already, Andrew says. Of course, as you can imagine, his only problem is how to get his copy of *Sporting Life* flown out, but apparently supplies have to be dropped daily anyway, so *plus ça change, plus c'est* very much the same old story, especially when it comes to holidays, I find. Everyone taking them and then coming back and telling you, and tans so common. Two a penny in the supermarkets, Maria tells me, and everyone just stopping and talking about them, instead of shopping. And then they have the gall to say they're not well off. Time was when no-one but the Duke of Westminster could afford two holidays, and then only if he took his own yacht. But—'

The Countess stopped, realizing she had gone too far.

'No, you're very naughty, Clarissa, you shouldn't have started me on this.'

Mrs Parker-Jones opened her mouth to protest that she hadn't, but shut it again when she realized that the Countess had called her 'Clarissa'. It was a first; as far as she could remember the Countess had never ever first-named Clarissa to her face before. It made her feel odd; almost, it had to be admitted, touched.

'Have you been on holiday?' the Countess wanted to know, staring at a slight array of brown on Clarissa's arm.

'Good heavens no,' Mrs Parker-Jones protested. 'No,

no, I've been weeding the mixed border by the bust of Beethoven in the sink garden, that's all this is. This is just a little Wiltshire tan. Not enough to make a sailor a pair of trousers.'

'It's so deep it almost looks foreign,' murmured the Countess accusingly.

'Oh no, I had it last year, I do assure you, it's not foreign at all, and it fades very quickly.'

'Where was I?' demanded the Countess, back to being ruthless because she really wasn't interested in talking about Clarissa Parker-Jones to her. Talking about Clarissa Parker-Jones to someone else was fine, but not to her face. It was boring, and worse, dull. 'Ah yes, I know where I was. I was just about to broach a subject.'

She put down her fine bone china teacup, Spode, eighteenth century, turquoise blue ribboning with very pretty faded flowers.

'Yes. Your daughter. Jennifer. Sweet girl, isn't she?'

Clarissa Parker-Jones's heart started to beat a little faster. So this was it, at last, the purpose of the visit. Jennifer had done something to the Countess? But what had Jennifer done? It must be something frightful, she quickly realized, or she, her mother, would not be here with the Countess taking tea with her in her very own home, and in the drawing room with the fire lit and the flowers arranged in artless designs.

'Sweet is not how I would describe Jennifer,' Clarissa said quickly. 'Buxom, firm, opinionated, very, very like her late father, Aidan, to that I would say a clear "yes". She always was, too, never at all like myself, either in looks or character. No taste at all, of course, but then since she is married to John Pemberton she doesn't need to have any taste, does she? I mean, when you're married to someone with fifteen racehorses in training, and a private art collection, you have no need of taste, everyone has it for you. No, sweet is not a word I would think of immediately when it comes to my dear daughter.'

The Countess looked at Mrs Parker-Jones, evenly. She was only too well aware of how frightful she was, and it had to be admitted she had been before she came, but not quite as aware as she was at that second. Any woman who was capable of running her daughter down in that manner should really not be trucked with. Alas, however, whether she had meant to or not Jennifer had gone too far in her letter to Mary, the writing in that letter was now on the wall, so *truck* with the Parker-Jones woman, the Countess realized, she surely must.

'I see,' was finally what she said, some few seconds after the Parker-Jones woman had finished speaking, and before she herself leant forward, poured them both some more tea, and spelt out her proposal for their mutual plan of action.

So mutual was the plan, and so completely in accord with each other were both ladies, that it was not long before both of them were pecking away at pieces of strawberry shortcake with small pearl-handled forks.

7

Bloss stared morosely at the Pemberton Cup and Cover. He knew it was historical, and he knew it was something that as the Pemberton butler he should be happy to clean, particularly since it was the whole reason why they now had a newly installed and over-effective burglar alarm, but for reasons which were all too clear to him nothing was making him happy that morning, but nothing, and small wonder, since he suspected that his lordship was trying to replace him. After all the loyalty, the waiting for motor cars, the accepting with a grateful expression first a motorbike and then a three-wheeler, vehicles that his friend the butler at nearby Bellington Court would quite frankly never have tolerated for an instant, after all that, it seemed that Bloss was going to be replaced by someone called Bert Ackroyd, if you please.

Not that Bloss was a snob. Of course he wasn't, even if he did say so himself. In fact he was the very last person who could be described as such, and he could give a for instance about that too. For a for instance, he didn't mind fraternizing down at the King's Arms, and he never spoke to anyone employed at the Hall as if they were servants, but almost always as if they were staff (with the single exception of a very nasty and randy maid who would, in his opinion, have been better suited to be a groom). He was always most careful to address everyone as if they were on an equal basis with himself, when everyone knew they couldn't possibly be. And yet, in spite all of this, and despite having moved with the times as no other butler he knew could have, or indeed would have, here he was faced with being replaced by one Bert Ackroyd.

Mind you, part of him wanted to know how his lordship proposed to bring about this enormous revolution. How would he tell her ladyship, for instance? They might not be the best of friends, the way his lordship and himself had been, in the not too recent past, they might not have a little, and quite successful, racing system going (small bets all of them, of course, but a system none the less), but even so he and Lady Pemberton were as one on many things, from how to deal with Mrs Dupont, the Village Voice, to how to keep the Countess away from the ball arrangements. In these things he and her ladyship had been as one, and while he could not be said to have the easiest of relationships with her, compared to that which he had always enjoyed until now with his lordship, nevertheless he was quite sure she would miss him should he not be there. Should Bloss be replaced by this Bert Ackroyd Bloss had no doubt that her ladyship would notice.

At least his lordship had had the grace to look embarrassed yesterday morning when the voice on the telephone demanded to speak to this Bert Ackroyd. Not even his aristocratic demeanour could remain untouched by self-consciousness as his butler handed him the telephone he had so ardently demanded.

Bloss himself had answered it, naturally, but it had been his lordship who had seized the telephone when

151

his butler had said, quite firmly and distinctly, that a Mr Ackroyd did not live at the Hall.

'Oh yes, he does, Bloss, yes he does,' he'd said. And then proceeded to apologize to the caller on behalf of this Mr Ackroyd. It seemed Mr Ackroyd had been 'unavoidably delayed', in spite of being a great friend of his lordship's, but that he had 'every intention of arriving', and that his lordship would give him the message and get him to call the agency back as soon as he saw him.

That was it, of course. As soon as he had heard the word 'agency' Bloss knew without any doubt at all that he was for the chop. He was going to be replaced by someone cheaper. It was obvious – the cost of living, plus all the new arrivals at Flint House, their brood plus Lady Tizzy's brood, it had all been too much for his lordship, and he was obviously being forced to cut down even on essentials, such as himself. (Bloss knew he couldn't be cutting down on any of the other staff, because they were all in tied cottages and had to work for a pittance at the Hall in exchange for the perk of having a permanent roof over their heads, free vegetables, free meat, and a corn-fed turkey at Christmas, plus a rather horrid pudding that if you weren't quick about it stuck to the teeth dreadfully.)

Of course he would have to tell Bloss today. Bloss knew that, and he also knew that his lordship was only too reluctant, because after the telephone call he had heard him muttering 'I can't do it, I can't do it', which was only to be expected when you thought that Bloss had been at the Hall even before her ladyship, and when his lordship had been a merry bachelor. They had had good times together too, he thought, his eyes misting over.

Bloss stood forward and blew on the Pemberton Cup and Cover. He had to keep himself busy until the axe fell. Of course he would find another position, and in a minute, but the idea of not being at the Hall was really very strange. After all, there were things at the Hall that only he knew. Things that no-one else knew, and not just about his lordship either. Information that he would now have no compunction in taking to his grave. Not for him the latter-day private income raised by some butlers, always ringing hateful gossip columns and informing on their employers, oh no. No, he had not been like some of whom he had heard, who paid their bookies' bills without a qualm by informing on aristocratic frolics. And even now, sore and hurt though he felt, even now he would not stoop to such a thing. He might make sure that the bag of oats was given to the horses, but nothing else. The buck stopped with him!

The telephone rang. Bloss picked it up.

'Ahem, it's all right, Bloss, I've got it!'

Bloss stared at the old bakelite telephone. It still had 'Pemberton 1' on it. Those were the days, the days of lifting up the telephone and saying 'Pemberton one', and how dear they had been. There was no doubt about it. His lordship always entertaining fascinating people, Bloss answering the telephone, no babies anywhere. Perhaps leaving now was for the best, yes, and it would be a far, far better thing he did if he did it himself. Suddenly Bloss was sure of it. The way he had been quite sure of his calling to butlerdom, to being the right hand of a very patrician person, to being someone on whom they could all count to enhance and make perfect at least one tiny corner of Old England and leave it properly polished and dusted.

'Yes, Bloss?'

His lordship lowered his ironed (by Bloss) copy of the *Sporting Life* and stared at his butler.

'Your lordship?'

'Yes, Bloss.'

'Your lordship, it has occurred to me, what with one thing and another, and another being one thing.'

Bloss cleared his throat again.

'Yes, Bloss.'

'As I said, what with one thing and another, and so on and so on. Life being what it is, and not at all what we hope it to be, it might be better if I wasn't.'

Pemberton stared at Bloss.

'Have you been having an early quickie? I mean, I don't mind if you have, but you don't usually sound like the Vicar until after six, Bloss.'

'No, milord, I have not had a quickie, but I do think all in all you should know that I know.'

The copy of *Sporting Life* was lowered even further.

'Good. Well, as long as you know that I know that you know, then everything's all right. Isn't it?'

'Not really, milord.'

Pemberton frowned. This was the longest conversation he and Bloss had exchanged without mentioning a sporting certainty for months.

'Probably might be a good idea if you did go and have a quickie, Bloss,' he said suddenly, after a long pause for thought, 'and then you can come back and spit out whatever's on your chest, and we can all return to the status quo, and you can mark this afternoon's card at "Ha'ddock", because I'm damned if I can see my way round it. Really.'

Bloss cleared his throat for a third time.

'What I am getting at, milord, is that I know all about Bert Ackroyd and the agency.'

Pemberton stood up at that. Things were getting out of hand when his butler could be heard mentioning a chap's personal arrangements in the library.

'If we're going to have men's talk I think we'd better go into your pantry, Bloss,' he told him, in a lowered tone, and strode ahead of him out into the corridor and from there into the snug under the stairs. 'You mustn't mention Bert Ackroyd in there, Bloss,' he said in a more normal but kindly tone, 'her ladyship might overhear. Can't have that. Not that I think she'd mind, not really. No, as a matter of fact, I don't think she would, but you know how it is with ladies, Bloss, they can kick up rusty if you let them in on things too early. But there's no two ways about it, it must be done. The knife must be plunged.'

'I know, milord.'

'I just can't afford to go on like this.'

'I know, milord,' Bloss agreed, nodding, 'and I am the first to understand. It's just a little hard, after all these years.'

'I know, Bloss, I know.'

His lordship put out a hand and placed it on Bloss's immaculately cut black sleeve.

'We've been through so much together, Bloss. But it's wartime conditions for the very rich out there. You just can't hang on to what you have any more, and six

children is twice as many as I bargained for, quite
frankly. You understand. You're such a good fellow. I
can't contemplate life without you.'

Pemberton patted Bloss's arm once more, but as he
did so he was suddenly appalled to see tears in his
butler's eyes.

'My dear fellow, I'm so sorry, how fearful! Don't tell
me, this is your best jacket?'

He removed his hand from the sleeve as if he'd been
electrocuted. But the tears remained in place.

Georgiana's return home had been, to say the least,
fortunate. As soon as she had seen that Gus obviously
wanted to be able to go his own way and do what
he wanted, when he wanted, she realized she really did
not have to sit about feeling too bad about her reunion
with Kaminski.

Except she did feel bad. Conscience, instilled by
Nanny all those years ago, dictated that she should
awake in the night and become covered in shame. How
could she have done what she did? Allowed Kaminski
to walk back into her life and have his wicked way with
her? Sometimes, such as when she was brushing her hair
very slowly in her dressing mirror and watching the
beautiful red lights in its dark brown mass, she would
literally blush, just remembering. The colour would
creep into her cheeks and increase to such a degree it
would filter down the front of her, until it was a positive
charabanc vee of colour. Other times, having been
woken by her shame in the night, and eventually fallen
back asleep again, she would re-awake in the morning
to a better sense of truth, and lie and remember, and

savour, their moments together, and it would make her curl over on to her front and clasp her pillow and smile, because really, if she was truthful, there had been a great deal to smile about between her and Kaminski.

Gradually, over the next days, she found herself blushing less and smiling more, until shame and conscience fled and hid their faces among the distant hills that could sometimes be seen from the gates of Longborough, and Georgiana would think only of how magnificent Kaminski was, more powerful, more intense, more electric than Gus, and even more different from herself than Gus (for it was always a requisite of Georgiana's that a man should be utterly different from herself). She thought of him as evening crept up to the side of her ancestral home, and she had nothing to which to look forward save Nan and Nanny at supper, and it seemed to her everything that had ever happened between them had happened in shadows, or with shading, however light.

Georgiana allowed herself a little frisson as she remembered how he had watched her in the dark of the bar as a man might who has just bought some new toy at a shop, and having wound it up sits back and watches it perform some particular set of antics, wondering idly all the time whether he will go on playing with it now, or eventually throw it away, tired out with its antics, last year's fad, last year's fashion. But therein, she realized, lay Kaminski's real fascination, for since he had rejected her when she was young and beautiful, she knew that he might, all too easily, do so again. Really, that was what was fascinating about him, particularly now that Gus no longer wished to stand before his easel enraptured by the texture of Georgiana's white skin, enthralled by her large eyes, and mesmerized by her aloof expression. Now that her lover had found someone else by whom to be artistically enslaved, Georgiana had in her turn a new need to enthral.

For if she was to be truthful, Georgiana craved someone else to be mesmerized by her, to be ready to be her slave, and she had sensed, even as Kaminski had left her to return to his current amour (Kaminski she knew from the newspapers and magazines always had a current amour), he was in precisely the frame of mind that she liked best in a man: he was ready to lie down and worship her.

And that was another thing which she had to face. Nowadays Georgiana had no time for women who wanted to be slaves to men, men must be slaves to her, and the moment they stopped, as Gus had very obviously stopped, then, emotionally speaking, it was time to move on. Her husband, Stranragh, had brought about the first real change in her too availing nature, and now it seemed to her Gus might have brought about not just a second change, but a complete cure.

Not that she didn't love Gus still, of course she did, she just didn't love him the way she had once, just as he quite obviously no longer loved her the way he had once, while still doubtless loving her in his mind, in a very little piece of his mind, the piece that wasn't completely taken up with Gus Hackett.

Georgiana continued to sigh a little, half to herself, and half to her looking glass, which she couldn't help noticing she was standing in front of for longer and longer stretches of time since she had returned from

London. But even as she re-fell in love with her own lustrous hair, she was all too aware that Gus would still be engrossed in painting his new model, the Junoesque girl from the village, tall and dark with a habit of wearing what she called 'cut-offs'. Without her clothes she obviously excited not just the artist in Gus, but the man as well. Unfortunately Georgiana had only had the one privilege, if it should be called that, of seeing her divested. Her strong tanned skin rippling over the old velvet of Georgiana's great-grandmother's faded maroon couch had been, to say the least, an upsetting sight.

Georgiana slowly buffed one perfect pink finger nail, as she carried on contemplating the facts of her life.

She was so different from her of the 'cut-offs'. No strong rippling skin, no large boned legs, and heavy fingers ready to grasp at every opportunity, her small eyes darting out from her face, assessing the value of every object around her. For only now, days later, when she was healing a little, could she begin to face how much she had hated seeing that girl with Gus when she had returned so buoyantly from the station that evening. It wasn't just that she had been quite, quite nude – and Gus had obviously just enjoyed her. It was much more that she had been sprawled all over Georgiana's precious studio room, her very own room that she had so generously loaned to Gus, and which he was now occupying, or causing to be occupied by someone who did not, and would never, let's face it, suit it in the least. Seeing a girl like that lying over a sofa that had once held the tiny satined posteriors of her ancestors had actually made Georgiana feel quite, quite sick. Do what he could with her, and goodness knows he had tried hard enough, Georgiana realized, Gus had not been able to change a hair of her head. She was, and always would be, Lady Georgiana Longborough. She knew now, and perhaps had known for some time, probably ever since she had taken up dried flowers, that it really might be time to move on to someone who liked her for what she was and didn't want to change every little hair on her head. Consciously dramatic as this thought was, Georgiana turned equally dramatically away from the looking glass and walked to her bedroom window, which overlooked the least pretty view. (Nan had bagged the nicest the moment she arrived at Longborough – 'You don't mind, Georgie dear, do you? I get the heebie jeebies if I can't see flowers.')

How restful, Georgiana mused, feeling quite gentle now, how restful it would be to be with someone who did not, by silence, and by anger, criticize her at every turn as Gus had and did. She must, she *had* to change her life, and the only way that she could, she reasoned to herself, would be through Kaminski, which was unfortunate to say the least, for he was the one person in the whole world she knew would never telephone or write to her. Indeed, knowing Kaminski he would even now have forgotten who she was, for he was the sort of dynamic character that forgets, and oh so easily, the person he has been with in a matter of a moment, just as, it seemed, he was able to remember, equally quickly, once he was reminded.

Bored with staring at herself, however beautiful a morning she might have on, bored even with her own thoughts, Georgiana picked up a copy of the *Daily Mail*. The showbusiness page featured a story about Kaminski and his new film. As usual the publicity man had decided to sell the readers a search and find story. This time, according to the columnist whose head was pictured at the top of the page, it seemed Kaminski was desperate to find strong athletic girls to play underwater divers in the film he was about to shoot.

For a second Georgiana felt a little tug of disappointment. Small and slight as she was, no-one in their wildest dreams could possibly do anything but laugh at her if she put herself forward as an underwater Juno. But, and it was the very word Juno that prompted her, there was someone who could be perfect for such a role: a large girl with thick fingers, and a habit of wearing cut-offs, who was even now taking up space in the garden studio.

Reaching for a pair of nail scissors Georgiana carefully cut, in a necessarily rounded fashion, given the shape of the nail scissors, the piece in question out of what was actually Nanny's paper. It made a small round hole that would have to be explained to Nanny, but nevertheless it would be quite enough for the lady who was even now baring her all for Gus's predilection, artistic and otherwise, to seize on the opportunity that Georgiana was about to lay before her. And so, Georgiana thought with satisfaction, a perfect solution could present itself. She could get rid of Miss Cut-offs and re-present herself to Kaminski, all in one move. Kaminski, who prided himself so much on his chess playing, could not have arranged things better.

The magazine declared from its cover an exciting new feature for the delectation of its devoted readers. It

161

seemed Annunciata Cauldron, the florist, was about to reveal all.

Elliott sighed with a smallish sort of pleasure. The kind of sigh that escapes a person who has, and only too recently, been through some equally smallish but quite vivid pain. Annunciata Cauldron was, besides James Beard and one or two others, an absolute hero. She was just what he needed on a damp morning in latish May, when Twinks was far from well. She had only just taken Elliott through her latest cure for tinea (lard used in places where she surely couldn't be serious). Apparently it had been used with great effect on someone in the village. Another smallish sigh escaped Elliott. There were sometimes just a few drawbacks to village life and recommended cures were undoubtedly one. Only last week Mrs Dupont, the Village Voice, had written out a cure for Fulton's seasonal hay fever which sounded and was rather worse than the affliction. Nettles crushed in spinach leaves. The cure penned in very faded looped writing ended: 'Apply to the afflicted part.' As Fulton had complained, and quite vociferously because his hay fever by now was much better, referring to his nose in such terms was too horrible, for even if his nose was a 'part' he didn't like to think of it as one, and once he did, well, he felt like staying indoors for the rest of his days.

Elliott lay back on the kitchen sofa, and, as the rain outside came down in stair rods, he flicked through the magazine from back to front, because that way it made everyone, even potters in very bright jumpers, look better. Finally, triumphantly, he arrived at Annunciata and her latest ideas.

Elliott poured over the pages, staring at the photographs of Ms Cauldron and her arrangements. Artichokes it seemed were in as firmly as cabbages with their attendant caterpillars were out, when it came to informal floral arrangements around the home.

Elliott stared at the large central colour photograph excitedly. He so badly needed a shot in his creative arm, what with Twinks having made a hash of the Duchess of Roseberry's wastepaper basket and matching pin tray, and Nanny throwing a moody because Bessie had spilt rose hip syrup all over Beau's newest Swiss cotton angel top. It had been that kind of morning all morning, and it was still only half past nine.

Elliott smoothed out the article on the marble-topped pasta-making surface, and held it carefully down at the corners with two weights. Artichokes. How glad he was that he had brought the magazine in from the stables. It would be hours before Twinks, to whom it belonged, would find it missing, and by that time the lard might have worked.

Artichokes with radishes and small stiffened marguerites worked in between the leaves would be just the kind of thing that would add the right tone to the double christening of Beau and Daisy-Marguerita at the beginning of September. Having to come to terms with the whole idea of twins had not been easy. At this very moment Elliott knew that Fulton was out getting the best possible exchange for his bronzed Golf convertible with wire wheels and limited stereo.

Of course ever since Beau's unexpected arrival in their world they had touched on the christening, most especially over the past few days, if only as a refreshing

163

change from the ball, and it seemed to both of them, at one and the same time, that their newest christening should not be an ordinary Waspish sort of christening. Not for them this time round, they had both agreed, just the Vicar and godparents with long names who, once it had been announced in *The Times*, would spend the rest of their days trying to forget that they were. No, for the twins, since they were a late spring double, they wanted something different, something to celebrate their doubleness, some sort of statement of fertility; not quite centaurs leaping, but certainly a Druidish sort of feel, with everyone retiring to a decorated barn, and people from the village dressed up while they turned spits with deliciously organic produce spiked on them.

'Come and see, won't you?'

Fulton stood by the door. Since Beau's arrival he had already started to affect different and very changed trousers, and at home, in the mornings, horn-rimmed half moon glasses which really rather suited him. They made him look a little more of the professor and little less of the antiques entrepreneur. Reluctantly Elliott turned from the double page on the artichokes and followed him out into the drive. Even though he would have preferred to have stayed out of the rain and in front of the magazine, in another way he couldn't wait to see what Fulton had exchanged for the bronzed Golf.

'Well?'

'Well.'

Elliott stood very still under his very small inflatable paisley umbrella which he knew had been a mistake, but which like all umbrella mistakes just would not

164

go away and get lost the way really nice ones always did.

Fulton breathed in and out.

'It's a Mobishi two-toned metallic Trekker with bull bars,' he announced, a little pointlessly since they were both standing in front of it. 'Well?'

'Well, I see what you mean.'

'Good.'

'The tyres are quite different,' said Elliott, staring.

'They're "off-road".'

'Is that why they've got that special white writing all over them?'

'Probably,' Fulton agreed uneasily. 'Heavy duty fogs,' he went on, pointing at them. 'Four doors, five seats, with an optional eight in scotchguarded Vylene Kiddicoated Velour. Eight-track CD stereo system for Nanny to play B. Potter's tales, and a sand shovel on the back door.'

'I hope we won't be needing that too often.'

'Now we are three, who knows? Or rather six, including Nanny.'

'Quite. I see it won the Paris to Dachau Rally,' Elliott said, reading the back window from one side to the other before turning to look at Fulton.

'Well?'

'Well.'

'Yes?'

'It's very – different. I mean, it's very different from anything we've had before.'

'That's what I wanted. Something very different from anything we've had before.'

'Oh well, if it's what you wanted. It's just that I rather

thought that you might have preferred that maroon
Porsche with triotonic scaling and slip diff that you saw
in the *Sunday Times* last week?'

'Of course I should have preferred the maroon
Porsche,' said Fulton shortly. 'But sacrifices must be
made. One glimpse at my bull bars and every headmaster
in England will be begging us to send Beau to his beastly
establishment.'

'I didn't know headmasters looked at your cars.'

'They look at everything.'

'In that case it's obviously the right choice. I mean,
it's got so much writing on it no-one could possibly
suppose we can't read.'

Even so, following Fulton into the house Elliott
couldn't help feeling that there was still a slight question
mark over the whole enterprise.

Over very strong coffee in their special window
overlooking the rain and the garden, Fulton knew
immediately.

'You're thinking something.'

'I know,' Elliott was forced to admit.

'You know you're going to have to tell.'

'Yes, I do know I'm going to have to tell.'

'Very well, tell.'

'If you're sure.'

'Well?'

'Well,' said Elliott, in a rush, 'if you really want to
know, I'm not sure that your new cardigans and your half
moon spectacles go with the heavy duty fogs, the bull
bars, and all that writing on the motor car.'

'How do you mean?'

'We-ll. The cardigan says solidity, dependability,

responsibility, and on a grey day, even disability, but the bull bars and the heavy duty fogs, they seem to be saying something else.'

Fulton nodded bravely.

'I know what you mean. You think I should perhaps change them for polo-necked cashmeres and shirts with very small collars and surprisingly short sleeves?'

'No-o, I don't think so,' said Elliott, carefully offering Fulton a home-made pistachio biscuit, 'no, I think you need some of those jumpers with pieces set in on the shoulders in very plain colours, corduroys, and shoes with bottoms in patterns that cake with mud at very inconvenient times, and then spill out later on someone else's floor.'

'You know, you are right. They're much more the thing to go with bull bars and fog lights and slip differentials. What a pity. I loved my cardies. Still, I suppose I could always give them to Twinks, she's very fond of anything woolly.'

Elliott stood up quickly. He didn't want to discuss Twinks, particularly not just after one of his best home-made biscuits.

'Let's talk artichokes,' he said brightly. 'I've had some nice Druidy thoughts for the christening,' he called to Fulton as he exited towards the kitchen. Then, passing Lady Tizzy in the hall as he went, he told her, 'You're going to be a High Priestess at the christening, how about that?'

'Can I have snakes in my hair?'

'Yes, if you want, or a viper at the bosom might be nice.'

167

'Not a real one though, a papier mâché one. I could get Twinks to make it.'

'Not before she's re-made the Duchess of Roseberry's wastepaper basket and pin tray you won't.'

'Twinks wasn't in a very good mood this morning,' Patti told Fulton as she joined him at the drawing room window, 'so I gave her the christening invitations to do for me. She'll like that of an evening, take her mind off everything.'

'I didn't know she had it on anything.'

'Oh yes,' Patti nodded, while expertly running her nail file around her long talons. 'Yes, her mind is full of tinea.'

'That probably explains the poor Duchess's waste bin. She got the coat of arms right, but the bit at the top was extraordinary.'

'Really? What?'

'It was a hand wielding something. As a matter of fact, now you come to mention it, it did look remarkably like a back scratcher.'

'Fulton?'

'Mmm?' said Fulton, his mind torn between the complications of exchanging his cardies for jumpers in army colours and shoes with complicated patterns on the bottom, and trying to interpret the extraordinary thing that Twinks had put into the hand at the top of the Duchess's coat of arms.

'How are you getting on with the ball, Fulton?'

'Like everything, as well as can be expected, if not less. The Countess has backed out, as you know, so now we're all back to apricot tones, but lumbered with cream and green for the tenting because it was already ordered

168

when she stepped in, and now she has stepped out, nothing to be done.'

'Our christening's after her ball, isn't it?' asked Patti carefully.

'Yes, why?' asked Fulton, surprised suddenly, which he prided himself he very rarely was with Lady Tizzy, because she was after all his wife.

'Nothing.'

'When girls say nothing they always mean something.'

'And when men say it?'

'It means everything. You don't want to have the christening until Nanny and her friend have finished copying the Duc de Berry gown so the babies are both matching, do you?'

'No, it wasn't that, it's just that I want our christening to be very special, and I wasn't sure it could be if it came after Jennifer Pemberton's ball.'

'They will be different. There will be no comparison. One so formal, pleated, tented, and matching, the other a sort of Wiltshire fertility gathering.'

'Have you told the Vicar?'

'Absolutely no need. The churchy bit will still be in the church, and if he doesn't like the Druidy feel to the party afterwards he can always leave.'

'That's all they do though, isn't it, vicars and priests, leave? I mean every time I feel like a bit of church, it's either closed, or there's a school play, or they've all had a quarrel and left.'

'They don't pay them enough, darling,' said Fulton, and he patted Lady Tizzy's cheek affectionately. 'If they paid them more they'd get a better class of person, more

169

people in the churches, better sermons, everything. After all, just because it's a vocation doesn't mean it can't be a job too.'

'What do you think about lady priests?'

'I can never tell the difference, quite honestly,' said Fulton, getting up to answer the front door. 'Why?'

'Nothing.'

'Not nothing again, surely?'

'Well, it's just that I was thinking I might as well go in for the priesthood, the way things are going, or not going, and what with one thing and another.'

Fulton stood by the door. He knew it. *Real Man* was raising its ugly head again. Torn between the front door and Patti, he nevertheless hesitated. After all, a certain person's going to *Real Man* affected them all, most of all him and his bank manager.

'Has he still not been?'

'Not according to Bloss.'

'And he should know.'

'Exactly,' sighed Patti. 'He should. 'Parently every time he drives up to the clinic, Bert – that's Pember's name at *Real Man* – gets out, goes in, and then comes straight out again saying there's a queue and he's never queued for anything in his life and he doesn't want to start now.'

The front doorbell was now insisting that it should be answered.

'You're not going to give in, are you, darling?'

'Of course not, I love you far too much.'

Fulton kissed his fingertips.

'And I love you too!'

What a relief. For once he really believed Lady Tizzy.

He knew that she really, really wouldn't do anything to hurt or distress him. After all she hadn't meant to have twins, or a boy, and now that she had, they had, and they had all three of them come to terms with it, it didn't matter in the least, in fact it was really very nice. Even so, it was most important that the whole episode at *Real Man* must now be closed down firmly.

Just before he opened the front door it occurred to Fulton that perhaps going to *Real Man* was a little like giving up cigarette smoking. A person needed an incentive. What Pemberton needed was an incentive, something he could, or they could, promise him at the end. Like a weekend away with the lady of his choice? Something that would make him feel brave, and able to queue. He must mention this to Lady Tizzy the moment he had closed the front door behind whoever it was that was now standing on the other side, and whose face Fulton rather unsurprisingly could not make out, seeing that he was standing with his back to them.

'Now what?' Elliott called from the kitchen, which was fairly cheeky considering he only ever opened the front door in an emergency, and then only if he thought the person on the other side would go away very quickly.

The 'now what' now turned round, and Fulton realized with a rush that it was no wonder he had thought the macintosh had a slightly familiar look to it. The wearer was Andrew Gillott, and he was holding an unmistakable bunch of flowers all done up with a mauve bow, which didn't suit them at all, since the flowers were florist's red roses of the kind that never open, even when you put their stems in boiling water and chuck in dozens of packets of cut flower food.

171

'I thought you were in China?' said Fulton, taking the flowers from Gillott as if they were for him, although they were both quite aware they were not.

'China's closed,' Andrew told him, while lighting a very strong-smelling cigarette and peering anxiously past Fulton as Fulton had noticed other men always did when they were feeling too excited for anyone's good, let alone his.

Lady Tizzy appeared at the drawing room door. Fulton did not need to turn and see this because Andrew's face told him quite clearly that it was so, lighting up quite dreadfully, and then also Patti's scent as always announced her presence long before she arrived on any scene.

'Lady Tizzy,' Andrew murmured.

'I thought you were in China?'

'It's closed,' said Andrew again, and his senses reeled before the sight of Patti in her plunging cocktail frock. It was just as if she was expecting him, which they both knew she was.

'I called on the off chance—'

'I always think people who call on the off chance are a bit off,' Fulton murmured, hurrying off with the flowers without telling Patti they were for her.

'What's he doing here?' Elliott hissed, peering through the crack in the kitchen door, and speaking above the sound of his new pasta machine.

'He apparently took it in his head to call because China's closed,' said Fulton, throwing the red roses into the double Belfast sink with single brass reproduction Edwardian tap.

'China may be closed,' said Elliott thoughtfully, 'but

172

by the look on Lady Tizzy's face she may well not be.'

'What do you mean?'

'You know,' said Elliott, picking up the red roses and ripping off the mauve bow which was useless even for Christmas presents, and running very hot water into the left hand Belfast sink.

'I can't bear it.'

Fulton sank down and rested his head on the marble of the kitchen top.

'Oh, it'll be all right. After all, she has promised; nothing doing until after *Real Man*,' said Elliott, shaking out the red roses and trying to unsquash their leaves.

'But this is the wrong man!'

Elliott turned and stared at Fulton.

'My heavens! You're right. Of course. This is the wrong man.'

They stared at each other.

'Better do something.'

'What?'

Elliott looked round desperately, and then shouted 'Help!' at the top of his voice. 'Help!' he called again.

'What's wrong with you? I must know what's wrong with you!' Fulton demanded, as he prepared to dash out into the hall.

'I don't know,' said Elliott. 'Think of something, that's all. Just think of something, and call an ambulance. It's the only thing that will stop whatever's going to happen happening. You know, we both know, when she gets that glazed in aspic look to her, disaster shortly follows.'

Only too anxious to oblige, Fulton ran into the hall.

'Help,' he cried out on Elliott's behalf. 'Help!'

He flung open the drawing room door, and saw at

once how right they both were. Lady Tizzy and Andrew were melting together already, and she hadn't even poured him a gin and tonic or herself some of the Emva Cream sherry that Elliott always got in for her.

'Help!' he went on.

They ignored him.

'*Help!*'

'Something the matter, Fulton?' Lady Tizzy turned towards him at last, and with great reluctance, as the pulse in Andrew Gillott's neck doubled its normal rate.

'Um, um – come quick. Elliott's hurt himself. Call an ambulance.'

Lady Tizzy seemed hardly to hear him.

'Oh, and a fire engine.'

That was it. The bolt of inspiration that he so badly needed. Never mind that Elliott might be dying of food poisoning from his own pasta, that would never disturb Lady Tizzy, not in that mood. No, but she did have an absolute passion for fire engines, and he happened to know her very dearest and unfulfilled wish had always been to call one.

'A fire! No, don't you call, I'll do it, I'll do it,' she cried, jumping up and looking at Fulton with sudden excitement. The gelatinous look dropped from her eyes, and her normal day-to-day expression of serene ignorance returned as she grabbed the telephone from Fulton, and then she stopped. 'Oh dear. Now what is it that you dial?'

'Nine, nine, nine?' Fulton suggested helpfully.

Slowly, with a pencil so as not to break her long red finger nails, Patti dialled the number nine three times, the expression on her face quite changed.

As Fulton saw that the other one, the one he always so dreaded seeing on anyone and everyone and most of all on Patti had quite gone, he half closed his eyes. What a relief. Yet another *crise* was safely passed. In the nick of time he had managed to pull the ass's head from off Patti's own pretty one, and she was his own dear Lady Tizzy once more, the silly expression quite gone. He turned back towards the kitchen. Now for the fire.

8

Jennifer sighed deeply as nowadays she had noticed she was wont to do. She had had a funny feeling about Pember for a few weeks now, as if part of him was missing, not just his mind, but a whole piece of him. It was a piece that she had once known and very much liked and it now seemed to her that it had been posted off and was living somewhere else, and what was worse, very possibly with someone else.

That was the feeling that she had had up until only a few minutes before, but the feeling that she now had was quite different, because she was sure she now had positive proof that Pember's foot had slipped from the straight and narrow. Positive proof was quite different from the funny feeling you got that someone wasn't quite with you, positive proof was the stuff of divorce and two years of waiting around in order to find out what you had to live on, and all sorts of beastlinesses.

A lump came into her throat at the thought of all the glee that her mother, and everyone they knew, would derive from her and Pember's getting divorced. It would be a positive tax rebate of emotional joy for them. Yards and yards of speculation, more yards than had gone into those beautiful cream and green tents that Fulton and she had had designed and ordered for the ball. Heavenly tents they were, tents that absolutely begged for people to set them about with magnificent floral devices and guests to come in their best jewels, and everything to be magical. But no more. The ball would have to be cancelled. She knew that now quite definitely. After all how could she dare to throw a ball, a perfectly private ball too, when she knew that her husband was obviously being flagrantly unfaithful and going to leave her for someone else, and she and her babies might end up penniless?

No, she would have to cancel everything. Pay for the tents, shut up shop, and wait for Pember to come and confess his all, which she was quite sure would be everything. Jennifer dug her rather too short tapestry needle into one of the floribunda roses that made up her new tapestry, and promptly caught her finger. It was nice to watch the blood, and then to suck her finger and taste it mixed up with that curious metallic taste of needle. Both the blood and the pain were appropriate, and besides, the pain stopped the tears coming.

Bloss stood by the door.

'You rang, milady?'

Jennifer looked up and across at him, and removing her finger from her mouth slowly shook her head.

'No, you know I didn't, Bloss. How could I have rung when I've just pierced my finger?'

'I'm sorry, milady. I was quite sure I had heard a bell. I must be getting like the late very great Sir Henry Irving, hearing bells where there are none.'

Jennifer didn't know what Bloss was babbling on about, so she frowned. She was so fed up with Bloss she could have hurled the cut glass decanter from the mahogany side tray at him. She had positive proof that

177

Bloss was on Pember's side, driving him around to meet this woman whoever she was every afternoon. Bloss was nothing more nor less than an enemy in the camp.

'You know I'm having to cancel the ball, do you, Bloss?'

Bloss stiffened.

'Oh, why is that, milady?' he asked with suitable caution.

'Because, Bloss, quite simply I have decided, with an eye to the future, we cannot afford it. Straightened circumstances are just around the corner, and I happen to know that it will be a complete waste of time.'

Bloss's face remained commendably impassive.

'I'm not a fool, Bloss. I know what is going on, you know. I know that Lord Pemberton is up to something, and it is only a matter of time before he comes and tells me. Whatever it is, he will have to confess to it, you must know that, and if you don't, I certainly do.'

Jennifer's words had come out in a rush, and she now flung off her embroidery spectacles and jabbed the canvas of her tapestry with abandon. Embroidery inside was beginning to get her down. So small and fiddly. Tapestry was better. And not only tapestry. Talking honestly was better. Much better, and much nicer, better and nicer, she thought with a rush, to have it all out in the open. A clean sweep with a new broom, and *voilà*, suddenly life was an open highway, no more worries, just decisions to be made and taken. And she had just made and taken one. No more ball, not for anyone.

'Your ladyship is very kind to confide in me this way,' Bloss told her carefully, choosing his words. 'Most kind.'

Outwardly calm he might be but not inwardly. His

mind began to race towards everything and everybody. He knew all too well that upon his next words depended a great deal, most of all his thoroughly cosy life at the Hall. Forget the new Pewgot. If he left the Hall, if there was a scandal, not only would he be replaced, the whole place would be replaced, and most likely not by a Lady Tizzy with a nursery full of by-blows, but by a modern sort of girl with power shoulders and fancy ideas about employing Filipinos for butlers.

'I very much appreciate your confidences in this. After all, milady, I have been at the Hall a very long time. Since his lordship's bachelor days, as you know, milady.'

Jennifer's eyes, so recently threatening tears, now narrowed and fixed Bloss with a stare, as she realized in a rush that he had really funny-shaped ears, a little like one of those new rabbits the children had brought back from Stanton. The tops of his ears turned right down, and quite a way too, but that didn't make him any easier to deal with, unfortunately. Having thoroughly examined the peculiarities of Bloss's auricles, Jennifer suddenly decided to stay silent, a little technique which she occasionally used.

'As you know, milady,' Bloss continued, 'I am and always will be devoted to both his lordship and yourself, and your continuing happiness is at the very heart of everything I do, even the silver.'

'Really, Bloss.'

There was no question mark to end Jennifer's short sharp exclamation, just a thick custard coating of sarcasm. Not too much, just enough, so that her inability to believe in Bloss's devotion shone through.

'Well, that is something,' she couldn't help adding, returning to her sewing with feigned interest.

'The question of finance, however rich we are, troubles us all, wouldn't you say, milady?'

Bloss sharply changed his tone, adopting one he was all too accustomed to hearing the horrid little accountants who so plagued his lordship using on rainy November days in the library.

'Expense is not stretched by small items such as the giving of balls, which after all, as your ladyship and myself are well aware, can be written off as advertising the Market Garden Company we are thinking of starting. No, it is the larger items, such as children, school fees, Nanny and her motor cars.'

Jennifer looked up sharply.

'Nanny's only got one motor car, Bloss,' she said defensively, because they both knew that this was a vulnerable area for both of them. 'Quite a small motor car.'

'Quite a small motor car with the newest reg,' said Bloss crisply and quickly, 'with limited slip diff, petrol lock, and foot mats finished in labelized rubber neutralizer.'

'She needs those for her special boot,' Jennifer put in quickly. 'It does spread mud so.'

'Nanny's motor, unlike the ball, cannot be put down to the Market Garden Company,' Bloss intoned.

'Yes, but it is necessary,' Jennifer exclaimed, just managing to avoid jabbing her needle into a new finger. 'I didn't know we were starting a Market Garden Company,' she went on.

'Mmm, that is why his lordship and I have been going

out and about together,' Bloss continued smoothly, while in direct contrast his mind continued in a ferment of activity. 'We have been doing business on behalf of the new projected company. Talking to local farmers, discussing produce. We want all our produce to be local rather than organic, which is a little too advanced for us, we thought. That sort of thing, milady. It was to be a surprise, I think.'

Jennifer shook her head.

'His lordship knows I don't like surprises. Hate surprises. People springing out of cupboards singing happy birthday, everyone wearing funny expressions as if they've just sat on a whoopee cushion.'

'Yes, but this surprise is a better sort of surprise than the normal kind, milady. A business surprise, something to tell you about in the winter when thoughts are turning to the cost of the central heating.'

But try as he might Bloss could see that her ladyship was not in a mood to be mollified.

'Well, if we're having to humble ourselves and go into trade, Bloss, we most definitely can't afford a ball, which is precisely my point, or one of them,' she told him crisply. 'Oh dear, here's my mother. I suppose you'd better let her in.'

Bloss and Mrs Parker-Jones were old allies, although no-one would have known it as he opened the door to her. Normally they exchanged smiles, and little facial grimaces that meant 'We understand each other', but today Clarissa was somewhat surprised when Bloss, who had among other things perfected his butler's nod over the years – curt, gracious, deep, very deep, everything depending on whom he was opening to – now delivered her one very curt nod indeed, before stalking ahead of her to the library door.

If Clarissa had had a clear conscience Bloss's nod would not have worried her, but the truth was she did not have a clear conscience, so Bloss's nod made her overly tight Rose Bruton hand-made ladies' cross-over all-in-one corset seem even tighter than when she had first struggled into it and done it up with difficulty that morning.

Just from his nod Clarissa knew that Bloss must know that she and the Countess had spent the previous week spreading a rumour among people of very important inconsequentiality, a rumour that more than hinted that the Pemberton ball was going to be a shoddy affair, all local County, no stars, pop singers, or minor royalty; and that the two ladies were actively, but actively, encouraging Lady Mary Stranragh, the Countess's daughter, to give a rival ball in Sussex, the Countess's old stamping ground, and with every chance of success, since it had to be faced Sussex was far easier to reach than Wiltshire if you were driving from London, and even if you weren't. And anyway was more fun for people who only wanted to pop in, and even those who didn't.

Bloss had his faults, as he was only too well aware when he was closing his eyes at night (when his daily sins floated in front of them and he realized that crimes such as watering down Nanny's sherry would have to be paid for), but disloyalty was not one of them. His first priority at the Hall was the Hall, its continuance and happy survival, and the ball at the Hall's being a flop was not going to be either happy or of continuing good.

182

It was by this point and this point alone that his curt nod to Mrs Parker-Jones was validated. He knew what he knew from Maria, the Countess's maid, his ally and friend whom he kept so liberally supplied with fresh young vegetables and fragrant and rare herbs, for precisely the same reasons that she kept him supplied with the latest up-to-date bulletins on the Countess's domestic plans and politics.

'Bloss seems out of sorts this morning,' Mrs Parker-Jones couldn't help remarking to Jennifer after he had closed the library door a little louder than normal.

'Mmm, and so he should be,' said Jennifer, not rising to greet her mother and sucking on her piece of wool before re-threading her needle. 'He's been conniving with Pember, and I have discovered it, and he doesn't like it. Not only that, but it seems we are having to go into trade like everyone else. No doubt it will not be very long before there are hippos below the ha-ha.'

'But the Hall isn't big enough for hippos in the ha-ha.'

'The Hall isn't big enough for most things, let alone what is happening at this moment,' Jennifer stated, and having successfully loaded her needle she now stared stony-eyed at her mother.

'How do you mean, Jennifer?'

Clarissa looked at her daughter uneasily. Her only child had a steely side to her that definitely came from her father Aidan's side of the family. Whichever, or whatever, side it came from, it had always surprised and discomfited her mother. It was the kind of obstinate determination that was so often displayed to such a frightening degree by thoroughly virtuous persons. Her mother knew only too well that Jennifer did not have a secret side to her as most people did. Some sad, delicate, or indelicate side that would make her vulnerable to sniggers or slight social blackmail. No, she was as honest as an egg, and just as binding.

'How do you mean?' asked Mrs Parker-Jones again.

Jennifer jabbed her tapestry, successfully stabbing the centre of a pink rose and making her mother start backwards slightly while at the same time glancing longingly towards the sherry bottle sitting so snugly, and not too far away from her, on the mahogany tray.

'How do you mean?' she asked for the third and last time, giving up the silent battle for an early sherry and staring instead at the top of her daughter's head.

'I mean,' said Jennifer, and she was careful to keep her voice calm, 'I mean there are things happening at the Hall that shouldn't be happening, which I am about to stop, including the ball.'

Mrs Parker-Jones's mouth, coated in two layers of Esther Lantern's Peach Perfect, dropped open, and stayed open until she remembered herself and quickly shut it. If she smoked she would have had a cigarette, but since she didn't, and never had, she opened and closed the clasp on her handbag instead.

'I am,' Jennifer confirmed, 'about to close the whole idea of the ball, as well as many other things. But I'm starting with the ball.'

'Why should you do that?'

'Why, Mother dear, because I am not in the mood to be made a fool of, that's why.'

The click, click, click of Mrs Parker-Jones's handbag doubled in speed. She hadn't felt so set back since her husband had dropped dead on the hearthrug on the day of Jennifer's coming-out dance. It was all very well for her to be scheming with the Countess to make Jennifer's ball a flop, but it was something quite other when Jennifer herself cancelled the whole idea. If Jennifer cancelled her ball it would make the Countess and herself look horribly foolish, scheming and plotting against something that didn't exist.

'You mustn't cancel the ball, Jennifer. Think of the dismay it will cause people, nice people, people who were looking forward to it. Think of the disappointment.'

'I have, and there will be very little or none,' she was told. 'No-one really wants to come to these things, not really. They all pretend they do, but then on the night they'll all cry off and the whole thing will be a disaster, so it's better if it doesn't go ahead. And anyway I shall probably be immersed in divorce proceedings by then, which will mean I will have to keep an eye on every penny, if only for my little nursery brood's sake.'

'Oh, but this is ridiculous, I mean to say, Pemberton – John – is worth millions. And you have no proof he has done anything wrong.'

'He was worth millions, but he won't be soon, and I don't need proof of infidelity. A woman knows.'

This last was uttered with such grim certainty panic seized Clarissa. Normally, day to day, she hated the fact that her daughter was richer, and took precedence over her, but now that Jennifer seemed intent on smashing her own position and committing social hari kiri, it was altogether a different matter. To be Lady Pemberton, to be the Marchioness of Pemberton living at the Hall was after all not nothing; to be an ex-Marchioness living in some village house would be really nothing. Mrs

Parker-Jones caught her finger in the catch of her handbag on what must be its hundredth click. The pain was nothing compared to the panic she was feeling. Jennifer must be stopped at all costs. She must be stopped from divorcing Pemberton, and whatever happened the ball must go on. The ball particularly must go on, which it quite evidently wouldn't, if Jennifer was thinking in terms of divorce.

Apart from anything else the ball simply had to go on, Clarissa realized in a renewed rush of emotion, because the Countess and herself had already set Lady Mary's ball if not rolling, certainly marching inexorably forward, and there would be no point to it at all if it wasn't given in competition with Jennifer's ball at the Hall; it would lose its point, its edge.

'No-one in our family has ever got divorced—' Clarissa began, deciding to take a different and more wholesome approach.

'Until you—'

'Until me,' she agreed, 'but then that's different. Besides, our divorce has not come through yet, and Andrew came into my life when I was very sad, on the rebound from grief you might say. I should never have made that particular mistake had I not been widowed.'

'How is Andrew?' asked Jennifer, not really wanting to know.

'Still being a walker to the Countess. She takes care of him most of the time. But to get back to this business of the ball—'

'No ball, Mother dear. None.'

'But why?'

'No. No ball. Absolutely no point to it, or indeed to anything now.'

Mrs Parker-Jones felt close to tears, and quite openly so. No early morning sherry, Bloss so very curt, Pember on the rampage, no ball, and Jennifer determined to get divorced. Her whole world seemed to be tightening around her in a sort of stranglehold, a worse tightening even than the Rose Bruton all-in-one.

'Good heavens, here's Pember,' said Jennifer, having seen his car from far down the drive. 'I wonder where he's been this time?'

She watched him climbing out of his new motor car. From this distance she could see he was looking really very sweet as always; such a shame she had to divorce him. She made to turn away when she stopped, having noticed Bloss hurrying down the front steps and making a line towards him, and realizing as Pember grew more apparent that he was not looking very sweet at all, he was looking most odd, and not a nice odd either.

Jennifer narrowed her eyes, watching intently. She saw they were having a short exchange of dialogue. No doubting what they were talking about, and it wouldn't be the Market Garden Company, she'd be bound. Suddenly she saw Pember put out a hand and leaning forward drape himself across Bloss. With a rush of guilt Jennifer saw Pember, her dear Pember, staggering and falling, even managing to bring his butler to his knees with him. She gave a low moan, dropped her sewing and rushed out of the room, leaving her mother to leap to the drinks tray and help herself to two large sherries in swift succession.

As Clarissa downed the second sherry she realized

she wasn't in the least bit interested in what was wrong with Pember, she was far more fascinated by what was wrong with Jennifer. The Marchioness of Pemberton was quite obviously out of sorts, as a girl who is about to cancel a ball and divorce her husband must be expected to be, but that didn't mean she should throw out the baby with the bath water, or in this case the husband with the ball. She had to persuade Jennifer to go ahead. That at least, whatever happened, she had to do, or the Countess and herself would become the laughing stock of people all over London, and most of all, dread of all dreads, of Lavinia Westington.

For Jennifer's friend Georgiana life was no easier. Having decided that she would put forward Miss Cut-offs for selection by Kaminski's casting agent, she now had to manoeuvre events so that they appeared quite natural, which wasn't always easy, because mad though Gus might be, he also had a strange almost unnatural way of knowing when it came to the preservation of his own pleasurable lifestyle, and the moment he felt Georgiana was distracted for even a single second from pursuing life as he wanted it lived, he would sense it, and come after her. Georgiana knew this the way she knew her first husband Stranragh would crouch outside her door watching her undressing, and then go away again leaving her untouched.

'I thought I would take a day off to go to London.'

Georgiana was aware that these were the most emotive words that she could ever pronounce in front of Gus. They had the kind of effect on him that the announcement of an infidelity might have on someone else. But happily this evening she had chosen her moment right, a moment when Gus, having spent a very long hot afternoon pursuing considerably more than the muse with Miss Cut-offs, was now downing his second California Dreaming, something to which Georgiana had had no hesitation in introducing him, knowing precisely how light his head was, and how especially helpless it would render him.

'That's a good idea, George,' he agreed happily. 'Very good idea. Go to London with Cynthia,' he agreed, his smile sliding off under the old faded wickerwork chairs in which they were seated in order to better view the sunset. 'Bring me back some more nice presents. Mmm?'

Georgiana didn't reply, because she had a feeling there was a limit to how many nice presents she wanted Gus to enjoy.

'But you've only just been to London, Georgie,' Nan complained, at the same time throwing a glance towards little George who was still half asleep even though it was breakfast time.

'I know, Nan, that's the whole point,' Georgiana agreed, happy that she did not have to cross her fingers, 'I have to keep going to London at the moment, because there's someone there who I have to see. It's about the future. My future, and little George's future.'

It couldn't have been truer, so Georgiana was well able to smile and nod at Nan and Nanny over their cornflakes and Weetabix, and clip her small crocodile overnight case smartly together.

'I'm taking Cynthia, you know Miss – you know

Gus's model with me. She's going up for a part in a film directed by an old friend. She's very excited.'

'It doesn't take much,' said Nan staring at two over-cooked rashers fiercely.

'You're not going to London on her motor bike, are you, Georgie?'

Nanny peered anxiously at Georgiana who shook her head.

'No, we're both going by train. Taking overnight things, just in case things get exciting. You know how they can in London.'

She smiled round the kitchen, but no-one was in the least bit interested.

Georgiana liked second-class travel on the train much the best, far away from the business men with large backsides spreading and early whiskies on the return. In second class she liked all the people knitting bright-coloured baby jackets, gossiping and playing cards, and the pleasant smells of too much Marmite spread between sandwiches, and onions chopped to make sliced plastic cheese more appealing. In contrast to the constant movement of the anoraks and the knitting fingers the views hurtling past the train windows appeared almost impossibly calm and green, even more so once set against the amiable chaos of the inside of the carriages, where the sound of gossip and office politics being aired was broken only by the intermittent demands of the over-patient ticket collector laboriously writing out bills for un-bought station tickets, as he moved slowly down the length of the train.

Georgiana smiled at Miss Cut-offs who lit a cigarette and held her right elbow with her hand to smoke it, which looked rather strange, and made Georgiana wonder why she did it, for just a little while, until she finally closed her eyes and nodded off. It wasn't until the sounds of paper cups rattling emptily and sandwiches being neatly re-wrapped for return journeys intensified, that she awoke to find that the train was stopping and they were in London.

As Cynthia trailed along beside her, her mouth so wide open in astonishment that her bottom lip seemed to be touching the hem of her leather micro skirt, Georgiana wondered what Gus would think of this model, by whom he appeared to be so besotted, if he could see her in London now? At Longborough Cynthia had obviously seemed distractedly exciting, a positive oasis of delight and beauty which Gus could enjoy when he wanted a change from Georgiana and his usual routines. In London, however, where beautiful leggy girls of every kind stalked the streets restlessly, moving in and out of the shops as with practised poise they dismissed each other's brilliant looks with one cutting glance, Miss Cut-offs looked stubby and ordinary, and pathetically provincial. With a nasty jolt Georgiana realized suddenly that the poor girl was too vastly ordinary to even take to the interview she had arranged with the casting director of Kaminski's film.

'I expect you're dying to work in London like everyone round Longborough?' Georgiana asked Cynthia over a coffee and Danish pastry, talking to the poor girl for the first time since they had caught the train together two and a half hours before.

'Oh yes.'

'I expect you'd like to work in a film?'

'Oh yes.'

'Except, perhaps you'd like to work in a shop first?'

'Oh yes.'

'I expect you'd like to share a flat and work in a shop?'

'Oh yes.'

'Good, well that's settled then.'

Georgiana nodded briskly.

'As a matter of fact I think I know just the place that's looking for people like you, and you should feel quite at home there too.'

It was a recently opened shop called 'Sunday Painters'. Cosily nestling in Pimlico, it seemed so perfect for Cynthia that within only a few minutes of talking to the friend of the friend who managed it, Georgiana was able to convince herself that this was what she had had in mind for Miss Cut-offs all along, a nice job in a painting shop. There was even a room for her to rent in the flat above, sharing with two Australians. Cynthia could start straight away since they were not yet fully staffed.

'Cynthia has modelling experience too,' Georgiana very sweetly told the manager, as Cynthia rushed off excitedly to telephone her mum and tell her she had a job in 'Lunnin' and wouldn't be coming home that evening.

Having left Cynthia in the unsafe hands of the manager of 'Sunday Painters', Georgiana walked off towards Knightsbridge feeling a little as if she had just sent a horse to the sales.

As she walked towards Kaminski's elegant apartment Georgiana examined her emotions. She knew what she had just done was not a nice thing to do, but she hadn't been able to help herself. The girl was so stupid, too stupid even to go up for a part of a deep sea diver, despite having swimming qualifications that would satisfy Jacques Cousteau. It was very naughty to have divested Gus of both his model and his infatuation, because now he would not only no longer be able to satisfy his lust, he would not be able to finish the painting, but then that was jealousy. What Gus would do when he found out what Georgiana had just done was quite another thing.

E.F. stared at Kaminski. He did not know what the great man would do to him if he found out that E.F. was knocking off his, Kaminski's mistress Sofia. Nor did he know how he had been able to do so for so long now, with such exquisite regularity, without Kaminski finding out. Sofia had constantly reassured E.F. with rather less exquisite but equal regularity, that she was not two-timing Kaminski, since Kaminski was currently not one-timing her.

'He's in his run-up phase, darling,' she explained to E.F. 'It seems you might as well be his best friend, of whatever sex, when he is in his run-up to a movie,' she continued with the total assurance of someone who had hardly known Kaminski at all before he cast her in her non-speaking, non-acting role.

E.F., who had known Kaminski for many a long and sometimes quite a short year, remembered concentrating on Sofia's magnificent if somewhat swamping prow while she talked such rubbish. The only problem was that when she continued, with the same hideous authority, to talk about Kaminski's attitude to his work with all that actressy confidence that E.F. noticed came so naturally to all the graduates of the American Warehouse School of Acting, E.F. found that despite himself, or more precisely because of himself, he suddenly, and quite quickly, no longer felt in the least bit amorous.

'This is so often the trouble with actresses,' he told himself as he waited for Kaminski at his newly leased apartment. 'They have everything,' he went on sternly, still to himself. 'Looks, figures, legs, bosoms, teeth, hair, everything except the one thing that could make the whole thing motor sweetly – an engine.'

Beautiful figures, beautiful legs, beautiful bosoms, beautiful teeth, beautiful hair, they were all as nothing without the personality to make them anything except a walking casting session. E.F. had once known a man who had an obsession with taking out beautiful girls. He was actually physically and mentally completely incapable of taking out anything that did not, had not, or would not appear at some time or another either on a billboard above Times Square, or on the front of *American Vogue*. Every first night, every premiere, every gallery opening, there was the luckless fellow with some new female confection. He had been the envy of everyone. He had money, and looks, and he certainly had the girls, which was why there was such consternation when he suddenly and quite accurately blew his brains out. No-one understood why he had done so, no-one that is except E.F. himself.

The motivation for suicide had been quite simple. The poor fellow had been too aware of his image to be able to be seen with anything less than the beautiful and in being unable not to be envied he had finally, and inevitably, shot himself from frustration and boredom. Of course the court had not understood this, but his friend E.F. had. He had understood it very well indeed, too well in fact, and even more when Sofia, of a morning, or sometimes of an afternoon, was lecturing him on some new acting technique or about something about which she knew less than nothing, and to say that Sofia knew less than nothing was to give her credit for knowing far too much.

Kaminski was on the telephone in the next door room, which was why E.F. had fallen into the bad, narcissistic, and self-absorbing habit of thinking. He peered through the crack in the door at the great man. He had been on the 'interruptor', as they called Mr Bell's famous invention, for a very great length of time for Kaminski. Not only that, but he had on his face a strange expression, strangely fierce and troubled, more like a charging rhino than a movie director.

'I'll call for you,' he kept saying. 'No, I said I'll call for you. Stay at the hotel, and I'll call for you.'

E.F. knew that he couldn't be talking to Sofia, because Sofia had moved out of the hotel and into the apartment with him, Kaminski, which was where he, E.F., had been increasingly less and less enjoying her. Sometimes he disenjoyed her in the early morning just after Kaminski had left on some location hunt which was of absolutely no interest to E.F. Sometimes he essayed to enjoy her when the great man was out re-lunching their producers. It was one of the greater perils of being a film director, having to be seen lunching and re-lunching your producers. Happily the lowlier half of a scriptwriting team had no such obligation, but if he was cute he could pick up some other rather prettier perks.

Except now that he had found out what a boring, uninteresting, untalented girl Sofia really was, E.F. found himself wishing, and oh so devoutly, that he had not taken up with the wretched creature. He hated being bored. Not quite as much as Kaminski hated being bored, but nearly.

Still, since Kaminski was intent on taking his elongated call, E.F. had too much time, and when there was too much time a person found himself facing those things that would not normally have to be faced, but which had to be faced if there was absolutely nothing else whatsoever on hand. Nowadays E.F. was finding being with Sofia about as interesting as being locked into a time capsule with an incomplete deck of cards. The girl could drive a sane man crazy, and personally he had never claimed to be sane. Never.

'In that case change hotels,' he heard Kaminski saying.

What was with this caller and hotels? E.F. peered once more through the crack in the door, and then seeing Kaminski's unchanged expression his heart froze. Oh no, it was that kind of call! Kaminski never ever took that kind of call, never made that kind of call, never admitted to being the recipient of that kind of call, and would never deal with that kind of call, except he obviously, from his expression, was about to, just had, and might even again.

Hezus Z. Christos, E.F. thought slowly, love surely was the greatest shaker and mover in the whole world.

No-one had ever had that effect on this man except one girl, and there had been so many others after her, and since her, he would never have believed that she could have still achieved so much in such a short time, over such a long period, with such a man.

'What's it with you and her? Not still?'

E.F. stared at Kaminski as the great man replaced the telephone. Just for a few uncomfortable seconds E.F. remembered what it was like to feel the way Kaminski was looking, to feel that kind of love, that kind of passion. The only time he had ever really been in love he had felt and no doubt looked as his friend Kaminski was now looking. His first, great love, the love his father had taken from him.

And that was another question that could spring to mind, if he let it. How much hate could a son have for his father? Sometimes it seemed to E.F. that every sea in the world heaped together, one on top of the other, could not match the depths of hate that he had for his father for taking his first love from him, snatching her from his own son, because he was getting old, and the young man's sun was rising as his was beginning to set. The poor young girl, what hope had she had? Dazzled by his sophistication, his charm, and his worldliness, she had allowed herself to be seduced, and then in some strange act of masochism, or perhaps even remorse, to become pregnant, and to die.

Of course, since it was such a good tragedy E.F. himself had not been slow to make immediate use of it. His first love became the basis of his first play, his first screenplay, his first novel, his first poem, his life. In fact it would be quite fair to say he had reaped not just a

197

good living from that first agonizing experience, but a small fortune. He had lived off it, out of it, and from it; it had been the great Ganges flowing through the centre of his life. But, nevertheless, and notwithstanding, he had made sure never ever to fall in love again.

This was something that he had always shared with Kaminski, in fact it was the very basis of their elegant friendship, their mutuality, their partnership: they both abhorred love and its endless, mindless, repercussions. Lust they admitted and were eager to pander to, and to enjoy. Dalliance was a high art in both their minds, but love, that which forces a man or a woman to forsake sanity and walk on hot coals for the rest of his or her days, was not for either of them. Except, now he looked at Kaminski in the bright light of a May London morning, and heard him hum a little snatch of 'Violets for her Fur' and saw him pull up his shirt collar a little tighter around his neck, and pause a little too long before turning back to E.F., it occurred to E.F. that maybe the two of them weren't going to have quite so much in common in this matter in the very near future.

'It's time to talk.'

Kaminski nodded towards first the coffee, and then the chair into which E.F. of a morning was wont to lower his frame in order that they could discuss the work in hand, and even write a little, something which, as at present, was difficult for both of them when they were working on a film which neither would choose to write, neither was particularly good at writing, and neither of them should be writing. However, judging from Kaminski's serious eyes, and the way he had his hands in their customary praying position, the tips of the fingers touching the top of his nose, judging from all that, the coffee having been poured and tasted, there were serious matters at hand.

'I'm bored with Sofia, E.F.,' Kaminski confessed suddenly.

It was E.F.'s turn to stare.

'I know, I know, you told me I shouldn't bring her over, and you were right. And now this other thing has come around once more. I realize it was, is, a mistake.'

Kaminski shrugged expressively. On a good day his shrugs could express more than a great actor's eyes.

'Even so, it doesn't have to be the worst mistake anyone ever made. I mean, she's very beautiful, and now she has lines in the film she seems very willing to work hard. She goes to the actors' studio every morning. You know?'

E.F. knew and only too well, and frankly if he heard Sofia mention it once more he thought he'd scream.

'I know you find her attractive.'

A long pause, then the praying position of the hands was being exchanged for the look of the King Emperor, the single hand up to the face, leaning slightly on the elbow, a blank, bored 'Will no-one bring me this man's head on a plate?' expression to the eyes.

'Take Sofia off my hands, E.F.'

E.F. stared. Oh, Hezus, Double Zed Christos, and he was only serious!

'I don't think I can do that, Kaminski, really.'

'Oh yes, you can, E.F.,' he was told, 'you can do anything. And have done.'

'Yes, but to be frank, I mean, Sofia, she's beautiful, she's lovely, but she does nothing for me here.'

199

E.F. put his hands a little too forcibly near the most tender part of his person, and then stared at Kaminski quite hopelessly.

'How do you know? You haven't even tried yet. You can't possibly know that.'

What could E.F. say? 'I have tried, and quite frequently, and now I'm finding it so trying I'm hoping not to have to try so frequently?' What? What, for heaven's sake? he wondered desperately.

'Just try, for my sake, E.F., really. Starting here, starting now. I have to go out, and what I want you to do is to take her out to lunch. She won't be down till well after midday—'

'Don't I know it,' E.F. thought with accelerating despair.

'Take her out to lunch, take her shopping, use whatever money you wish, I'll put it down to the movie, and then take her to the hotel. You know, Lexingham Gardens? And do what you can. I know you can, and if you can't, try.'

'I'm getting older, Kaminski. This kind of thing, lunches, sex, shopping, it's less interesting to me, you must have noticed that?' E.F.'s voice was rising in panic, and they'd both noticed.

'No.'

'What "no"? You must have noticed. I've grown quieter, older, more – more sensitive.'

'Shopping, lunch, sex, no-one is ever too old for, E.F. It's just a fact.'

'No, really, Kaminski. Really. I have changed. It's since I spent so much time up in Vermont with Alicia, my new wife—'

'I know your new wife, E.F. I was at your wedding. I was one of your witnesses.'

'Since we bought the house up there, ever since, I keep noticing the garbage in cities more. Every time I go to a city I think I'm going to enjoy myself, but I can't, because I find I keep noticing the little things too much, waiters' shoes, the napkins having little marks, small hairs on hotel pillowcases. It's pathetic, but it's true.

'And the same goes for the women I meet in cities. I mean take Sofia. I notice the small hairs at the back of her legs that she forgets to shave, and the way after a glass of wine her lipstick wears off, that kind of thing. I don't mean to, but I do, and it has a limiting effect on my hormonal activity.'

Suddenly Kaminski wasn't listening. He was back in front of the mirror adjusting his collarless shirt, and smoothing his jacket sleeve. Finally he turned towards E. F. and patted him on the arm.

'Don't worry, you'll be all right. When it comes to the crunch you'll be great. You'll have a glass of champagne, and she'll give her deep throaty laugh—'

Oh God, why did Kaminski have to remind him of her laugh? If only he knew how much E. F. had grown to hate Sofia's deep throaty laugh. Nowadays it reminded E.F. of nothing more than an outside drain.

'A couple of glasses of champagne—'

'A minute ago it was one, now it's two?'

'And you'll forget about the little hairs on the backs of her legs, and the faded lipstick, and how she keeps talking about herself. Come on. Have fun. And don't forget, keep her amused at the hotel until

201

well after five. I have extended business back here.'

Kaminski snatched up the keys of his rented Porsche and headed for the door. E.F. watched him walk outside into the street before crashing his head against the suede-covered walls of their rented study. Goddammit times five thousand! Sofia. And all afternoon. And on orders from the King.

What would he do? The last time he had voluntarily made love to her had been hard enough, but now, now that he absolutely had to keep her occupied, what would he do? He walked up and down the gloomy brown room. The only thing he could think of was that he could tie her to the bed, and then pretend to faint. Kaminski and he had put that in a recent comedy they'd written together. It hadn't worked too well, even in a comedy, which was probably why the picture never got made. Oh that such a day should come to him, that he should be desperate to think of some way not to have to make love to a beautiful girl.

And what was almost worse, that wretched girl calling Kaminski up like that, right out of the blue. Not only had it cut their working morning to shreds, but Herr Direktor had not even noticed that magnificent speech he had just made to him. Quickly E.F. went to the desk, and started to scribble a reminder of the images he had used. 'Waste not want not' was what his mother had written in his autograph book when he was young. He had been so embarrassed by it, and her, but now he was grateful. No better adage for a scriptwriter.

'Waiters' shoes, napkins, small hairs on pillowcases, etc.,' E.F. noted in his algebraic handwriting.

The gist of that speech would be perfect for the marine

biologist when he fell in love with the beautiful city slicker with the power suiting who arrives on Jumby Island to buy him off. Two candles on the table, some pasta on their plates, and two minutes' screen time could pass very pleasantly with that speech. But not thanks to that bastard Kaminski, E.F.'s sometime partner, his elegant friend, his bosom pal, oh no. At that minute he was far too besotted with that patrician Mata Hari from the English shires to even notice a beautiful speech, even if it hit him on the side of the head.

Kaminski had mixed feelings about meeting Georgiana. He was too sophisticated, too well versed in the art of love not to have mixed feelings, and not to be only too well aware of them. He might feel charged with adrenalin at the sound of her voice, charged with anticipation at the thought of meeting her for lunch, and quite helpless with desire when he finally saw her, but he was not fooled.

Georgiana was no longer the helpless kitten who had never had a love affair. The young slender girl whom he had only to dress and take out, put back, or leave, at his will, had gone for ever. She was a young woman now, a young woman who knew the frisson that sexual power, rather than just being made love to, could give her. That was the true tree of knowledge. He had noticed straight away that she was only too aware of the effect that she could have, and might continue to have, on Kaminski. Now she was cool where before she was uncertain. She had been shy – three years before she had been so shy about love she had blushed to drop her robe even a little – but now he realized that when he made love to her he was in competition not only with his former self, but with her past, as he had never been before. Georgiana had a past now.

And yet, as he watched her sipping her glass of champagne, her long slender legs draped with care, her long fingers clasping the fluted glass with delicate appreciation, he realized that self-confident though she might be she was still not so self-assured that she had lost her charm. Charm after all was based on not knowing you had it, an inner uncertainty that asked, indeed demanded, that the person you were with reach out to you so that two people could become one. People who were charmless were like the very rich, desperately dull because they knew what they had. Georgiana's eyes still told Kaminski that she needed his presence to reassure her that she was as alluring as she undoubtedly wanted to be.

Looking at her in her full-skirted suit with the nipped-in waisted jacket, and the dull turquoise blue silk shirt which they both knew showed up the colour of her eyes to perfection, Kaminski was only too happy to remain where he was. Soon he hoped he would be a great deal nearer. The only question in both their minds was, for how long?

9

The Countess was feeling greatly, horribly irked, and by no greater person than Colonel Bentley, her co-patron of the Field Mouse Rescue and Rehabilitation Centre. It wasn't that she wasn't used to feeling irked, because she was, what she wasn't used to feeling was irked with Colonel Bentley. He had started off as a rather pleasant sideline in her life, telephoning her on rainy afternoons when her knees were feeling far from well. Posting little cards to her to remind her of their mutual duties to the dear little creatures. Cracking the whip behind the out-workers who were making Dormouse Units out of recycled winter woollies and old plywood boxes, not to mention working on the design of their charity card, three dormice bringing their gifts to the Infant. (Couldn't be sweeter.)

Just lately, though, things had begun to change. Colonel Bentley had started to call frequently, and most inconveniently. This last time, the evening before, he had blustered up to the gate just when the Countess was doing the one thing in the country to which no-one but no-one admitted, namely watching television.

All right, she had been watching television upstairs and not down, but even so the pressure was the same, what to do if he had seen the blue light flickering from far off down the drive, and then what to say if he was so rude as to mention that he had? In the end she had plumped for complete evasion. It being Maria's evening off (which was why her mistress was glued to her television) the Countess had every reason to pretend that she wasn't in, and not to answer the door, but that had not been enough for the Colonel, oh no, he had had to push open the front door and shout 'Cooee!' leaving the Countess with nothing left to do but lock the door, leave the television on and pretend to be her own maid.

If that had been an end to the matter, all well and good, embarrassing though it all had been, and still was. But no! The wretch (he must be a bogus colonel), not content with pushing open the front door and strolling into the hall, had prowled about the downstairs rooms while the mistress of them remained helplessly aware of his prowling and quite unable to do anything about it upstairs.

'Blast him anyway!' said the Countess out loud, just as Maria, the real Maria, pushed open the drawing room door in the accepted manner of all maids, namely with her derriere, followed closely by the rest of her bearing a tray. (There was no other way to open a door if you happened to be carrying a heavy tray, the Countess knew, because she had actually tried it once or twice, just to see.)

Maria didn't pause in her progress towards the mahogany table upon which she always placed the coffee tray.

'Colonel Bentley's at the front door,' she told her mistress at last, straightening up.

This was too much.

'Kindly inform Colonel Bentley I am not in to him,

206

or to anyone to do with the Centre, until further notice.'

Maria nodded, and stood expressionless for a few seconds before deciding to speak.

'He's brought a thing with him.'

'What sort of thing?'

'A thing for the mices, a little 'ouse,' said Maria, becoming suddenly a great deal more foreign than she normally was, which she always did when she was excited.

'He can leave his little house in the hall, and I will call him about it,' said the Countess coldly. She had a horror of people who opened doors and prowled around other people's houses. After all, anyone could be doing anything, and they very often were, even watching telly. But quite honestly, if a person couldn't be doing anything in their own house without a person such as Colonel Bentley coming upon them, then it really was time they all did join that dreadfully Common Market.

'Her ladyship wants you to leave the 'ouse in the 'all.'

The Countess could hear Maria putting on her most stringently acerbic voice, the one she always used to Andrew if he came up the drive drunk and, alas, in time for dinner.

'But I want to know if she—'

'Her ladyship wants you to leave the 'ouse in the 'all,' the Countess heard Maria repeating, and she herself nodded again, vigorously, in approval.

There was the sound of the hall door being what the Countess imagined must be re-opened by Maria, but she was wrong. The hall door was not being re-opened by Maria, it was being opened by someone else, by Clarissa Parker-Jones, for herself.

'I had to see you!'

Because she had come in, Colonel Bentley had taken it upon himself to follow her.

'I wanted to have your opinion about the house—'

With one nod of her head the Countess froze Colonel Bentley out of the door. Another nod and Clarissa Parker-Jones was welcomed in, and immediately set to pouring coffee.

'That man!' said the Countess, breathing fire, so that even Mrs Parker-Jones looked nervous. 'The impertinence of him. I shall find out all about his colonelcy, and I'm quite sure he will prove to be no more a colonel than I am.'

Clarissa wanted to say 'Never mind that, wait till you hear the real news', but she couldn't, so she sat down opposite the Countess instead and, crossing her double-gusseted nylon-tighted legs, waited. She knew it might take a little time for the Countess to come back to her. She also knew that she would, and when she did it would be well worth it. There was something about bad news that made the teller of it feel very important. Even Clarissa realized that despite hating to tell the Countess what she undoubtedly had to tell her, she nevertheless felt tremendously important.

'Jennifer has cancelled the ball.'

The Countess stared. 'But she can't have!'

'Oh, but she has, she has cancelled the ball, and now she is talking about divorcing Pember.'

'It can't be true.'

'It is true. I have only just come from the Hall, and I do assure you every word is true. Pember collapsed in the drive, and Jennifer lost her rag and accused him of

208

infidelity, maintaining that the reason he fell over in the drive was that he was too tired to walk. She had some insane idea that he had come straight from his love nest, would you believe? I mean Pember of all people. So reliable. Why on earth should she possibly think that he was maintaining a love nest? Do you know, sometimes I despair of my daughter? She seems to find it so difficult just to maintain the status quo. And as for the ball. Why throw out the baby with the bath water, I ask you?'

'Yes, why is she?' agreed the Countess, for once almost silenced.

'Because,' said Clarissa slowly, 'she says if they have to halve everything she'll need the ball money to clothe and feed the children because men always get very tight-fisted once they decide to ditch you. I told her that.'

'Well, you were right, they do, but not men as rich as Pember. Judges always take a very dim view of very, very rich men divorcing their wives. Just jealousy really, they know rich men can afford to do what they can't. She'll get a very good settlement, she mustn't worry.'

Now Mrs Parker-Jones knew true panic. Suddenly Jennifer's divorce was real. The Countess was making it real, so real that for one brief second Clarissa saw herself following Jennifer out of the court, holding her arm sympathetically as they both posed for the photographers, pausing to smile in a dignified way for the television cameras before 'politely declining to say more'. She even saw the headline. 'Marchioness Uncovered Love Nest', and then the sub-headline – 'Collapse In Drive Told All'. One second later found her wondering whether to wear her navy blue trilene two-piece with the knife pleats, or the dove grey and mauve mottled coat-dress with dove grey hat and self-matching hat ribbon? It was difficult but not impossible to decide.

'Since you're getting divorced too, you may well both feel like making it a double,' the Countess observed tartly. 'This is a pretty kettle of fish,' she added, half to herself, because not only did it place her in an awkward position as far as her daughter's ball in Sussex was concerned (no point to Mary's ball if there was no rival really, everything would be very flat and unexciting) but, and this was a very real but, since she knew that Pember undoubtedly had not just a love nest but a nest full of babies at Flint House, the fat had quite obviously hit the fire, and it looked as though they were all going to get it in the eye.

There was a long pause as both women saw the end to their cosy chats together. No more planning and plotting. The two balls, all those people they had spent hours listing into tidy columns, Very Important, Less Important and so on, had all suddenly come to nothing because of Jennifer.

'Of course she does realize that once she divorces Pember, although technically she will remain a Marchioness, she will no longer live at the Hall, no longer command the same respect, the same service from others – she will in fact be a back number? It's always something that girls forget, you know, in their sudden flurry of self-righteousness when they find out that their husbands have been doing what all husbands do, namely having a little enjoyment without them. After all, it's always gorn on, you know, always. Never been any different. Never known a naturally faithful man. It simply doesn't mean the same to them, wouldn't you say?'

210

Clarissa leaned forward and placed her coffee cup in front of her. Lately she and the Countess had grown, if not together, at least less apart. They had a cautious if enjoyable alliance, which was a new and fascinating hobby for both of them.

'I do so agree with you, although I will say for Aidan,' she told the Countess, 'I will say that he never did stray, you know.' She felt a little rush of un-accustomedly genuine tears flood into her eyes. 'Not once.'

'Was he very fat?' asked the Countess with interest.

'Yes, as a matter of fact he was,' said Mrs Parker-Jones, surprised, and the tears stayed at the front of her eyes, not attempting to flow down her cheeks. 'He was very fat indeed.'

'Ah well, that would explain it. Very fat men aren't unfaithful very often. They have too many meals to think about, and of course they dance very well, so they're usually very romantic. Freddie, my husband, was quite fat, a Master of the Greys and Greens, all that sort of thing, wonderful dancer, but he never strayed, despite all the temptations thrown at him in the field and at hunt balls. No, he was very special. I miss him. Always will, always have.'

The two women looked across the years at each other and smiled. There was a short pause, and then the Countess reopened proceedings.

'So, what to do about this pretty kettle of *poisson*, then?'

'Must just bring Jennifer to her senses. Tell her to start interesting dear Pember more,' said Clarissa firmly. 'She can be terribly boring, Jennifer, and not at all

211

attractive. Time to pull up her socks and put on her suspenders and do her stuff—'

She stopped, realizing too late that a little too much of her original background had popped out before midday. She looked at the Countess, waiting for immediate censorship, or at the very least sarcasm, only to find none was forthcoming.

'Quite right,' the Countess agreed warmly.

'She has taken long enough to settle into the Hall and its ways,' Clarissa continued.

'Quite right,' the Countess said again. 'Although perhaps you might not be the person to tell her all this. You know how it is, daughters and mothers. I have only to tell Mary that she looks lovely in mauve for her to burn everything mauve, or give it away to Juanita. It's always the same. Might it not be better if the advice, whatever it may be, came from another source?'

Clarissa looked sharply at her new ally. She was right, of course. One word from her and Jennifer would get divorced straight away, if only to spite her mother. And that was something that Mrs Parker-Jones wanted about as much as she wanted bunions.

'Would you . . . could you say something?' she wondered.

'If you think it's a good idea, I surely will. I have known Pember since he was quite a little boy, you know, quite, quite little. Perhaps it might be a good idea if I explained the birds and the bees as they undoubtedly are to the Marchioness. Girls take infidelities, even a hint of them, quite badly. And really, as I say, they needn't. Most of the time men are only interested in seeing if their bodies are in working order. They just can't help being curious, it doesn't mean a thing, and of course women take it so very badly when they needn't at all. I always say the difference between men and women is that men will do anything for a new lover, and women will do anything for a good one. By the way, I must mention Andrew.'

'Andrew.'

Clarissa felt dull at the very idea of her soon to be former husband.

'Just must, I'm afraid. You see, I think he may have found another interest. Has he given you that impression at all?'

Clarissa's bosom, size thirty-eight on a warm day, now grew to forty plus as she swelled in indignation. The very idea of Andrew being unfaithful to her, and before they were even divorced, was appalling.

'Do you want me to have a word with him too?' asked the Countess delicately. 'After all we don't want him to rock the boat before the decree comes through. You don't want to find him back on your hands, and if some other woman's husband names him in his divorce, that could well happen.'

'I shall be most grateful.'

'Good. Well then, that's that. Only thing we have to do now is get the Ball rolling again, and if I do my work, that should take care of itself.'

The Countess smiled. So much to do, so many people to see, the whole of Wiltshire in turmoil. No doubt about it, but she was going to be kept very busy. The whole discomfiture of the evening before, the embarrassment at finding herself being spied on while watching television, Colonel Bentley and his intrusion, everything had

213

passed, and she was now very much herself again.

'Heigh ho, heigh nonny no,' she told Mrs Parker-Jones, who didn't understand at all.

If Elliott was in doomy form, peering out of the kitchen window he could see quite, quite clearly that Lady Tizzy was in far worse than doomy, she was in private hell. He knew this from the general un-made-up pallor which she was presently disporting round the garden, not to mention the over-natural bushy look of her hair. It was impossible to ignore Lady Tizzy when she was experiencing the mean reds. Even from outside her mood, like the currently cloudy weather, seemed to penetrate every corner of Flint House.

'You're right, Elliott, I am feeling decidedly iffy.'

As Elliott stared sympathetically at Lady Tizzy he noticed that her lips seemed to be protruding even further than normal. The idea suddenly crossed his mind that she might once have been a trumpeter.

'Feeling iffy's beastly.'

'Yes, well, just now iffy's exactly what I am feeling. I mean, I'm sure I know just how Kipling felt when he had looked on his twin thingies and found them just the same.'

'I've always found that a bit hard to believe, that if business. Try reciting "If" to a starving man.'

Elliott's eyes narrowed with vague indignation and then he let them roam at random round the garden which Twinks was meant to be helping maintain, and obviously wasn't. It seemed to him that the garden at Flint House was reflecting their life more than somewhat. Tidy lawns perhaps, but the flower borders were just a mass of confusion. Some things going in one direction that should be going in another, other things going too far up when they should be going sideways, and among it all the wild outside creeping in stealthily through the undergrowth.

'*Real Man* has been a flop, Ely-ot.'

Elliott looked sideways at Lady Tizzy now. If it wasn't for the babies, Beau and the girls, he really would feel like flinging her out on her ear, even though she wasn't even married to him. Her love life, which should be as calm as a mill pond, was chaos, not so much a mill pond as a positive stew pond, full of carp thrashing about. First Pemberton, and then that policeman she had a crush on, and then Pemberton again, and now Andrew Gillott who was anyway meant to be being the Countess's walker, not Lady Tizpots' lover.

'How d'you know *Real Man*'s a flop, anyway?'

'Bloss rang me in a flurry.'

Patti dropped her voice, and removed a finger, the nail of which she had just bitten in a particularly tense manner, from the side of her mouth.

'Yes.'

Elliott had noticed that Lady Tizzy always said 'Yes' as a punctuation when she had managed to grasp a very uncomfortable idea and was just about to explain it at length for Elliott's discomfiture.

'Yes, Bloss rang me in Fulton's car. We have an arrangement. I wait for him to ring at midday and then he calls me and pretends to give me the fodder order for the week.'

'So that's why you keep disappearing into the great outdoors in the mornings. I must say I had wondered.'

Patti nodded sadly. Matters had come to a pretty pass, they both knew, when she was missing the re-runs of 'Wiltons and Company' – an everyday story of a shopping mall – in order to take a morning call.

'Bloss is very clever, really,' she went on in a thoughtful voice that hinted a little that he might not, even so, be currently being quite clever enough. 'You see, what happens is he puts in an order for more fodder for the horses, oats and bran and so on, and I take it down, and then when he's quite happy no-one has picked up the other receiver he quickly tells me the latest about *Real Man*.'

'Which is?'

Patti burst into tears quickly.

'Terrible. Poor Pember. Bloss finally got him to go off to the agency, and he was quite fine, it seems – you know, chatting and joking and everything – until he actually got there disguised as "Bert Ackroyd", you know, all tramps' clothing, not at all Pember. Even so, nothing bad happened until he got to the door of the building when there was a man coming out looking terrible, all green around his gills because he was quite obviously all blue elsewhere.'

'Well, he would be,' Elliott agreed, feeling really quite faint himself.

'And Pember saw him, and it was just too much. He began to – you know, pass out, and only just managed to drive himself home where he actually did pass out in the drive which was worse than anything because he was still disguised as Bert Ackroyd, you see.'

Elliott frowned.

'I don't understand,' he said, continuing to frown.

'Why was – why was how he was dressed anything to do with anything?'

'Because Jennifer saw him!'

Patti nudged Elliott hard. Really, he was being so thick. He needed a good dig in the ribs to wake him up and make him see just how awful everything was.

'I still don't understand. I wear funny clothes sometimes but that doesn't mean anyone thinks I've been especially naughty.'

'Oh, Elliott, really, that's just how you are; that doesn't count at all,' Lady Tizzy insisted. 'Anyway, it's different; you're not naughty like Pember. So there was poor Pember dressed as Bert Ackroyd, and even though Bloss saw him first, it wasn't enough, because Jennifer soon joined them, and there was Pember all in a heap wearing funny clothes, so Jennifer immediately took it that he had been being a very naughty boy with someone else instead of trying to be a good boy and all responsible as a father and everything, and now she's going to divorce him and not give a ball. Bloss told me this morning, just now. And that Pember told Bloss it was all my fault for making him go to *Real Man* in the first place, and that he felt like never seeing me again, even though he hasn't been seeing me anyway. So you see why I feel I've looked on Rudyard Kipling's twin thingies and found them both the same?'

'Sort of.'

There was a long silence while Elliott stared straight ahead. It could be reasonably admitted that Lady Tizzy was right to feel that she had looked on Kipling's twin thingies and found them just the same. Things having

217

been sort of the same at one point, now could hardly be worse.

If Jennifer divorced Pember he might well marry Lady Tizzy, and if he married Lady Tizzy she would have to divorce Fulton, and they would both live at the Hall, and Fulton and he and the babies would be parted for ever, particularly Elliott, because he wouldn't even have visiting rights and be able to talk smocking with Nanny and potting with Bessie.

'This is just like something that happens in Monday's paper – in Penge.'

'Where is Penge?'

'Just a little to the left of most things,' said Elliott, giving the sort of deep sigh that only a man stretched to the end of his tether could bring to a situation.

'Oh, Elliott, what shall we do?'

Tears were brimming and about to make a watery trail down Patti's cheeks. Elliott removed a handkerchief from his pocket with a sigh. The sigh came first of all because he knew if he gave his handkerchief to Lady Tizzy he would never see it again, and it was one of his best, and second because he knew that giving her his handkerchief would never stop her crying, and there was something about girls crying that made him want to shout at them, because when they cried they made him feel so especially helpless.

'We had better go in now,' he finally said after Patti's sobs had died away a little, and he had given them both a Polo mint to suck. 'And we had better tell Fulton everything, and find out if he has a solution.'

'Oh, do you think he might have, Elliott?' Patti wanted

to know, pushing his handkerchief deep into her top pocket.

'Certainly. I mean, he has just finished reading *Wisdom and its Consequences*, so you never know, he could have found out something useful.'

Patti gave a dry sob. On hearing it Elliott felt a vague sort of lump of terror come into his throat as he thought of their babies who would just now, at that very minute, be coming back from their walks, two in the pram, and one toddling. It didn't take much imagination to picture how pretty and adorable they would be looking.

Nevertheless, if Fulton had managed to learn from *Wisdom and its Consequences* their bacon might not be altogether cooked, just a little too crispy maybe, but not burnt to a frazzle. He took Patti's hand and walked into the house with her, praying hard, which despite his deep belief in an all-seeing all-hearing Great Central Force, he nevertheless feared might be just a trifle optimistic, because it had to be faced the all-seeing all-hearing Great Central Force did seem to have been a tiny bit deaf of late. Please, please God, help things get sorted out, Jennifer and Pember and Lady Tizzy particularly, and soon, please. Immediately soon.

Georgiana stared around the house. Or was it an apartment? She didn't feel like asking, principally because she had a feeling she was going to find out anyway, so that asking might be just a little *de trop*. She felt safe despite being quite on her own with only Kaminski and a secretary in another room, as a girl must who has a very good nanny looking after her little boy, and a

219

common-law husband far away in the country, and a set of wonderful excuses to visit London.

She imagined that she must after all be in a house, because she couldn't sense a bedroom anywhere near, and she knew there was an upstairs because she had seen one when she jumped out of the taxi on arrival. She had always loved being alone in a house. Sometimes at Longborough, when she was a little girl, she had seemed to be alone for days and days on end while her parents went away on a visit for more, and still more different hunting with more, and still more, different friends.

While the servants listened to very loud radio comedy shows in a kind of religious rejoicing at the absence of the master and mistress, Georgiana would wander round the many rooms, hiding in cupboards from no-one at all, talking to her dog, encouraging him to jump over obstacles in the attics. Reading alone in her pony's stable while with eyes open he slept, and the comforting sound of rain outside made their two presences together inside a poem of cosiness. Being alone had been, and perhaps still was, in her mind anyway, one of the great luxuries.

She stared at what she could see of Kaminski's presence in the brown suede-lined room. Books, books and more books, but not paperbacks, all hardcover books with nice bindings, many of them old, some of them from the London Library, all for the film, she supposed. Flowers arranged by someone else were extravagant and beautiful, and crowded into square-cut vases in the approved fashionable manner. A paper knife with a strangely foreign-looking cypher, which must belong to someone with Russian blood, a leather folder with the initial 'K' beautifully engraved; inside the folder the first correctly typed pages of a script.

Georgiana sat down behind the partners' desk but instead of opening the folder she closed it, not bothering, not even for a second, to pause and read what was written on the expensively typed pages. She was not a reader of other people's letters or diaries, or scripts for that matter, any more than she could ever have brought herself to look in someone else's bathroom cabinet. It would have upset her to think that she had ever even known someone who did things like that, although knowing that Nanny did it, and Nan for that matter, didn't bother her at all, because they were old and allowed to be different. And anyway that was all they had, things like that, letters to steam open, other people's lives upon which to speculate now that their own were just a little still. So she closed the folder without giving its contents even a first glance before the leather slipped back over Kaminski and E.F.'s latest work. Only the 'K' for Kaminski remained for her to read.

This, in contrast to the script inside the folder, she did scrutinize, picking it up and turning it towards the light to see how deeply the 'K' was etched on the leather. She traced the letter with her finger, just a little sensuously, thinking from the chicness of it that it must be French, before putting it back and carefully reading the listings on the telephone beside the numbers. From these, since they were many and varied, she was at last able to ascertain that she was actually in a house and not an apartment.

She yawned, carefully putting her hand in front of her mouth, and then because Kaminski appeared still to be busy, despite having been told that she had arrived by the secretary in the other room, she picked up the internal telephone and rang 4 for the housekeeper and asked her to bring her up a glass of Evian water.

From the spyhole inset on the other side of the suede-covered door Kaminski had been watching Georgiana all the time she had imagined she was quite alone, and reluctantly allowing himself to be enthralled. She looked so detached from everything she was doing, not bored, but detached, as if she knew time was passing, time had passed, and time would continue to pass and really what she did or did not do would make not the slightest difference to everything happening around her, now or ever.

His hidden eye was Kaminski's camera, and he was self-conscious enough to know it. He knew he could not have directed Georgiana better in the scene, moving around, touching everything and yet not really looking. If she had been Garbo in *Queen Christina* she could not have effected a scene without words so well. But now she had rung for her Evian water he would have to go through to her, and become part of the same scene he had been so silently, and it had to be admitted, excitedly witnessing. Becoming part of a scene meant that it at once ceased to be directable. After all it was the number one rule that direction went out of the window once emotions became too heavily involved, and as he walked into the library-study and smelt Georgiana's curiously lemon-tinged perfume, and saw her long fingers carelessly release a leather-covered book, and her eyes, with their new detached expression, look up as she heard him make his entrance into the room, Kaminski felt

222

himself sinking into a quicksand of emotion that he really didn't want, and yet he would not, and could not, resist.

The truth was he longed for the Georgiana whose first lover he had been, who hadn't known her power over him, and whom he had therefore been able to leave behind as he was able to leave a canister of film, or an old script, quickly moving on to some newer, and therefore more interesting project, or in the young Georgiana's case, some newer and more interesting affair.

In truth once he had flown back to Los Angeles Kaminski doubted whether he had cast his mind back to Georgiana more than a few times, and then only to celebrate her contribution to his film, and the fact that their affair had proved to be the inspiration that he had so needed for his re-make of the Bolst classic. But that was all. Really, nothing more, nothing less than a mental comparison had been made, while watching rushes, or talking to his faithful editor, which was why when he saw her sipping her cocktail at the bar of that hotel he had been so astounded at his own emotions. Then and there, within a minute or so, he had wanted to make love to her, and without a doubt he saw that she felt the same, and yet the person whom he saw, whom he had once made love to, who had enchanted him with her indoor picnics was quite gone, replaced by someone quite different, more powerful, seemingly detached. Someone capable of dominating him where he had once dominated her. How he longed for the person he had once known, and yet he could not but stay to become enthralled with the person who had come to replace her.

'I see you have a new prison.'

She looked at him smiling, but the look in her eyes was just a little mocking.

'You're staying.'

There was no question mark as far as Kaminski was concerned, but he was all too well aware that there might be a considerable one from her point of view.

'This is very different from your last prison, Governor Kaminski,' she continued, ignoring him. 'Actually, I think I rather liked the last one a little better. Charles Street. More chic, the interior more faded, the neighbours a great deal more prestigious for having always been there.'

Kaminski felt that odd sense of panic that comes to everyone when someone with whom they are currently impassioned makes a reference to something in their mutual past, however brief, which they are meant to remember and can't. She was obviously caught up with this analogy of prisons, but he couldn't remember why.

'You used to lock me up in Charles Street and throw away the key, remember? Only the maid was allowed in and out while you and E.F. went away filming and came back with things for me to wear. My "prison clothing" I used to call it.'

He couldn't remember, so he gave up, not bothering to hide the fact that he was not even going to try to.

'Here – look, Kaminski – there isn't even a fireplace where you can smash your drinking glass for luck, for instance.'

Georgiana turned a full-circle, indicating the whole room with one long graceful gesture as she did so, all suede, no fireplaces, nothing but the chicest and newest

224

of everything, steel, glass, leather. Only the desk was old, but even that had new handles, she noticed with amusement, and was all polished up and vulgar in a way that would have made her mother wrinkle her nose and say, 'Why they always insist on doing that one will *never* know.'

'I'll have someone smash a hole in the wall and make one, if you wish.'

Georgiana smiled, but this time only slightly, because they both knew that Kaminski was perfectly capable of not only ordering but carrying out such a thing. He was after all a director, and once they had the go-ahead directors could order anything, more than generals really, which was rather funny when you came to think of it.

'It would look strange though, wouldn't it, with suede on the walls? Besides, it would have to be a log-effect fire, and that kind of fireplace is hopeless for smashing glasses.'

'Can you stay the night?'

Too soon, he had said it too soon, but what could he do? He couldn't stand another afternoon like the last one, when they had made love brilliantly and passionately, and then she had left him rather too promptly to catch the four forty-five (how he had come to hate that time of quarter to five) back to Wiltshire and her painter.

Georgiana could stay the night, as a matter of fact she wanted to stay the night, but she wasn't going to tell Kaminski that, and nor would she for some time to come, if at all. She preferred both to keep him strung along, and to keep an avenue of escape open. After all they might not even love each other by the end of the afternoon. She knew now that these things happened, and quite often. People met and made love, were passionate about each other, ready to die each for the other, or commit murder, or suicide, and then just as quickly they were dying of boredom at the very thought of each other. Allowances had to be made for this. No, she couldn't tell Kaminski that she was able to stay the night, she couldn't, and what was more she wouldn't.

Besides, she liked seeing the dying hope in his eyes, and the way he turned away from her aware only of her power over him, not of his over her. She would never let him be aware of that again, not ever. He must always be at her feet, quite, quite crushed, begging for mercy, squirming and wriggling with anxiety as to whether or not she loved him. Anything else, anything less than that and a man became bored. That at least she had learnt, not just from Kaminski who had left her, but from Gus who might as well have.

Indeed it might be preferable to be left – the clean break, the sudden change of existence – rather than suffer the dull little ebbings away, the little pieces taken out of you, like the birds that robbed the scarecrows around the fields at Longborough, taking pieces of their bodies to build up their nests. Nothing would ever be the same again between her and Gus, so that being so, she thought, as she saw Kaminski walking towards her with a certain look in his eyes, that being so, she might as well change everything in her life.

'You rang for an Evian water, ma'am?'

The maid at Charles Street, in the old days, when they had last been lovers, had been small and dark and foreign, and eager to be on Georgiana's side, approving always of her affair with this famous director. A very young girl with an older man was after all to be approved of, providing the older man was rich. To continental eyes it was a perfect match, and the maid had cried when Kaminski had left Georgiana, perhaps because after Kaminski had left her Georgiana had found it impossible to cry for herself.

Now as Kaminski advanced towards her, so full of purpose, Georgiana could only remember that time of growing up. The pain of the ending of that first affair, and how afterwards she had walked, so often, past that house in Charles Street in the months that followed, wondering to herself, over and over, why she had meant so little to someone who had meant so much to her.

The memory made her turn away from Kaminski towards the window that overlooked the outside street, a street that held no memories, only passing people, people hurrying, people strolling, people standing waiting for someone, none of them knowing that she was watching them, to distract herself, to take her mind away from the past, away from the pain.

Kaminski watched her, her back turned towards him, the long dark hair on her shoulders moving slightly as she sipped the Evian water, and he wondered, as he so often did with women, whether he would be in love with her if he understood her? Probably not was his usual answer to this most unanswerable of questions, and yet with this one, perhaps he would. Suddenly he found his heart literally sinking at the thought of how much power she could have over him. If he came to understand her, if she came to possess that kind of power over him, he would never be able to leave her, not for a second. It was a terrifying thought. He could never allow such a woman out of his thoughts, or indeed out of his sight. He would want her with him all the time, beside him when he filmed, beside him when he walked, ate, or slept, he would talk to her for the rest of his days, and that would still be too little.

'A lifetime's talking will be over.'

That was a line of his and E.F.'s in a film they had written, or was it E.F.'s? What did it matter? It was true of so few relationships. To be with most people was to be alone and shivering with loneliness. *Huis Clos* was the greatest film ever made about hell. Hell was indeed other people, and heaven was too. Heaven was looking across a luncheon table at someone and laughing and laughing, and knowing that they saw the same colour in that laughter-making thought, the same exact vision, and when the laughter stopped the silence that followed did not have to be filled, because the relationship was a prism.

Still watching Georgiana sipping her water Kaminski challenged himself to walk out of the room and leave her. It would be so easy, and make life so easy for him. He could leave E.F. to Sofia, make the movie, go back to the US and forget about this grown-up version of what he had once just played around with. It was easy. He could leave her. It was easier than easy, he only had to walk across the room, put his hand on the door, and slip out into the hall, walk to the outer door, let himself into the street, and it would all be over. Outside there would be cars, and streets, and people, and restaurants, and trees every now and then, and dogs on leads, and umbrellas that were about to be put up, and taxis to be caught, and shops with models facing outwards so people would look inwards. It was all so easy, but then she turned and he saw the look in her eyes, and it was very grown-up and very tender, and he realized that for that moment she was feeling older than him, and the idea made him giddy. She knew better than he did that he was caught, and that the look in his eyes was no more the look of a man who could walk out of the room, across the hall, and let himself out into the street than it was of a successful man of great fame. It was the look of a dog in a pound, and only one person in the world at that moment was capable of paying to get poor dog Kaminski out. But would she? Or would she leave him caged up, his nose against the bar, longing always for that one voice that would say 'I'll take him'?

'Shall we go upstairs now?'

Before it had been hotels, first hers, and then another that he rather liked, but now it was his room, and yet she walked up into it as if it were already hers, as if she had already re-decorated it, made it over as the Americans said, and as women always did when they moved into your life, changing everything except the man, and sometimes they changed him too.

Kaminski pulled down the blinds. They were strangely old-fashioned and made of stiffened cream holland with insets of old-fashioned cream lace. They reminded him of Russian trains, of his grandmother, of samovars, of the old days when he was a little boy and wore silk suits, before Paris, and then America.

'I want to take you to Paris,' he told her before they started to make love, and he found himself wrapped up in the mystery that was passion.

'When?' she murmured between kisses.

'Tonight,' he told her casually. 'We'll take a train. It will be wonderful.'

Georgiana said nothing. There was, after all, very little to say. It was a long time since she had been in Paris. She couldn't remember how long, but as Kaminski pulled her towards the great draped fourposter that dominated the room she sighed with pleasure at the idea of the beautiful streets, the women in their smart clothes, the pavement cafés, the restaurants, and as they began to make love it seemed to her that she could even hear an accordion playing and Edith Piaf singing. So great was her desire to escape from Gus and her life with Nanny and Nan at Longborough, the voice of the famous Parisian sparrow could have been that of a siren.

10

It had been a fine morning all over Wiltshire, and it was continuing to be so, so fine that even Clarissa Parker-Jones had been forced to pause and reflect about how strange it was that no-one had ever become used to calling her 'Mrs Gillott'. They had all, to a person, had to be reminded that she had changed her name, and now she had, pending the divorce, quickly changed back to 'Parker-Jones' once more, no-one had really noticed at all.

Of course, having been through so much with Andrew, marriage, and putting up with him, and so on, it seemed only fair and reasonable that she should, even after her divorce came through, retain the Honourable bit of his name. It wasn't that she mentioned it very often herself – indeed hardly at all unless it was to do with the cup she presented in the village and they wanted to know what to put on the posters – that sort of thing. No, she didn't fling her handle around, or insist on it or anything, but now she was faced with the decision as to whether or not to give it up, she realized she couldn't. It wasn't that she was a snob, far from it; with a great-grandmother who had been known as the Belle of Bishopstrow, how could she be? No, it was that she had come to realize how much other people enjoyed titles and handles and things. Shops loved it, even quite big ones, and then of

231

course there was a certain satisfaction to be had from people taking the Honourable to mean that she was an M.P., as in the Right Honourable, and asking her advice about their rates and things, which she was naturally quite happy to give whenever she could, and it was pleasant to see how grateful they were for even a little crumb of comfort.

All of which thoughts, as she sat on under her old apple tree with an approved clematis climbing through it, led her to contemplate the ghastliness of life if Jennifer, her only and fairly beloved daughter, divorced and became the ex-Lady Pemberton, the former Marchioness of Pemberton.

Clarissa sipped an indifferent cup of coffee as she freely imagined Jennifer living in the village, squatting in some little eight-bedroomed house of the kind that people frequently turned into antique shops, bringing her children up to go to the village school. Heavens, how sordid it would all be, even before Clarissa's friends started ringing her up and commiserating with her. 'Ghastly for you, Clarissa, and on top of your own divorce, so public always. You haven't been having much luck, have you?' She could just hear the voices, and the hidden delight that would be behind them, and imagining them made her foot swing up and down, and her hands grasp her coffee cup until the knuckles showed a little white. She had to stop Jennifer being headstrong and doing whatever she wanted when she wanted. It all came from being an only child, but with her father being so over-weight what possible chance had Clarissa to have had more?

She cleared her throat out loud several times, and

allowed her imagination full rein. Christmas would be so different, for instance. Spending Christmas in a village house would hardly be the same as spending it at the Hall with the security of a butler and staff. Clarissa took out a handkerchief and blew her nose very hard. Jennifer was impossible. Why couldn't she just turn a blind eye like every other decent wife? Why not forget about finding Pember in the drive dressed in funny clothes? Why not accept his story that he had merely been going around disguised as someone called 'Bert' in order to find out how many people would be interested in his new scheme for marketing local rather than organic produce? But no, that would be too easy for Jennifer, she had to plump for the big one, for disgust and divorce instead.

The telephone, small and plastic, rang from under a nearby philadelphus. Clarissa hurried to it. She hated to admit that she couldn't do without a telephone within a few yards of her, even in the garden, so she always took the trouble to hide it beneath the freshly planted philadelphus.

'Are you in the garden?'

It was the Countess, vibrantly alive and full of news, Clarissa could tell because she could hear her smoking on the other end of the telephone line, one of her small gold-tipped Turkish cigarettes that came in different colours, no doubt.

'No – I'm not.'

Clarissa hated to admit that she was in case the Countess didn't want her to be and rang off, or made one of her little remarks that could, at times, be so cutting.

'That's funny. You sound as if you're in the garden. Telephones are so sensitive, I find, I thought I could hear little leaves and things rustling, but perhaps you're flower arranging?'

'Yes, flowers and leaves, something special,' Clarissa lied.

'Things are going from bad to worse,' the Countess related with relish. Clarissa had often noticed that the dear Countess seemed to enjoy bad news almost as much as she didn't enjoy good. 'Jennifer has been to see a lawyer, but only one, and in Stanton, and they don't count. Mary, my daughter—'

'Yes—'

Clarissa knew only too well that Lady Mary Stranragh was the Countess's daughter, and had no need to be told.

'Mary has apparently decided to cancel her ball! How she found out about Jennifer's scandal—'

'Pember's scandal—'

'Exactly, how she found out I wouldn't know. I have to take the train to London straight away and sort things out. She can't cancel, not now Jennifer's cancelling. I just don't understand the young now, really I don't. Nor, as I say, can I understand how she found out about Pember in the drive in funny clothes. It's too awful.'

There was a sudden and very long pause as at either end of the Wiltshire line both ladies came suddenly to realize that perhaps after all they did know how the London-based Mary could have found out. Bloss.

Lady Mary stared fixedly in the mirror at her hairdresser. He was being boring, dull and egotistical, and if he had been doing anything except her hair she thought she

234

might have had the greatest pleasure in kicking him in the shins, but since to do so meant turning round and getting her hair in even more of a muddle, most unfortunately she couldn't even attempt such a thing.

On and on he was going about doing many and varied, if not various, other boring people's hairstyles for 'your dance'. She had corrected him two or three times with 'ball' when he said 'dance', and then had finally given up and lit a cigarette instead, which she knew he couldn't stand.

The trouble was Lady Mary could not bring herself, at any point, to tell him that she was about to cancel the stupid ball and go to Scotland for a very long sabbatical instead. For heaven's sake, she hadn't even told her wretched husband yet, and just as well since he was in New York handing out invitations to every other friend on Wall Street, as far as she could gather.

There was no getting out of it, however, none at all. She had to cancel. The whole point of giving a ball had been to put Jennifer and her mother's noses out of joint for the first and last time, and now that Jennifer was getting divorced instead, the whole thing had to be wrapped up, and as soon as possible.

Lucius, her one-time lover, had tried to persuade her otherwise last night over supper, but of course he had been quite unable to do so, because in the end even he could see that if the whole point of a social occasion had been taken away, then that was blasted well that.

'Couldn't you just give the ball for some new reason? For the sake of enjoyment, say?' he had asked a little plaintively at one point.

'Really, Lucius.'

That's all she had said, and that was all she'd had to say. After all, who had ever heard of giving a social arrangement for enjoyment, of all things? It was like being asked to give a wedding and have the guests not bring any presents, just themselves, because you were fond of them and liked them, and that sort of thing. It was perfectly laughable, and perfectly ridiculous at the same time, and she only hoped that she had made it plain both to Lucius and to Juanita who was listening at the door that it was probably the silliest idea that she had ever heard mooted, if that was the right word.

Anyway, enough of that, except that even thinking about cancelling things was almost more work than getting them up, so it was really no good pretending that the subject would go away by saying to yourself 'enough of that'. So instead she thought to herself 'besides that'. Besides that, and besides wanting to scream at the hairdresser and murder Jennifer, and her mother, and so on and so on, besides all that, and if that wasn't enough, she knew that when she arrived home for luncheon she would be in the unenviable position of finding her mother waiting for her, something that neither of them would enjoy at all, but which had to be endured.

The Countess was indeed waiting. She stared uneasily at Mary's freshly coiffured hair. It had a funny bit at the top which looked rather silly. She had obviously said 'yes' to the funny bit at the top when she had meant to say 'no', always absolutely fatal with hairdressers. Happily Mary was not someone to say 'How do you think I look?' because if her mother had been forced to answer that she would have had to say 'A bit silly' and there would have been all hell to pay, no doubt of it.

236

'I don't see why you have to cancel your ball, just because Jennifer's getting divorced and everyone will want to come to yours after all,' the Countess said, almost as plaintively as Lucius had the previous evening. 'After all, it was not the whole point, was it, to give one on the same night as Jennifer? That was just part of the point, not the whole point.'

'If you can't see the point then there's absolutely no point in going on talking about it. Besides, there's another reason why I have to cancel, which is another point,' said Mary with grim determination.

'Which is?'

Mary sat down opposite her mother. Her one oddly coloured eye and her other more normally coloured one stared with vengeful fervour at her mother.

'John is not paying for the ball. He is refusing to help out, and today I have had a letter which makes it quite plain that I can't manage to pay for it on my own.'

The Countess stared at her daughter, and then lit one of her small Turkish cigarettes, and took a leisurely puff. Stranragh, Mary's second husband, was notoriously mean, but not so mean surely that he wouldn't pick up the tab for a ball that could do them both nothing but good?

'How are you to cope, then?'

'How I was going to cope,' Mary told the Countess, and she put her head on one side as her tone turned to one of heavily light sarcasm, 'how I was going to cope was with the insurance money from the Chi Chi china dog, which Juanita stole. That was what the letter was about this morning. They won't pay out, even though I'm covered for theft.'

237

Juanita stole! The Countess's puff of smoke, she didn't know how, slipped smoothly out towards the perfumed air of Mary's drawing room without pause, a miracle of self-control in the circumstances.

'She denied it, of course, but I sacked her anyway. You might have noticed, I have a Filipino cousin of that butler I sometimes use instead. Quite nice, except she does smile a little too much for my taste, but then one can't have everything, or indeed sometimes anything, I find, when it comes to maids.'

The Countess's mind raced towards the sacked Juanita, and then turned back and raced towards Mary and her insurance money.

'That Chi Chi china dog was very valuable, as you probably know, and the insurance company had agreed a figure, a very substantial figure as it happens.'

The Countess leaned forward in expectation of finding out how substantially valuable that ghastly ornament had actually been. Quite a few thousand perhaps, if Mary had felt able to give a ball all on her own without Stranragh kicking anything into the kitty. Several few thousand pounds perhaps; more than several few thousand even, perhaps?

'It was valued at over fifty thousand pounds in the current market. Well worth Juanita stealing, as it happens.'

The Countess gasped, choked, and eventually, overcome with emotion, stubbed out her cigarette. Fifty thousand pounds! That ghastly relation of Freddie's ploughing her way through all those catalogues and peering at everything with her eyeglass had been more

than a dull and boring expert, she had obviously been a
dull and boring genius.

'Things Chinese are very valuable nowadays, not just
because China's shut, but because they have lost the will
to create things for the people they killed off years ago,
you know, a bit like the English. That red Chinese box
of yours must be quite valuable now, I should think.'

If the Countess could have blushed she would have
done. The red Chinese box was currently sitting in an
upstairs room filled with old buttons and pieces of lace.

'If it has a phoenix in flight on the side I should pop
it straight in to somewhere and have it looked at for the
insurance, if nothing else.'

The Countess sipped her perfectly horrid glass of
sherry and tried to conjure up the decoration on the side
of the red Chinese box now filled with buttons. Did the
wretched box have a bird in flight on the side? The sherry
began to burn her insides as she suddenly couldn't
remember whether or not the box, full of buttons or not,
was still in place in the little sewing and ironing room
in her house. She thought it was, but then, on the other
hand, she had been in a bit of a tearing hurry on her way
to the races the other day when a wretched woman from
the village in a faded green quilted coat had called asking
for bric-à-brac.

Being in a flurry and the drawing room being full of
an impatient Andrew puffing and panting and waiting
for the off, the Countess had instructed Maria to find
something, anything, to give the silly woman. That being
so, it was perfectly possible that Maria, who had first
been directed towards the attic and found the ladder too
giddy-making, and then towards what she would insist

239

on calling the 'utility room', had snatched up this perfectly boring box, emptied it of its buttons, and given it to the equally boring do-gooder Mrs Dupont – always it seemed and ever known to the surrounding countryside as the Village Voice.

'Why is a phoenix in flight a good thing?' she managed to ask Mary eventually, in a low, quiet, controlled voice.

'Because it means it was made for an empress,' Mary replied in the ever-patient way she now adopted towards her mother, and which her mother thought was nasty and made her feel old, but about which she could do nothing whatsoever at all. 'Anything made for a Chinese empress is very rare and special.'

'Well, it would be,' the Countess agreed, her mind now completely made up. She must return to Wiltshire immediately, and find the red box. She could ring Maria, of course, but Mary would be sure to overhear, and to admit that she didn't know where the red box was, or whether it was still in the so-called 'utility room', would not only make her feel terribly old, it would make her seem terribly old, and that would be twin evils of the most hellish kind.

Watching her mother leaving, and climbing with just a little difficulty into a taxi cab, Mary sighed and wondered. 'Do nothing to cancel until you've heard from me,' her mother had said. Fair enough, she would do nothing, particularly since the invitations were still sitting in their boxes, their engraving shining with lovely glossy black, the words 'Lady Mary Stranragh' set in beautiful flowing type, their left-hand corners uninked with any names of friends, acquaintances, enemies, or other bodies. Not that she was going to tell the Countess that, by any means, for this was her revenge on her mother for breaking the Chi Chi dog and not telling her, and for letting her sack Juanita, who would now have to be enticed back from the beastly new family who had taken her on and re-installed, and a very large and handsome endowment deposited in her Post Office account to make up for the whole unfortunate incident.

Happily her mother had no real knowledge of things like insurance. She would never know that it would be impossible to claim on the Chi Chi dog, since most claims were impossible anyway, but particularly when it had been broken beyond repair. Now the silly old bag would be sent back to Wiltshire on a wild-goose chase, and serve her right too.

It had seemed like such a perfectly lovely idea, to give a ball in opposition to that frightful Jennifer Pemberton's, but then everything had got so out of hand. The final straw coming when she had had to do her own house-work while waiting for the new maid to arrive, had found the Chi Chi dog, and putting one and one together had realized that it was Mamma who had broken the dog and hidden it, the day she had thought to arrive and depart from Mary's study without trace. (She forgot small things like leaving the butt of a Turkish cigarette in the ashtray, and the bill from lunch screwed up in the wastepaper basket.)

How could Mary know it was her mother and no-one else who had broken the dog, Stranragh had wanted to know when he called from New York at five o'clock that evening? Simple, she was able to tell him, very simple, dreadfully simple, because Juanita never dusted!

241

'You know I always have to get in the Belgravian Dusty Company to do heavy housework, every other Thursday and all the months with an "r" in them, darling,' she was forced to gently remind him. 'Juanita only does and opens doors, she doesn't actually *do*, and one doesn't and can't expect her to.'

'Ah yes, of course, darling. But if you get her back what will you do with the Filipino?'

'I will keep her to iron. She's very good at ironing.'

'But do we have that much ironing?'

'Really darling! With Scotland! Of course we have that much ironing.'

'Do we send laundry south?'

'My sweet, how on earth do you think one gets the napkins so stiff? Have a nice day, bless you.'

Mary replaced the receiver. Really. Imagine Stranragh even suggesting leaving the napkins in Scotland to be done. What were things coming to when he thought that even a possibility? And where he thought they found peppercorns, Bath Olivers and Belgian choccies in the Highlands she wouldn't know. But that was men for you, completely impractical, which was why they had to be sent off to offices to run goverments and businesses and so on.

When they were first married, (both on their seconds of course) Stranragh had not gone to an office, but Mary had pretty soon altered that. A husband at home was one thing to which she could never get used, and was never going to either. She picked up the telephone once again. Lucius. The dear darling, he must come round at once. Now that he had left Hugo they had so much to talk about. As she dialled she smiled at the thought of the discomfiture she had put her mother through. She didn't even really care whether or not she had a Chinese box, she just liked to think of her beetling back to Wiltshire to find one.

'As it happens I shall keep the invitations,' she told Lucius later when they were cosily dining together. 'They will come in useful for my "at homes" for the next fifty years.'

'You were going off the ball anyway, weren't you?'

'Mmm, absolutely. You know how it is, you order the invitations to be engraved and while you're waiting for them to be engraved you draw up the lists of guests. You study the lists of guests, you mark them "a" and "b" and so on, and it all seems very nice. You imagine your dress, your friends, the orchestra, the band, the food and the flowers, and when the blessed things finally arrive you've enjoyed it all so much in your head—'

'You might as well not give it at all?'

Mary nodded. 'Oh dear. We always did feel dreadfully the same about everything, didn't we?'

Lucius nodded. It was true. They had.

'Love is such a pill, isn't it?'

Without exactly meaning to Lucius leant over the table and kissed Mary briefly on the lips, and Mary quite suddenly remembered a great many things that she had previously forgotten about Lucius, about herself, about all three of them, Hugo and her and Lucius. Very nice things. Very beautiful things. Very good things. It was Capri where everything had gone so wrong. But now it was no longer Capri, it was Knightsbridge, and they were alone, just the two of them. How heavenly.

*   *   *

The Countess's journey home was more of an odyssey than a journey really. Thanks to the train service which wasn't she spent three hours waiting for a connection which never transpired, and was forced to hire a taxi, which also wasn't, just one of those broken down cars that are always pretending to be taxis in the country and which might as well be pumpkins for all the comfort they afford. She didn't arrive home until near enough midnight to make it nothing but selfish to wake Maria, so she had to let herself into the hall, quite alone, having paid a fortune to the cabman. When she was finally able to sit down in her own dear home, it was hardly surprising that she found it quite easy to burst into tears.

It was pathetic and dreadfully old-ladyish, but she hadn't been able to resist it. The tears were from relief mostly, and frustration a lot, but she had felt a great deal better after them, and having poured herself a really lovely stiffy she nipped straight upstairs (although nipping was a little out of her range nowadays) to the wretched utility room to retrieve the button box.

Except it wasn't there. No box, only a great many buttons, and all piled in neat stacks. Shirt buttons in one stack, brown coat buttons in another stack, navy blue coat buttons in another, and so on. The ironing table upon which clean clothes were placed after starching had now assumed the rakish look of a casino.

The Countess looked desperately round, wondering as she did why she was doing so, because she knew now, and for certain, that the red Chinese box had gone to the village bazaar to be sold for a few pence in aid of the Vicar's Watercolour Classes and the Annual Wildflower Award.

244

The thing to keep was calm, she told herself, as she wobbled slowly downstairs to the hall again, and back to the drinks table for another stiffy. She must keep calm, calm, calm. Except she couldn't, and for a very good reason, perhaps even fifty thousand pounds' worth of reasons. Having given up any attempt at calm, she tried to assemble her thoughts. Just because the box had been given to Mrs Dupont for the bazaar didn't mean that the bazaar had taken place and the box been sold. The Countess eyed the telephone on the kitchen wall as she paced up and down and through all her many rooms. It was both too late and too early to telephone the Village Voice.

She sat down at the kitchen table. Sitting at the kitchen table gave her an odd feeling, the feeling that she used to have when she was a child. She thought she could almost smell the fine flour that her mother's cook would use, and feel the sides of the rust-coloured bin in which the flour was stored. Everything was home-made in those dim, dear, long gone, past and gone, days. Nothing bought at all. What a wondrous thought that was. And also very nice too. Nice that one had known those things, even if they were gone now; they were there in her mind, whenever she wanted them. Now she put them away and allowed her eye to fall upon Maria's little notice board. So many little reminders. Maria was a good maid. Faithful and loyal, despite everything really.

Suddenly there it was. The notice of the bazaar. On Maria's board as large as life, and when she read the notice, twice as horrible.

CHURCH BAZAAR it said in very, very faded

home-done printing, on very, very funny thin yellow paper of the kind usually only used by firms who wanted to wash your cars for you and added ANYTHING ATTEMPTED NO JOB TOO SMALL, which if you ever had the misfortune to brush with them made you want to alter it to EVERY JOB TOO SMALL.

U

CHURCH BAZAAR IN AID OF WATERCOLO/R CLASSES AND GRAND WILD FOWERR COMPETITION!!!!!!!!!! SATURDAY TWENTY SECOND MAY. ALL WELCOME. DOGS NOT admittED EXCEPT BY REQUEST TO BE GRANTED BY THE REV!!!!!!!

The Countess sank back on to the kitchen sofa. Saturday the twenty-second of May had been and gone two days ago, and so too doubtless had the Chinese box. She put her hands up to her face but because she'd had two stiffies she felt no inclination to cry whatsoever. There was nothing like a touch of the Laphraoig for drying up the tear ducts. She had no intention of crying, so she bit her lip instead.

'Countess.' Fulton nodded importantly into the receiver of his old black bakelite phone as if he was greeting his old friend in person.

'You've got to help me.'

'Naturally.'

'I knew you would.'

'Naturally.'

'It's Maria. She's given my Chinese box to the bazaar, and she shouldn't have.'

'Of course she shouldn't.'

246

'She should have given – something else. At any rate, you know that dreadful woman, Mrs Dupont. Can you get it back off her for me? If I try she'll only smell a rat.'

'It's valuable?'

How grateful she felt towards Fulton for saying that in that way, the Countess thought. He knew at once.

'Very.'

'Leave it to me,' said Fulton smartly.

'By the way, how are the babies?'

'Valuable.'

They both rang off understanding each other completely. How refreshing, and how *comforting* true understanding was. No need to say words, or be or do anything, no cheapness, no crowing at another's discomfort. Fulton was there in one, and of how many people could she say that? The Countess continued to wonder as she staggered off to put herself to bed in broad daylight. She'd had no sleep whatsoever since the late-night discovery of the disappearance of the Empress's Box, as it was now known in her mind.

As she sank between her sandalwood-smelling linen sheets, grateful for the heaviness of her Colefax and Fowler curtains keeping the bright morning at bay, the Countess put all thoughts from her mind except that which would best induce sleep.

Fulton was a miracle worker. If he did succeed in retrieving the Empress's Box, then she would reward him heavily. A dozen of those ghastly papier mâché trays of his with matching wastepaper baskets and inktrays, spill boxes, or whatever he wanted. She would order dozens and dozens of them. She fell asleep contentedly designing and counting them as Fulton at last found Elliott in the kitchen where he had been all the time.

'We have got a knotty one here.'

'Not another knotty one, I can't bear it,' Elliott moaned, slapping his Grant loaf hard so it hurt both him and it. 'Oh-dear-I-shouldn't-have-done-that, now it won't do a thing. Will nothing go straight for us at the moment?'

'I'm not answering that without my lawyer.'

'The ball, Patti and the fearful Gillott, Pember, *Real Man*, Bloss and Jennifer, Mrs Parker-Jones, the divorce, Mary's cancelling – is there anything more that Wiltshire can throw at us?'

'Mmm, 'fraid so.'

Elliott stooped, banged the hateful Grant loaf into the oven, banged the oven door shut, and then straightened up feeling much better.

'Very well, tell me, but if it's something too knotty I shall tell you something you won't want to know either.'

'Really? What about?' asked Fulton, momentarily distracted.

'About Twinks and lard?'

'Not before midday, thank you. In brief. The village bazaar has been given, and during the proceedings a person or persons unknown has sold to another person or persons unknown, whom we don't as yet know, the Countess's invaluable Empress's Box.'

'How do you know it's invaluable?'

'Because she would only say it was valuable.'

'Oh my heavens. So what now?'

'We must get it back.'

'We must get it back? And get Pember to *Real Man*, and Lazy Tizzy out of bed and wanting to live life to the full again? And rid of Twinks's tinea? And the ball in or out on time, whatever balls are meant to be?'

' 'Fraid so.'

'You're afraid? I'm scared stiff. Does our little Countess know what Mrs Dupont's like? Does she know that the world is round? Once Mrs Dupont knows we want something from her, or indeed from someone else, she will do her level best to make sure that we never ever, ever get near it ever, ever again.'

'I don't think she knows exactly, but I think she might have guessed or she wouldn't have asked, would she?'

Elliott shook his head slowly.

'Do you know, Fulton, if life goes on at quite this pace for quite this amount of time again, I think I shall probably quite give up.'

'I can quite understand your feelings.'

'A plan must be made.'

'Not *another* plan!'

'Mmm.'

They stared at each other, and Elliott, noticing that Fulton's eye was flickering first in one direction, and then in another, knew without being told that Fulton already had a plan in mind. What it was he couldn't guess, but the tell-tale flicker was all it needed. Mrs Dupont, the Empress's Box – the game was on and would be fought for all it was worth, even if it meant chucking the Grant loaf at the Village Voice and knocking her for six and stealing the wretched box back while she lay prone on the floor.

'I think I might have an idea, dot, dot, dot.'

11

As soon as Georgiana was boarding the train to Paris, and the night outside the windows was dim and black around her, and she had a glass of champagne on one side of her and Kaminski reading on the other, she wanted to go back to Longborough and her son. Stars shone ahead in a night sky, an oddly quiet London was being left behind them as the train started to move out, and all she could wonder was not at the delight of it all, the private apartment, the new luggage, the beautiful shoes that Kaminski had just bought her and fitted himself, but how her little boy was, and if he was asleep?

She knew that her sudden concern came from nowhere, and was because she was feeling helpless and trapped. It was also a direct result of her usual helplessness in the face of happiness. Happiness was not something with which Georgiana knew how to cope, any more than she knew how to cope with her small son. The fact that he would not miss her for a second, that his face lit up when he saw her, only to light up just as much for Nan or Nanny, or even Gus for heaven's sake, didn't diminish the urge she had to feel miserable that she was leaving him behind for a few days.

Kaminski and she had made love. That was all that had happened, and for the first time in her life Georgiana realized she had known serenity, and been completely happy, not the slipping away kind of happiness that is there for a few brief seconds, a little pause in the game of life, but total immersion. The sounds from outside, Kaminski moving around the room, for one long hour nothing could disturb her inner peace, and so it had taken some time (some time that had of necessity to be spent telephoning home to make excuses for her absence) for her to search and find some reason to be unhappy. Having found it in her absent child, she lay back and allowed it to hurt her. After which she found she could be happy again, even though serenity had fled.

'Don't you want to read?'

Georgiana shook her head and allowed herself another sip of champagne. Ahead of her lay Paris and delight, behind her lay only dried flowers, endless days of Gus, and more Gus, his moods, and his dreadful domineering ways. Nothing but nothing she had ever done had been right, not ever. Not even when he had decided to be unfaithful, not even then had she been able to be right, because she had disturbed his painting, if you please, and by so doing had deprived the world of a great work. No wonder she was going to Paris with Kaminski, no wonder she was being unfaithful to Gus, who hadn't even bothered to marry her and make her little boy legitimate. Really when she thought about it the whole thing was ridiculous, and why she had gone on as long as she had putting up with Gus and his selfish demanding ways she really didn't know, and never had.

Dried flowers, and Jennifer's invitation to the ball, that was how it had all started, that and Gus not even sending her a postcard from Israel, not a line, not a telephone call to say how he was. That was when she knew what kind of person he must really be deep down, the kind of person that could travel halfway round the world and not bother to think of the people he had left behind. It was all Nan's fault, had been Nan's fault, spoiling him like that, her only little boy, and now George was going to be another only little boy, if Georgiana wasn't careful, growing up to be as domineering and selfish as Gus.

'Are you sure you don't want to read?'

'Quite sure, thank you.'

Georgiana sipped some more of her champagne and swung one beautifully silken leg sideways on to the next seat so that she was posed carelessly, and beautifully, but not exactly opposite Kaminski any more. This was in the hope that he would stop looking up at her every five minutes and asking her if she didn't want to read.

'Why don't you want to read?'

She stared at him, but only after a small dissatisfied pause during which she stared first out at the dark night and the lights of the small towns the train was speeding through, and then eventually back at this tall distinguished man with his new look of besotted gentleness.

'Probably because I don't really like reading.'

Kaminski stared at her.

'That's not true,' he said, still besottedly gentle.

'Oh, but it is,' Georgiana insisted. 'I only really like magazines. I hate reading long books and waiting for the end to come, which usually is terribly disappointing anyway. I like films,' she added, as a sort of token gesture, since she was sitting opposite one of the world's greatest directors. After which she turned and stared out of the window at the darkness and the lights once more, as if the scene beyond the carriage was a movie which Kaminski had interrupted her watching.

Kaminski put down his book, and picked up one of her ringed hands, and kissed it.

'Very well,' he told her. 'You win. You have my complete attention.'

Looking at the seriousness of his complete attention Georgiana smiled mischievously, and promptly forgot George and remembered once more that she was in love.

Kaminski tried to forget the warnings of his partner.

'Going to Paris with Georgiana? Are you crazy? She'll bury you. Anyway, what am I meant to be telling our esteemed producers, in your oh-so-obvious absence? That you have taken temporary leave of all senses save the one that can only lead you into very deep and unpleasant waters?'

'Gone on a reccy, E.F.'

'What is a marine biologist going to be doing in Paris, Herr Direktor?'

'The same as everyone else – making love!'

'But you can make love in London!'

'E.F., you can fall in love in London, but if you want to become lovers you must go to Paris.'

Kaminski knew every yard of the old quarter of the sixième arrondissement where he used to live with his grandmother, her samovar, his mother, her sacrifices, and the large émigré community that always found its way to their apartment on Sundays.

'First you cross the Pont des Arts,' he instructed Georgiana the following morning, when they had arrived at the Georges Cinq, dined, made love, ordered breakfast in the middle of the night, made love again, slept, ordered breakfast once more, made love once more, and finally drawn the curtains to admire Paris outside the windows of their sumptuous suite. 'But you must wait until about twenty to six in the evening, or like this morning, about twenty to eleven in the morning, when the air is very, very clear, and you can lean on your elbows and wonder at the beauty of the river. The *bateaux mouches*, the painters setting up their easels, the old men with their medals pinned to their macintoshes walking their wives' poodles, the sense of coffee being brewed all over the city, glasses being polished in expectation of lunch, and lunch itself, already planned, and smelling quite wonderful. That is the warmth, the excitement of Paris, and you can feel that, you can sense that, just by standing on the Pont des Arts at the right time of day.'

Georgiana stared at herself in the mirror. She was looking wonderful in a new coat of a brilliant yellow with a matching dress beneath, well, not exactly matching, but toning, a vague pattern to its silk, its silk matching the lining of the coat. Yellow made her dark hair shine and she knew it, and smiled at herself, her eyes half-closed, before turning back to Kaminski who was waiting to put on her hat for her.

'Women always wear their hats too far back, particularly English women,' he said, holding the prettiest little confection poised on the tips of his long fingers. He stared very seriously down at Georgiana, and she knew it must be the look that he had when he was staring at his actresses (he was famous for never using a viewfinder or staring for hours through the camera). He lowered the hat on to Georgiana's head, and she stared at him as seriously through the half veil, remaining perfectly still, one leg poised in front of the other as a model will stand, as he stepped backwards to judge the effect.

'That,' he said, 'is as near to perfection as we will arrive at this morning.'

She looked so vulnerable. Not as young as she had looked those years before when he had first fallen in love with her, but vulnerable and uncertain, still looking to him to tell her not just how she was, but what she was. It made Kaminski love her more, he thought wretchedly, knowing that she was no longer the girl he had first taken, that she was now as vulnerable to the passing moment as the rest of them. His once-upon-a-time brief affair, the sprite who was never going to grow up, had grown up, and the mystery was that instead of resenting it he loved her more, because she had somehow 'coped' – that was one of the words she used a great deal – she had 'coped' with the growing up, and it had made her seem if anything infinitely more vulnerable and more tender.

'We never got near you, you know.'

He murmured this really more to himself than to her as he was turning away, thinking she wouldn't understand.

'Didn't you? I never saw the picture.'

He smiled. It amused him when she made these little attempts to Americanize herself, to widen her horizons, to be less the person she was, and more the person she thought he might like, using words like 'picture' and 'ice box'.

'The actress looked right, but somehow for me and E.F. she wasn't ever quite right. You know when you trace a drawing, and then you lift it up, and then you try to put it back on top of the drawing again, it will never fit? That's what happened really. You were there, the original drawing, and we drew deftly round you, quite deftly, and we lifted it up and we took it across to the actress we had chosen, but it was never really a fit. There was always the memory of you, and of course once we started to edit, the more we edited, the more we remembered, and we couldn't be free of our memories. E.F. and myself. It wasn't just my own feeling. We were neither of us ever happy with the movie. But it didn't matter. It was a great hit, and everyone said so, even Pauline Kael, so it must be true. Only E.F. and I knew it wasn't what it should have been, and now I at least know—' Kaminski bent and kissed Georgiana's lips very carefully under the tiny veil, 'that it was never, ever, going to be possible.'

They walked out into the late spring sunshine. Paris was already well ahead of London in her summer finery. Beauteously bedecked with trees, her wide avenues, her long vistas, her elegant buildings allowed humanity to stroll through, past, up and down her, and while *gendarmes* waved their arms and lovers strolled, Kaminski took Georgiana's arm as she automatically waited on the sidewalk for the doorman to signal a cab.

'Ah no, not in Paris, in Paris we walk,' he told her, and they set off together at what Kaminski called 'a lovers' walk', where two people stroll down an avenue, looking around all the time, pretending great interest in everything, but even as they look away from each other

257

they are never really taking their eyes from their real source of interest, each other.

Even walking as all lovers do, with a beautiful young woman on his arm, even so for Kaminski every pace was a memory to be visited, his mind strolling ever faster ahead of every step they took, remembering, savouring how he had felt then, wondering what he would have thought of himself now? The cafés where he had first sat writing scripts in carefully learnt American. The long hours spent in the more expensive cinemas that had helped him to appreciate not just the language of film, but the economy of American dialogue.

'Shall we walk on, or shall we stop for a coffee?'

Georgiana nodded. 'Let's stop.'

They sat down, the waiter arrived, and Kaminski ordered.

'Might I have a patisserie as well?'

'Before lunch, and just after breakfast?'

'You have forgotten how greedy I am,' she said, but she did not seem in the least apologetic because it was so obviously not true, and anyway she was too slim to be 'greedy'. That was another word Georgiana used that Kaminski wouldn't think of using, and that E.F. wouldn't understand her using – 'greedy'. The patrician English habit of over-emphasizing to deflate any criticism they feared they might be about to incur. She knew she wasn't greedy, but since she was afraid someone else might think she was she quickly said it about herself before anyone else might or could.

The coffee arrived, and a patisserie was chosen by Kaminski for her, one with apricot, the kind he liked and he therefore wanted her to enjoy. Georgiana began at once, delicately cutting at the pastry with a fork, but eating quickly and appreciatively, but for once Kaminski did not watch her. Instead he let his eyes roll outwards to the avenues, to the crowds, to the women so chic and so navy. Only Paris could sport such women. Although it was an old thought it was one that Kaminski could not help savouring. How irritating for women who were not French to see what a French girl could do with a simple pleated skirt, a long thin piece of silk, and a plain cardigan. It was irritating and it was fascinating, even to Kaminski, for he knew however beautifully he dressed Georgiana he would never be able to give her that particular sense of chic, and nor could she acquire it.

Perhaps she felt him thinking this because she sighed and said for him, 'Let's go. I can't bear to see so much style in such a very short time.'

Kaminski looked at her and smiled. Style didn't seem to matter when she smiled at him like that from underneath the little veiled hat which was perched so perfectly over one beautiful eye.

'Come here,' he commanded as they left their table.

Obediently Georgiana stood in front of him as Kaminski tilted the hat forward a little more, arranging the precise angle with such finesse that the two gentlemen seated at the table behind them applauded. Kaminski turned and acknowledging their appreciation made a conductor's bow, as from a podium. It was a moment of sublime warmth and elegance, it was a moment from a picture by Renoir, the yellow of the hat and coat, the gentlemen seated at their table, the light steam on the windows of the café, the tall, middle-aged man in his collarless silk shirt, his French-cut jacket, his

Italian trousers and his English hand-sewn Lobb shoes, but most of all there was Georgiana, glossy-haired, large-eyed Georgiana. She did not bow as Kaminski had done. She had no need. She knew the applause was for her. Kaminski might be the conductor, but she was the music.

The carpet of memories unravelled itself towards Kaminski as they drew nearer and nearer the Pont des Arts. Always at that point, when he crossed the Place de la Concorde and started the long walk towards his beloved river, towards his own (everyone who had ever lived near it claimed it as their own) his own bridge, he would start to feel as if he was a little boy. Not as he had felt then, all those years before, bewildered by the newness of it all, not understanding much of the language, not realizing that they were going to live there for ever and ever, that it would be his forever home, but as if he was a little boy now. As if the whole of his idyllically successful life only made sense if he returned to this most beloved spot in the guise of a small boy, seeing it for the first time, holding it to him. And as he walked towards it at last, his beloved Pont des Arts, as a painter might wish to fade into his palette, or become the colour on his canvas, Kaminski wished that he could become part of his bridge.

He was grateful for Georgiana's silence. It would have been quite terrible if, having arrived at what she knew was beloved for him, she had at once demanded to know something, or tried to talk. But she seemed too interested to even attempt to talk to him, standing behind a painter watching him, looking down the river at the boats, looking across to the steps where the children were playing, brightly clothed, their piping voices carrying on the warm summer morning, floating up towards the pedestrians on the bridge. Kaminski turned towards the archway behind which lay all his boyhood.

He knew there was no avoiding a flashback, a device for which Kaminski himself had once upon a time had a particular fondness, but which just recently he had, of necessity, avoided.

It had always seemed to him that his grandmother had been the great beauty of the family. Somehow she had managed to come from Moscow, bringing with her a maid, a samovar and a daughter who was healthy and could work, and had set up house in the ancient unfashionable rue de Seine, in the bohemian quarter of Paris, and carried on as she would have done had she remained in Moscow. She commanded and people came and brought, and attended to her as if there were not just the three of them living in the apartment, but fifty-three of them.

When he pushed open the door the apartment had always smelt the same, of the strong cigars and cigarettes of other émigré visitors, of the musk used in the oil put on the lamps, of his grandmother's perfume. 'Ma patchouli' he thought she called it, but her usage of some words was always so difficult to understand it made little difference what it was called, only its scent seemed to be more overpowering and have greater force than any of the other scents that mingled in the air. And that's how she had been: more overpowering, more present than either his mother or any of their visiting relatives.

'You will be a great man, Sashie.'

She had never said that to him, but like a great actress, she had thought it. She had looked it in her eyes. 'Don't speak the dialogue, look it.' Perhaps it was from her that he had really learnt direction. She had never commanded, she had looked. One look towards his poor beautiful mother, and she ran. One look towards the long-suffering maid, and she sighed and went. One look towards Sasha, and he climbed on her knee.

She had told him stories when his mother was out 'at business'. Stories about the old days, about troikas, and about lovers who ran away, and about parents who ran after lovers, and about fortunes lost and brains blown about, but because he had been only seven he had not understood a word.

He had *remembered* all the stories, though, saved them up in his mind, without exactly realizing it, because that is what happens when you are only seven: you listen and you remember. Then when he grew older, not a great deal older, he gradually realized that they were poor when they shouldn't be, and that his mother did not go out to a business, all dressed up in her beautiful clothes. Her beautiful hand-made crocodile shoes took her to hotels like the Georges Cinq where she lunched or had tea with gentlemen who were staying over in Paris, gentlemen who enjoyed conversation and erudition, and sophistication, as well as making love. Once he had sensed that what his mother had to do to keep them was not what other mothers in less beautiful clothes did, who shopped in the neighbourhood market on Sunday mornings, and bemoaned the lack of good cheese and wore black clothes for most of the year. Sasha knew that he would do well to remember those stories of his

262

grandmother's, so that one day, please God, his mother would never have to lunch or have tea with some gentleman she had never met before ever again.

How young he had been, and how old too. Just the look of that courtyard above which they had lived for so many years, and above which his grandmother had declined as his own star began its ascent, brought him recollections of painful intensity. His mother crying and crying some nights, and some mornings too, and not even his climbing on her knee and bringing her flowers stolen from the side altar at the great church of St Germain brought a halt to the tears.

'Oh Sashie, Sashie,' was all she ever said, and he put his arms up to kiss her and found only the wet salt of despair.

His grandmother ignored the tears which she must have known were shed. She looked only straight ahead, not at the way they were, but the way they might be once again. He was to rebuild their fortunes, her eyes told him, he was to be the person to bring back the old days and make everything as it had once been.

'Are you going to be famous? It would be a good thing if you were famous. Fame is important if you are as unimportant as we are now.'

How poor they had seemed to each other! But to other people, people in the neighbourhood, the concierge, the shopkeepers, the café owners, they must have seemed rich. His grandmother who would wear beautiful lace clothes in summer, and fur-lined cloaks in winter. His mother who never wore anything but the most fashionable and expensive that could be arranged, and never could wear anything less, if she was to continue to take

263

tea or lunch with rich and successful men. He himself was always in something silk. Silk shirts and trousers, silk vests even, all made by the wretched but devoted maid, ever and always called 'Pompom'. (It wasn't until they were burying her with the greatest honours that Kaminski realized with a shock that 'Pompom' had been christened Katya, and that she had even had a surname as well.) How exotic they must have seemed to their neighbours, and yet how deprived to themselves.

As soon as his reading of French became tolerable Sasha read from the newspaper to his grandmother. Everything was to do with fame. People had to be famous to be anything at all. It wasn't enough to be what they were, they had to be seen to be what they were. So if a writer was to be read, he must be read about. If a director's film was to be seen, he too must be seen. Even then Sasha knew that it was a fraud, that it was all a pretence, that it was only what you did, not what you were seen to be doing, that really mattered. The end was Art, the path, littered and often dangerous, was fame.

When he was out of favour, or there were womanly things that they wanted to talk about, or visiting relatives who needed a great deal of quiet to explain their need to borrow money from his grandmother, Sasha was always sent down the three flights to the courtyard with the lettuce. There he would stand for sometimes up to an hour, swinging the container that held the leaves until not only were they dry, they must have been nearly cooked, and until such time as Pompom eventually leaned from the great tall windows above him and waved her handkerchief as a signal that he could now come up.

Paris had been planned to be just a temporary resting

place for the family before they sailed in splendour to New York and greeted the Statue of Liberty as they wanted, in fine furs and with a savings account waiting for them at the Chase Manhattan Bank, except that every month that might have seen their savings grow saw instead their growth in comfort. As fast as his poor mother lunched and attended teas, and *thés dansants*, and other euphemistic occasions of sin, their life grew more elaborate, and more expensive.

Rugs and icons were bought from poorer relatives, Russian was spoken more and more, and French and English less and less, as if with the rugs, and the heavy wall coverings, and the filled larder, and Pompom in a full frilled white lace apron with a matching cap, as if with the growth of such visual splendour around them his female relatives were able to convince themselves that they were once more in their beloved Moscow. But for Sasha it was different, as it must always be when you are first seven, and then eight, and then ten, and you speak French and English more and more, and you are known in the neighbourhood as 'petit Sashie', and then 'Sashon', which is even more affectionate.

The neighbourhood became his own. The pastries that were unsold at the end of the day, the single flowers that were left at the side of the bucket, the hardened chestnuts that had been cooked and then not bought, they were all his at a certain hour, and to each and every person who gave to Sasha, he gave back, because he would entertain them with his stories of the others.

So at the patisserie Madame would be regaled with a story of how the flower seller had been found cheating on his wife, and the flower seller with the story of how

Madame at the pastry shop had been left by her husband for a woman who made lighter profiteroles (only to return when he found the young lady's brioches sadly wanting), and the chestnut seller with stories of the money spent by Americans in the bookshop on novels of a kind that would cook his chestnuts without his needing to light the fire. Instinctively Sasha came to realize that so long as he entertained people, he could get his own way and make his life easier and better.

'Basically every artist is a whore at heart, dying to please, and then be paid,' E.F. would joke.

When Sasha-Sashie-Sashon grew older, he would only occasionally accept a free pastry from the smiling 'Tante Tatine' and then only in deference to her great art, her feather-light pastry, as a courtesy to her. Further down the little winding street he would make sure always to buy his flowers and his chestnuts from his so-dear boyhood friends, and in return, now he was older, they would amuse him with stories of the neighbourhood, which was how it should be now that they could no longer ruffle his hair.

Eventually the bookshop became his permanent second home, more than the student cafés, far more than the apartment where his grandmother still held sway and even Sasha as yet could not compete with her.

At the bookshop American was spoken, and all the time. American businessmen would cross the river to buy from the owner, always returning to exchange their eagerly bought volumes when read, because all of the books that they chose were not of the kind that their wives would like to find them reading, and were banned in America. Coffee was served, and at all times, by the owner of the shop, and small biscuits handed around sometimes. From secret reader, and occasional buyer in his holidays, Sasha rose to permanent assistant at the shop, developing a taste for appearing to be a wry, withdrawn personality, which was in fact an imitation of the owner of the bookshop, the father figure in his life, the man whose personality through adolescence and into early manhood he started, subconsciously at first, but later quite consciously, to assume. This personality was later to become 'Kaminski', for Kaminski was not the surname of Sasha's family, but the name he assumed, the name of their best customer at the shop, a Monsieur Kaminski who arrived every Wednesday afternoon with a small leather briefcase which he would empty of last week's volumes, beautifully unmarked but assiduously read, and promptly fill again with new books with which he would return the following week. He was the shop's best customer.

'Monsieur Kaminski read more dirty books than anyone I have ever met or hope to meet,' Kaminski told Georgiana as they stood outside the shop, which no longer sold books, but towelling and sheets which could be monogrammed to the customer's own preference, which the French liked very much because they thought of such linen as being very English. Very occasionally there are English things which please Parisians very much, and which they imitate, always stressing how '*Anglais*' they are, while happily staying very '*Français*' themselves.

To recommend the books it was necessary of course to read them, and so his reading became omnivorous, and his taste catholic. He read Sartre and Camus, of course, and was impressed. He read James Joyce, and was enthralled. He read Tolstoy and Dostoevsky, and was envious. He read a great deal of purple prose, and was amused. But all he really dreamed of was making films, and all he was searching for when he read was to see how he could recreate these stories in a film.

Film was his secret vice, not approved, not even countenanced at home in the apartment, where no-one, not even their visitors, had ever attended a movie house, and where he was still expected to read Pushkin out loud to his grandmother, although mercifully only on rainy days. But like all secret vices, he knew, and came to accept, that it was gradually taking over his whole life.

When his mother discovered his predilection she took him out to lunch. Sasha wore a suit that had been altered for him. The restaurant was fashionable. To their table came many and interesting people, and because Sasha was eighteen he noted that they all, to a man, greeted his mother with that affectionate but possessive manner that men are wont to use towards women whom they have known intimately, and feel they might know again at some future date.

His mother had been beautiful to Sasha. At seven and eight she had been his madonna; now at eighteen he realized she was getting a little older, there was a slight pleating underneath the chin and her beauty had become more fragile. She spoke gently, her Russian accent giving her French a charm and an originality which the mature son could appreciate in the elegant surroundings of Le Vefour. Although he was only eighteen she deferred to him, nodding to the *sommelier* to give him the wine list, and letting him talk to the avuncular figure with his riband and his spoon about the perfect accompaniment to each of their courses without interruption.

'Let us lunch here.'

Kaminski stopped in front of the door of a discreet, now fashionable restaurant. With the discreet and fashionable pale shades of cream and the beautifully displayed menu inside, it could only be Paris.

Because it was early they were found a table in the best corner, and because in Paris Kaminski was justly famous, they were treated with immediate deference.

Classical French food and wine remains classical, but tastes change. The mussel soup that so delighted the revelling Sasha on his return from a student party would doubtless now seem coarse to Kaminski's refined palate. Even so, he was able to select a menu that was similar enough to his memories of the lunch that day, all those days, so long ago.

'Sasha must not go into the film business.'

When his mother eventually made the purpose of the luncheon clear, he could hear only her mother's voice behind everything she said. His grandmother could have been standing behind the daughter's chair.

Sasha loved his mother, but no longer with the pain and passion of the little boy, only as he would love someone about whom he had read in the bookshop, and in whose plight he would take a three or four hundred-page interest. He felt no volcanic feelings of resentment towards her for her way of life, nor did he pity her. Life had been hard on her, but it could have been harder. At eighteen his dispassion allowed him to free himself.

But now? Kaminski stared at Georgiana. That day so long ago, how had he been able to be so mature? And why was it now that he was able to be so immature? Sitting opposite this beautiful girl with her yellow coat and dress and her small veiled hat he was feeling all the volcanic possessiveness that he should have felt at eighteen.

That day so long ago, the menus, the sunshine, his mother's little hat, it was clear and iridescent in his mind's eye.

And she had worn yellow.

Georgiana nodded for the thousandth time. Kaminski had never talked so much or so interestingly to her. He had even held her hand differently; lightly, more affectionately, as if she was a human being with a soul, not just a girl with a great pair of legs, which was how most men held your hand.

And yet she wished he would stop talking, because the more he talked, and the more his eyes filled with memories of far-off days, the more he became Sasha, and not Kaminski the great director, the *auteur*, the man who commanded and was respected. The more he became short-trousered, and vulnerable, and she saw what it must mean to him to be rich and famous, and not vulnerable the way he had been, the less he fascinated her.

She wanted to tell him to stop talking, to stop filling in the gaps for her, to stop staring down the years, or looking up to them, to stop searching for the places where someone had once stood who stood no longer, and go back to how he had been in her eyes when they had caught the train the previous evening.

But it was too late. Not only was he now at her feet, he was also insisting on becoming smaller and smaller in her eyes, and she didn't want that. She didn't want him to be small and sorry, she wanted him to be arrogant and hard, and forceful, and not little Sachon who chewed on hard chestnuts when he was hungry. She wanted him to be a tall man with expensive suiting.

After lunch as they strolled back to their hotel to make love Georgiana tried holding Kaminski's hand differently, and as they walked she prayed. With luck, once they had safely crossed the river, left behind the Left Bank, he would once more become Kaminski again.

12

In order to enter the sitting room of number two Cheap Street, it was necessary for Fulton to duck his head. He was feeling pretty fed up with the world in general and Wiltshire in particular, so it would not have surprised him if he had knocked his head on the wretched lintel and knocked himself to the floor. Try his best as he had he could not find a single person other than Nanny, Twinks, Bessie, and the babies who would speak to him at that moment. The Hall was on non-speakers after the proposed cancellation of the ball. Not only were Pemberton and Jennifer not speaking to each other, they weren't even speaking to Bloss. Which seemed strange because how do you ask your butler to bring in your spritzer, your coffee, or your champagne if you aren't speaking to him? On the other hand it might not be quite so strange, now he really thought about it, for Fulton had already noted that should persons cease to speak to each other, they more often than not became mute to everyone, and deaf to all entreaties.

Certainly Jennifer had been acting most strangely towards him of late, and he had been more than a little embarrassed by her, so much so that he had been forced to put on his thinking cap and worry as to how he had actually been or was being towards her to make her behave towards him as she had been. Insinuating is how he could at best describe it; at worst she had been positively possessive in her manner. Try as he might Fulton could not find out what he had done to deserve such a change in manner. Perhaps something said when consuming too strong a Pimms? A little nod too many, or a handshake that had lingered too long? Something must have happened for her now to treat him quite openly as if they had had a raging affair. (Somehow in the popular mind affairs always 'raged', although personally he would have thought it perfectly possible for an affair to be quite gentle without a rage in sight.)

The worst of it was that Jennifer having convinced herself that she had somehow, or he had somehow, or they both had somehow been naughty, it now seemed that even Pember was convinced, albeit surely with a great pinch of salt, and hence the non-speaking status to which Fulton had been raised. It was all desperate. There was no other word for it. For what had he in actual fact done? Nothing. Only help to arrange a perfectly private ball, and now he was supposed to talk this ninety-year-old woman covered from top to toe in Honiton lace out of the Empress's Box. What more, he asked himself, as he shifted his position in a thoroughly over-polished and persecutingly uncomfortable Windsor chair, what more could life in Wiltshire throw at him?

'She's attached to it summat dreadful,' the old lady's granddaughter informed Fulton primly after the first twenty minutes had passed in appreciating the Honiton lace on her grandmother's blouse, and the horse brasses around the fireplace.

Fulton would have loved to have said 'But she can't be, she's only had it a week' but he didn't because they were farming folk, and everyone knew that when it came to farming folk you had to tread so softly even the fairies couldn't hear you.

'Of course she must be,' he agreed coolly, 'most attached.'

''Sup to you, 'course, Gran,' the girl shouted now at her grandmother. 'Don't let me 'fluence you, know-what-I-mean? You wanna sell your box to the gennelman for more than I paid for it 'sup to you. Just 'cos I gave it to you for yer ninetieth don't mean you have to hold back on selling it to him. You could buy yerself summore horse brasses and all, if you have it in yer mind, but 'sup to you. 'Course it is.'

She swung one socked high-heeled shoe upwards as she spoke and nodded primly towards Fulton.

'I'm sure the gennelman means no harm, Gran, no matter what you first thought.'

This last was an oblique reference to Fulton's calling on her the previous afternoon when she, with the natural old world courtesy of Wiltshire folk, slammed the chained front door in his face.

'She's been watchin' too much telly on the box with the sound up too high, nothin' but robberies and such like and all local, it's not nice the Health lady keeps tellin' her. Better off gettin' stuck into her lace and she would and all, as the Health lady says, but she keeps gettin' her hook caught in her hearin' device.'

Fulton eyed the Empress's Box resting contentedly on Granny Moore's knee. She had not one but both hands on it.

'I'll open the box.'

'See, she likes her box. Bless her.'

274

The socked stilettoed shoe swung upwards in triumph once more. The granddaughter smiled smugly.

'Bless you, Gran. You keep your box.'

'I'll open the box!'

'Bless her!'

'No, no I won't, I'll take the money!'

The old lady nodded towards the telly. Fulton straightened up, but only for a second before sliding down once more to subnormal height thanks to the over-polished Windsor chair.

'Very well, Granny Moore, if that's what you want.'

As quick as lightning, Fulton counted out ten very clean and ironed ten pound notes and put them on the small three and a half-legged oak table to the side of him.

'There we are,' he said in the forced jolly tone that he always found himself using towards people named Granny.

'She dunno what she's sayin', thinks she's on the telly. Open the box, take the money, that's the one she thinks she's on. You want to keep the box, Gran, could be worth a great deal of money to you, that could be. Our mam says that could be an investment for yer, that could. What's money when it comes down to it, except money?'

The old lady leaned forward and gave Fulton the box.

'No, I'll take the money,' she said happily. 'You open the box,' she told Fulton.

Fulton could hardly believe it. Luck was coming his way at last. An all too rare feeling of serenity and happiness pervaded his whole being as he took the box from dear old Granny Moore and she took the money and promptly counted it out, licking her fingers tenderly between each note.

'I tell you you dun better to keep the box, Gran. Could be an investment for you, like I told you. Never mind.'

She leant forward to her grandmother.

'I'll have summa that then, seein's you're not keeping the box, and seein' as how I paid for it in the first place. It's only fair,' she told Fulton, who didn't think it fair at all, but then life never was, and it was pretty silly to expect it to be really.

It was only when he reached his car and slung the wretched box on the seat beside him that he remembered to look for the bird, the phoenix in flight on the side of the immaculate red lacquer. The sight of that alone would make it worth all his while, both for the Countess and himself.

13

Jennifer stared at Pemberton her husband, as far as she was concerned soon, pretty soon, to be ex, with something very close to hatred. What a sausage! Did he really expect her to accept his story that he had been caught going round dressed as a sort of tramp person because he was doing market research for his and Bloss's newest money-maker the Local Rather Than Organic Garden Produce Company, rather than doing research of a more intimate kind that gentlemen of his age were somewhat inclined to do if not watched?

'Really, I am no longer the innocent person that you once knew,' she hissed, and then hesitated, shooting a look towards the drawing room door, but since the handle was not moving and she couldn't hear Bloss snuffling she presumed they must be more or less alone and she could go on regardless. 'I am no longer the innocent person,' she repeated, 'you first met and married. I have' – here Jennifer raised her chin slightly – 'I have actually read magazines. *Cosmo*. That sort of thing. In the hairdresser's. I do know to what people, men, especially middle-aged men, I do know to what they can get up! There are certain habits to which once a marriage is well under way they can resort unless either caught or actively discouraged.'

Pember had his back turned to her, a sure sign of guilt, she supposed.

'You can no longer expect to treat me like a fool, Pember.'

'No, well, I don't suppose I can, Jennifer,' Pemberton admitted with his usual candour. 'Even so, I don't think you want to know the truth; too painful by far for both of us. You know how it is: if you tell someone how things are, it never goes down very well. Always ends up all ends to the bottom and nothing to do but chuck the whole thing in. The truth is never really a good idea, you know, it never has been. Quite apart from anything else, d'you see, it changes so from day to day, one day it's the truth and the next day it's altogether something different. Last year's notion is never this year's fashion, besides there are other things more important than the truth.'

'Oh, really? And what, may I ask?' demanded Jennifer bristling. 'And if you think this sort of eyewash is going to stem the tide of my indignation I do assure you it is not. Oh no, by no means. I demand to know the truth, Pember. Why, why were you dressed up like a less than fascinating tramp driving Nanny's car at the time of day when most gentlemen are to be found reading *Sporting Life* and putting on bets with their butlers?'

'Very well, Jennifer,' Pember said, breathing in and out quite slowly because he had an idea that too much oxygen at too early an hour might be harmful and cause a sudden rush to the brain. 'Very well, you have as they say in popular newspapers asked for it, I'm afraid, and I only hope you don't get what you don't deserve. The reason as you have undoubtedly guessed was not just

278

the pursuance of the Local Rather Than Organic Garden Produce Company, the reason was—' He paused and gave another slow breath in and out as an opera singer might if he was given the time. 'The reason was I have too many children!'

'What! Do you expect me to believe that? A man of your wealth, three children? What kind of turpitude is this?'

Pember frowned, puzzled. He wasn't quite sure of the meaning of 'turpitude' himself even, so he was equally sure that accuse him of what she might Jennifer could well be barking up the wrong tree.

'My father used to say that economics and women don't mix, but I'm not so sure. Sit down, Jennifer, and let me tell you about money.'

'Do I have to listen?'

'As a matter of fact you do if you wish to find out why I was dressed up as Bert Ackroyd and driving Nanny's car at ten o'clock in the morning.'

Jennifer sat down very suddenly and spread out her dog skirt evenly around her as if it were a crinoline, and then by way of comfort she took one of her dogs on her knee just in case the news was so hideous she would need to bury her face in its fur.

'Money is a very difficult thing to understand, Jennifer. You are an intelligent girl, which was one of the reasons why I married you, so I know you can bring yourself to understand modern economics, probably as well as any Chancellor.'

'Pember? Is this going to take long?'

'About as long as the Chancellor on Budget Day,' her husband told her evenly as with quiet triumph he saw her eyes sliding off his face and gliding towards the rose garden outside the window. He had already lost her interest. What a bit of luck! 'Do you know how much money it takes to run this place?'

'Lots,' said Jennifer shortly.

'Precisely. Lots.'

Once again Jennifer's eyes were drifting like petals on the water of his eighteenth-century raised goldfish pond towards the garden and then back towards the top of her dog's head, and then out towards the garden again, and then down to her tapestry where they stayed fixed with an expression of increasing longing as Pemberton proceeded with his economic lecture in such a measured tone that the dog had started to nod off before he was halfway through.

'So you see, if one child's education in ten years' time, given the steady growth of the cost of living, is going to cost me a hundred thousand pounds and that's before he decides to go to university, three children will therefore cost me three hundred thousand which on tax paid at my level is a million pounds. And then there's Bloss. Bloss we know we can't do without, most definitely. Bloss is paid ten thousand pounds a year which is nothing by today's standards, and he has kept his salary down for the past fifteen years which is more than can be said for Nanny.'

Jennifer's gaze transferred itself to Pember for the first time now for some minutes.

'Well, but, Pember, if you think we have too many children you must expect to pay Nanny a decent wage.'

'Bloss is on ten thousand a year, Nanny on six thousand a year, which at present tax levels makes it necessary to bring home forty thousand, and then there is the garden, which at present tax levels needs to generate an income of more than fifty thousand which over a period of the same ten years given the same spiralling costs will mean at least half a million pounds, and that's before we put any petrol in Nanny's car or the lawn mowers or indeed, Jennifer, come to the horses. We maintain a stable of ten to fifteen horses in training which at present costs more than the garden.'

Having defended the need for Nanny Jennifer's mind switched itself back to her tapestry. She was glad she had abandoned her embroidery for the minute, because her tapestry was nearing completion in not one corner but three. Soon she would be on to the hare and the flowers which would be much, much more interesting.

'So all in all, without taking into account our other houses, and their upkeep, it is necessary to think of the household of the Hall as needing four million pounds over the next ten years, and that's with only three children.'

Even Jennifer had to sit up at that.

'Four million pounds. Goodness, Pember, that does sound rather a lot,' she said a little faintly.

'Sound rather a lot?' said Pember, dropping a small stub of pencil with his bookmaker's name in gold on to the table beside him. 'Sound rather a lot? It is more than a lot, Jennifer, it's a great deal.'

He stared ahead of him, wishing that he hadn't decided to make any calculations, wishing that he had never taken it upon himself to instruct Jennifer in the art of what everything cost.

'Pember darling, you look quite white.'

'I feel quite white.'

'That's the worst of all possible worlds. To look quite white, and to feel quite white.'

Jennifer leaned forward to her husband and touched his arm. He didn't appear to have seen what she had just done, or indeed even noticed. She had not touched him for some few weeks, not even when she kissed him good night.

'We'll manage. You mustn't worry.'

Pember turned his now dulled gaze towards his wife. Four million pounds.

'Jennifer, I have suddenly realized that there's nothing left to us except prayer. We must pray that Bloss and I somehow or another can make a go of the Local Rather Than Organic Garden Produce Company, or else we'll just have to move out, camp in the grounds and generally live off cheese parings, if we can get any, which I very much doubt thanks to the decline in cheese-making in these parts.'

With some difficulty Pemberton struggled to his feet and stood swaying a little. His mind was made up. The sacrifice must be made. He would have to go under the knife, and that afternoon, chop, chop. He needed a stiffy to strengthen his purpose, but it wouldn't make any difference. Whatever happened, he would have to go over the top at *Real Man* and cut the caper, that was all there was to it.

Even so he agonized on secretly to himself. If Jennifer knew that that was only the half of it, which thank heavens she did not, heaven knows what she would think.

282

If she knew what and whom he had to support at not just the Hall, but at Flint House. If she knew that it was not just four million pounds that he most likely needed, but more properly six million pounds, then she would probably strangle him with her dog skirt.

'Pember, what is it? You look quite ghastly.' Jennifer ran in front of her husband to attract his attention. 'You look as if you want to faint.'

'I do want to faint, but I can't, not until this afternoon, and then I shall have good reason to faint.'

'What's happening this afternoon, Pember?'

'What's happening this afternoon, Jennifer, is I am going to go to that place which I was going to go to when I was all dressed up and calling myself Bert Ackroyd. You wanted the truth, now you have it. I am going to go to *Real Man* where I was going before, but now I am not going to bother to go as Bert Ackroyd. Thanks to your demands for the truth I don't mind if I am seen or it is discovered that the seventh Marquis of Pemberton was spotted going to *Real Man* in his normal clothes, far from it. Now I know, now I have done my sums, now I understand just how hard it is for common man to make ends meet I am going under the knife, and in doing so I shall be setting an example not just to all of Wiltshire, Jennifer, but the Third World, Catholics everywhere and Fulton Montrose-Benedict-Cavanagh in particular.'

'Is that what you were really doing, dressed up as a tramp?'

'It certainly was. I wanted to keep this hidden from you, to protect you from the cruelties of life, but you insisted on the truth and here it is, millions of pounds' worth of the truth, unvarnished and painful. Particularly painful.'

'Oh, Fulton says it's not that painful.'

'He's been? Why has he been?'

'Because, Pember, he and Lady Tizzy have been procreating too much, as we seem to have done. Perhaps it's the water from the River Wylton? Do you think that's what it could be?'

'No.'

'Well, it doesn't matter. As a matter of fact I gave him the cutting from the *Parishioner*. You know how it was, with twins, things were hotting up a little for them, weren't they?'

'They certainly were,' Pember agreed. 'They certainly were. So there you are, you see what I mean? The need for *Real Man*.'

'But I never realized that's, well, that's where you were going, Pember darling. I wish you'd told me, I should never have been so worried.'

Pemberton turned and stared at his wife, his hand on the eighteenth-century door handle, his eyes on his wife's face. 'Whatever happens this afternoon, Jennifer, I want you to know that I loved you.'

Jennifer flew forward, her dog skirt billowing out behind her.

'Oh, Pember, I do love you.'

Pemberton stared down at her.

'No you don't, Jennifer,' he said suddenly. 'You love another, you love Fulton. I've known it for some time and now I have proof. Why else would you have been so worried about him going to *Real Man*? You can't expect me to believe you were worrying about the cost of things at Flint House. Why should you? You never worry about the cost of things here, so why should you worry about the cost of things at Flint House? No, you were thinking about the dangers to yourself and your lover, that is what you were thinking about, Jennifer.'

Jennifer screamed. There was no other word for it, Pemberton realized as the sound reverberated around the room. It was a scream, a long, hard scream, and it was as full of menace as anything he was likely to hear.

'That is not true!'

Jennifer stamped her foot. Pemberton had hoped to put her off the scent, to call the hounds off, but all it seemed he'd done was reveal something he had only half believed, namely that his wife's interest was elsewhere. Never mind his own interest elsewhere, a chap's wife was a chap's wife.

He put out his hand and pulled Jennifer to him.

'There's a little time before the place opens after lunch,' he said suddenly, 'time that I could profitably spend with you, Jennifer. Yes, just time enough to take you upstairs,' he said with sudden determination and relish.

'No, really, Pember, I don't think—'

What Jennifer had been about to think was something that neither of them would ever find out.

Only Bloss, with some satisfaction it has to be admitted, was witness to the spectacle of his lordship dragging her ladyship up the great staircase to their boudoir.

He gazed after them with interest. It was not often his lordship felt like anything like that before lunch nowadays. Things must be looking up.

He turned back to his snug underneath the stairs. Luckily enough for all of them the Local Rather Than Organic Garden Produce Company, having been invented for amatory rather than serious business reasons, had now turned into a positive fact. The accountant had become quite excited (not a very edifying sight at the best of times), and it seemed that Bloss, at any rate, quite by chance had fallen on his feet. It looked as if Local Rather Than Organic Garden Produce was really going to take off, with all the local gardens, the Hall included, coming together to sell off those vegetables and fruit that local people normally only gave away to reluctant visitors. Now instead of heaping weekend guests with old cabbages and chrysanthemeums they would heap up Bloss's smart new van and his driver would take them to a central point where local people would buy them, which would make a refreshing change from Londoners putting them in their dustbins on Monday mornings.

There is a hand that guides us all, Bloss told his new bottle of Malmesey, as he put back the time for lunch thirty-four minutes. A hand that guides, a path that makes itself clear, a purpose that we can know not of . . . He paused, wondering where exactly he had memorized this charming thought, but couldn't quite place it. It was either the *Golden Treasury of Positive Thoughts*, or the mini-Bible translated by the Cantering Cleric, a sometime television personality who had had a short success as a wine snob on an early evening programme which Bloss had been in the habit of watching while his lordship changed for dinner, and her ladyship fussed over the children.

He'd liked that programme, but of course they'd taken

it off as they took off everything with nothing offensive in it nowadays. Ridiculous now he came to think of it. After all, there surely must have been enough people prepared to be offended by recipes and interviews with wine experts for it to run and run, but no; it seemed it had offended no-one so off it had come.

The first glass of Malmesey had gone down so well he followed it with a second, which he sipped. Life had been so tense lately, so very tense, that he had taken to drinking Malmesey which he found immensely soothing. With his lordship, from what he could gather from outside the door, off to *Real Man*, and her ladyship and he not only speaking to each other but enjoying each other too, which didn't after all always go together, everything in the garden was becoming just a little more roseate even though as yet the goose could not be said to be hanging high.

The telephone in the snug rang. Bloss picked it up. It was her ladyship's mother, Mrs Parker-Jones. He had actually found her a house, quite near the Hall, something with which he knew she would fall instantly in love, but he was not in the mood to convey this to her, since her ladyship's mother had not been in a very nice mood with him lately. He knew of what she suspected him, and it shocked him to think that she could even imagine him as capable of deception. Even so he was generous enough, and warm enough, thanks to the Malmesey, to forgive her for being so suspicious, and worst of all, for getting it wrong. He would never give away his or anyone else's secrets to anyone. It was not in his interests. Besides, his way was to get his own way, no matter what. Even if it meant flying by the seat of his striped butler's pants, he proposed to get it, and the newest reg. If Mrs Parker-Jones had suspected him of telling the world her secrets, fair enough, but no, she had suspected him of trading in them, and dealing, and taking advantage, which was something else.

'Hallo, Bloss.'

She sounded positively guilt-ridden, like the father in the last act of *La Traviata*.

'Yes.'

There was enough of the wounded butler in his voice to make Bloss stand back and gaze in admiration at himself in the cracked mirror that stood behind the silver cleaning materials.

'I wonder if I could speak to Lady Pemberton?'

'I'm afraid her ladyship is otherwise occupied.'

'Perhaps you could tell her it is her mother?'

'I'm afraid not, Mrs Parker-Jones.' He knew what to do with the 'Mrs' as opposed to 'Lady' when dealing with a caller. He could say that for himself. 'But I could leave her a message.'

'Is she somewhere special?'

'Her ladyship is on the nest.'

It must have been the second glass of Malmesey, but there it was, the fact was out and who cared? She had, after all, asked for it.

And to give Mrs Parker-Jones her due, she called back again an hour later without a murmur.

Fulton and the Countess stared and stared. It would be no exaggeration to say that they could not believe their eyes. There it was on the side of the box, the phoenix in flight, just as Fulton knew it had to be if it was to be at all valuable.

'That's what Mary said, a bird on the side,' the Countess mouthed into the heavy silence that followed both of them putting on their glasses and staring at the side of their treasure.

'That makes it worth fifty thousand pounds.'

'So Mary said.'

'Now what,' said Fulton, but not as a question and quickly removing his specs before Maria came in with the coffee.

'What do you think, Fulton?' The Countess was misty-eyed. 'The nicest thing about this is, I don't need the money,' she said, sighing.

Fulton agreed silently while his finger traced the outline of the bird against the red lacquer of the box. He knew exactly what the dear thing meant. It was the nicest thing known to have an unexpected source of money and just when you didn't need it. It made you feel as if life was just a piece of cherry pie with fresh cream from the dairy, after all.

'You can take it to one of those ghastly firms that advertises, Fulton,' the Countess told him excitedly. 'You know, auction houses, quite horrible. All full of people telling you what is valuable isn't and what isn't valuable is, all depending on whether you're buying or selling to them or from them. We'll sell it to them knowing it is what it is, and so we'll get more gold for it than the Empress ever wore round her neck. And then I shall give the ball!'

Fulton stared at her. 'You will?'

'Why not? After all it was my idea in the first place.'

It hadn't been, but that was beside the point really, Fulton thought quickly.

'Yes, I shall give the ball and Mary and Jennifer can pass me both their guest lists and everyone can come. I shall give the ball at the Hall, and we can pretend it wasn't ever going to be anything but mine in the first place.'

'What about all the invitations?'

'What about them? As long as I am the first to receive everyone the world will get the picture. I will be Wiltshire's fairy godmother. We'll have tents and fireworks and everything will be as it was going to be in the first place full of zest and fun, just like the old days when people entertained each other for no better reason than that they wanted to see each other. No charity organizers, no causes, just fun. What a change that would be. On one condition only, though.'

Fulton stopped smiling and his heart sank as he saw all too clearly that familiar look of relish come over the Countess's face.

'One condition only.'

'You have a slip put in the invitations?' Fulton guessed, delaying the dreaded announcement as long as possible.

'Not even warm, but put in one anyway.'

'You want Lavinia to do the flowers?'

'Cold. So cold you must be freezy cold.'

'Don't know.'

'Yes, you do.'

'No, I don't.'

Fulton knew he did, but he couldn't bring himself to say the words. The Countess stared.

'Provided we change the colours back to cream and green, not peach, Fulton, cream and green.'

Fulton could have said, 'But Twinks has just dyed all the tablecloths and napkins in a rainwater butt' but he didn't. After all the main thing was to get on with the ball.

'You know what I think? I think cream and green is most tasteful, I just thought peach was more summery. If you want cream and green, who am I to stop you?'

'No-one,' the Countess agreed cheerfully. 'Now come along, you wizard of the Empress's Box, let's go quickly out to dinner before Andrew gets back from China and decides to come with us.'

'I thought China was shut.'

'It is,' the Countess agreed as she pulled on her small gold-embroidered jacket. 'It's what I call the pub he goes to because like China it always seems to be shut when he wants to go there.'

With which she took Fulton's arm and they both headed out towards her motor car and a thoroughly convivial evening.

'Tallywhack and tandem again?'

Elliott looked across at Fulton and was only too glad that it was he who was bending down to get the Grant loaf out of the Aga. Fulton did not look as if he could bend down if he tried, or rather he looked as if if he did try to bend down for anything at all, he would just keep on going and end up in a heap on the floor.

'Just don't speak to me.'

'I wasn't going to.'

Elliott nodded and put some highly organic muesli in front of Fulton.

'Twinks has already heard, if that's what you're worried about,' he told him. 'Actually as soon as you told me about the box, as a matter of fact, we both guessed the Countess would take over. In spite of only just finishing the cloths and napkins she's perfectly prepared to return to the butt from whence she came and plunge the peach-toned cloths in green. As for the rest – cream's easy.'

'How's Lady Tizzy?'

'Deeply boring.'

Fulton carefully removed a rather strangely shaped nut from his bowl and put it on his side plate.

'You sound like the Countess.'

Elliott sat down opposite him.

'Lady Tizzy is not at her best when she's being deprived of what she calls her "curranty bun", or what you and I call her *"raison d'être"*. You know Pemberton's gone at last to you know where?'

'The whole of Wiltshire knows he went.'

'And now of course he can't. Before he couldn't, because he couldn't *in case*, and now he can't because he *can't*. If you see what I mean?'

Fulton nodded. He knew only too well. He had also seen Lady Tizzy's wastepaper basket full of old Del Monte tins. When Lady Tizzy got into one of her pets and felt neglected no-one could get her out of her bed, and when she wasn't lying in her bed feeling neglected then they couldn't keep her out of other people's beds. Let's face it, they couldn't win.

'At least he's been,' said Fulton at last, after a long

pause during which he tried, as was his wont, to see the best in everything, including Wiltshire. 'I mean at least Pemberton has been to *Real Man*, and now therefore there are going to be no more school fees to lose yet another night's sleep over. I mean at least there's that.'

'Oh, there's that all right,' Elliott agreed, slicing a hot piece of loaf and buttering it quickly. 'There's that. I just hope it works, that's all. It doesn't always.'

'That we can't think about. We must just cross our fingers.'

'That is not a method that would have worked with Pemberton and Lady Tizzy.'

'Oh really? I believe they're trying it in Africa with tremendous results.'

There was so much to do. The flowers, the napkins, the matching tents (thank God they at least were still cream and green). Fulton's mind ran over all the details. The lighting, the staff, the candles, the floor, the fruit, the garlands for the poles, the help from all the surrounding villages. People to park the cars and bring the guests to the door or back from the doors – busboys he thought they were called in America, but never mind. They would need hundreds of them, and then there was their clothes. A beautiful dress for Lady Tizzy, a green frock for Twinks, so much to do, so many places to go, so many places they had been, but it would all be worthwhile providing the weather was clement, the food didn't melt or stayed hot, the staff the same, the guests ditto and all to keep a handful of the upper hundreds happy for a few hours in Wiltshire. Except that wasn't all it was about, really. People would come and go away again and after only a few hours nothing would be the same, no person would remain unchanged, someone would have fallen in love with someone they shouldn't, someone else with someone they should, at the very least new paths would be sought, and old paths, sometimes of righteousness, fallen from, but whatever happened nothing stayed unchanged, and nothing remained the same. As the Countess would say, 'On with the motley!'

'I've never quite understood what the motley was, and I have never quite dared to ask before,' Elliott ventured with unforced modesty, at the same time realizing that he should not have eaten his hot buttered bread quite so hot or quite so buttered.

'The motley is the crowd that follows revelry, and what a crowd will be gathering next month, Ely-ot, *mon vieux*.'

'Do you think if we buy Lady Tizzy a stunning frock she will climb out of her sulking bed and come and join in the game of living once more?' Elliott wondered.

'Mmm, I do, but first let's you and I visit Nanny and Bessie and the girls and Beau in the nursery. That at least is all safe for the moment. No nasty divorces, Jennifer back with Pemberton again. Lady Tizzy not where she shouldn't be, the ball going ahead after all, and with both the *crème* and the *crème fraîche*. So to the nursery we must go to watch our babies grow and grow. Ignore that; my mind's gone.'

'Are you sure you're up to it?'

'Of course I'm not.'

'You look just a little cream and green still.'

'It's only to be expected.'

Fulton smiled as a quite irrational feeling of serenity crept over him. He would take Victoria up in his arms and swing her round and Nanny would cluck. He would give Beau and Daisy-Marguerita a finger to hold, and they would hold on to them terrifically tight which babies always did, and all would be well. Everything, endless worries, making papier mâché spill boxes and trays by the dozen, keeping their mother somewhere near the straight and narrow, their father from making more babies, keeping everyone from everyone except when they were meant to be with each other, it would all be worth it.

'Just must re-paint those finger plates,' Elliott murmured, as they passed into the nursery and the door closed behind them.

But Fulton never even heard him. He was too busy holding out his arms to Victoria.

14

Kaminski stared at E.F. He was quite sure he'd heard him right, which was why he was staring at him.

'When did they cancel it?' he asked in his quietest voice.

'Last night, just after you didn't get back for the third time,' E.F. said, and he unwrapped a large bon-bon from the nearest bon-bon dish which was very near since they were seated in the kitchen of the apartment. The previous evening Sofia had given a ghastly gathering that she fondly imagined was a dinner party.

'I doubt that it's anything to do with when I got back,' Kaminski said eventually.

E.F.'s fist crashed down on the table. 'You should have come back when I told you. Jumby Island has just had the H bomb dropped on it. All our work over the last months gone. Do you realize what this means? We are without a film!'

Kaminski stared at E.F. He was right. In fact he was very right, and yet somehow it didn't matter in the least either that he was or that they were without a film. The situation they were in was serious. It meant they would have to go back to Los Angeles and begin again. Trading, trading, trading.

'It's nothing to do with my not coming back, E.F., but everything to do with that sleeper taking sixty-three million in the past week. That's what it has to do with, E.F.'

'Look, what is this sleeper anyway?' E.F. said more to himself than his director. 'Man, woman, woman. We can rework our script. Forget Jumby Island, the fact that he's a marine biologist, increase the women to two not one, make the island an apartment in Manhattan's East Side, and *voilà*, we have ourselves a nice little "me too". We can get back to Los Angeles by Monday with a rough-out, give it to Pan to type – that takes all of two minutes – and sell it by Thursday.'

Kaminski looked across at E.F. He could see all the advantages from his partner's point of view, but only from his partner's point of view. What about from his own point of view? Kaminski gave an inside sigh and thought back to Paris and then forward again to Georgiana who would now be back in Wiltshire with her son and his father. He had no wish to stay in England any more, he knew that he must leave at once, but he knew also that wherever he went from now on it would have to be with Georgiana, she had become his talisman, his good luck charm, his icon. Supposing she forgot him once she got back with the painter? Supposing she wanted to stay with her son? Supposing she didn't come through with the invitation to the ball? Perhaps she had merely suggested that they meet in Wiltshire at this oh-so-social occasion so that she could have time to think of how to be rid of him?

He'd panicked when she'd left him, waving one graceful hand out of the window. It had seemed to him that her gesture had in it all of *adieu* and very little of *au revoir*. It seemed to him that graceful though it was

297

it had only been a perfunctory gesture, a gesture she had made out of *politesse*, and having made it she couldn't wait to get on with her old life once more, as a bored actor at the end of a long day's shoot will run back to his dressing room unable to wait to put on his own clothes again, be himself. It seemed to Kaminski that the object of his passion settled herself into her first class seat and kissed her hand to him to say goodbye for ever.

Georgiana stared at Gus. They had been away from each other five days, but he seemed now not merely a stranger but quite definitely an ex. Ex-lover, ex-common law husband, whatever it was that in the present complications of her life she should call him.

He had not been happy at having his current model Miss Cut-offs taken from him, so with his usual ruthless egoism he had found out from Miss Cut-offs' mother where she was working in the art shop in London, and talked her into returning to Longborough, where she was now it seemed being put up in the stables and being called upon to model for him whenever or however he wished. It was all true, everything they had ever said about painters. 'You'll marry the Earl and we'll see about the painter later.' That was a line from a book she had read, although which book she couldn't at that moment quite remember. It was just that the truth of it kept running around her head as if it was a jingle she'd heard on Nanny's television. 'You'll marry the Earl, and we'll see about the painter later.' There it went again, and again, and again. Had she married an earl, any earl, would she not just be hunting her horses and going to the Bahamas in the winter and generally being herself instead of being as she was the ex of a painter and the why of a cinema director? (Why did she go to Paris with him? Why had she thought him so fascinating? Why had he seemed so changed away from London, away from all her familiar haunts, hotels and shops? Most of all, why had she let him tell her all about himself? Not even his name was his own. It made him seem unreal, as if he himself were just the product of the cinema and not a great man.)

'Gus?'

'Mmm?'

Gus looked up from the morning newspaper that he only ever read at night with the particular frown that he always conjured whenever someone else took the initiative and he was forced to stop doing whatever he was doing and realize that there was someone else on the planet beside himself.

'I hope what I am going to say is not going to make you unhappy?'

His eyes had returned to the paper now, and a beer was being lifted to his freshly grown beard. Georgiana thought how strange it was that men mocked women for changing their hairstyles, when they themselves didn't just change their hair, but their whole faces, and almost as frequently. The beard had obviously been grown in tune with the new affair with Miss Cut-offs.

'We're not making enough money, Gus.'

Nowadays his work on 'The Lady Loves' series was always late, and the quality was not what it was, as even Georgiana had noticed. No, as a matter of fact she had been the first to notice. The company who had paid him were not keen on increasing his money to keep up with the cost of living, but neither of these facts seemed to matter to dear Gus. Only Miss Cut-offs, his studio, his other paintings, and George for five minutes in the morning and five minutes at night, that was all that was of any interest to Gus.

'Gus, we are not making enough money, not to keep all of us, you, me, Nan, Nanny, the gardeners, George, and all the other costs. A place like this eats up money, Gus, and we're eating it up, but not enough of it is coming in. You know the dried flowers? Well, they haven't really taken off, too many people doing it.'

Gus looked up at Georgiana once more and then down again. She might as well have never spoken. For one unnerving moment Georgiana faced the fact that Gus was not very nice, that the father of George was a selfish, egotistical person whom she would have done well to avoid, and by whom she should certainly not have had a baby, not even one.

'I have been offered a temporary job, helping out in Los Angeles, that film director I was doing the reccy in Paris for? He has offered me a job as personal assistant just for three months, but very well paid. I think I should take it, don't you?'

Gus still said nothing, but turned the paper over. How old the news looked by evening, Georgiana observed to herself. It all seemed like something from the day before the day before, nothing fresh about it at all. A bit like herself and Gus, so yesterday. Maybe even a bit like Kaminski and herself too. They might soon be just yesterday, but that was something about which she could not think.

'Yes, well, George, you might as well do what you

want,' her soon-to-be-ex told her without managing to look up from his newspaper, and not registering the slightest interest in his voice.

'I've brought you back something from London,' Georgiana told him, not waiting for him to pick up on his lack of interest, which would be disastrous.

'What?' Gus said looking up, just slightly.

'Open it and see.'

Eagerly he opened it. A silk vest from Jobbit and Taylor. The very best that they could possibly produce, and of the kind that gentlemen who had gentlemen of their own to lay out their undergarments currently and always had favoured. Smooth and silky next to their moneyed skins, it was so far from a hair shirt to render guilt, about money or anything else, a foreign word.

Georgiana knew that Gus would not wear it as the assistant in Jobbit and Taylor would have fondly imagined as he was stuffing the short sleeves with bright white tissue paper and boxing it up with tightly pulled string. Gus would wear it as a tee shirt. She could see straight away that the colour she had chosen had found favour. A particularly soft blue that would make Gus look harder, leaner, and browner, at any rate to Miss Cut-offs. But as he stroked the expensive item Georgiana could see that it was not himself that Gus was visualizing in it, but the newest occupant of the flat over the stables. It would go beautifully with her hair and eyes, he was thinking. Georgiana smiled at the top of Gus's head. He was so obvious, totally, horribly obvious, so much so that it was quite amusing.

'Why are you smiling?'

'Nothing.'

Georgiana turned away quickly. Jennifer's ball was now going ahead as arranged; everything was falling into place. She had time to make arrangements, to talk Nanny into following her out to Los Angeles with George. (An ideal opportunity would present itself when Nan and Gus made their annual pilgrimage to his grandpa's grave.) Kaminski would meet her at the ball, and then they would leave discreetly together, and in the aftermath, the days that followed, few people would notice or even care where she was or how she was or with whom. She thought of her dress. When taking her to Manuel Manonas to be fitted, then at least Kaminski had seemed to be himself again, no nonsense about being Sasha any more, and he had chosen for her the most beautiful ball dress, a piece of perfection in the palest of pink taffetas, yet another copy of a Winterhalter painting, something which was so popular for balls at the moment. With it she was going to wear the family tiara and her hair up for the first time for years, not scooped up but folded into her neck in the manner of a prima ballerina dancing *Swan Lake*. The shoes to go with the dress were out of this world, all tiny straps and things which made her slender ankles look even slimmer.

She moved easily away from Gus, her head filled with the scented thoughts that she so liked to preoccupy her, and as she did so, her soon-to-be-ex-lover Gus looked up from his newspaper and stared after her. Georgiana did not see the look on his face as she left the room, leaving behind her a slight aroma of 'A La Recherche'. It was probably just as well.

15

She had arrived. Bloss's undoubted star of the newest reg, and she was sitting gleaming outside the staff entrance at the Hall, as near to the door as Bloss could park her. He liked to think he had easy access to her, so that in between his other duties he could nip out and run a duster over her, the new love of his life, a bright red gleaming Pewgot Starduster complete with limited slip diff, rubberized steering wheel and stay-put mats with pale grey Vylene Kiddi-coated Velour seat coverings. With her two-toned matching driving fascia and her featherlite jack and spare pliers and plastic first aid kit, she really couldn't be more lovely if she tried, Bloss thought, stepping back to admire her for perhaps the forty-ninth time.

Heaven only knew it had given him joy enough to be able to order her up, so much joy that now she had arrived his heart felt near to bursting, especially when he allowed his eye to travel down to that glory of all glories, that plum of all plums, the newest registration, and he hadn't even driven her down to the King's Arms yet. But then there hadn't been time; the Hall had been in a positive whirl for the past weeks, whirling and whirling towards the great day, and now the great day was here along with the Pewgot. Bloss's favourite cup, the Pemberton Cup and Cover, was full to overflowing, and no denying it. Having run a duster over his little beauty he now strolled round to the side of the Hall to admire the tents which had been put in place the previous day. Amusing to see how his old friend the Countess had won the day. The tents were a most tasteful cream and green, and one had to admit the dear lady had a point. Their palely tasteful colour went quite exquisitely with the faded stone against which they were set.

Bloss folded his arms. When you looked at a fine sight like that you had to agree that England was still England for all that people had tried to spend the last few years trying to turn her into Mesopotamia. No, when you saw tents on a lawn and faded bricks and roses rambling and the pink of the dawn being followed by a sky coloured the palest of blue, when you saw no garish colours and heard no gun killing a skylark for no better reason than to eat it, you knew you were in England. From Land's End to John O'Groats they had done their best to make life hideous, but they had not quite succeeded everywhere. Wiltshire was still Wiltshire, and would remain so, if people like himself and the Countess had anything to do with it. They stood for walks on Sunday afternoons, tea on the lawn, a retriever at the heel and a tent with pleated silk. They would not let Wiltshire go under. Tax might come and go, but there would still be an English heaven if he and the Countess had any say in the matter.

And now tonight to the Hall would come the cream of London Society. As soon as the Countess had taken over the organization of the ball there had been two lists put into operation. One she had entitled 'the Cream' and the other 'the Cream Fraîche', in other words, old money and new. Thanks to one thing and another, and politicians in particular, the first was a slimmer volume than the second. Nevertheless, the fact that it existed at all was heartening to those like Bloss who preferred the older wines. On the other hand the second list wasn't as bad as it might be. It was far thicker, but it was of interest, and the two could mix, and would always mix, to the benefit of each other.

'*Bloss!*'

Jennifer stared at him in fury.

'I've been calling you for hours, where have you been? Not polishing the Pewgot again?'

'Just checking the stanchions on the tent pegging, milady,' said Bloss quickly. 'The slightest weakness and they can come down and cause you and your guests endless entanglements, let alone the insurance. You can imagine.'

Jennifer might have been able to imagine. She probably would have imagined if at that moment she was not intent on hoping against hope instead of imagining.

'Are you all right, your ladyship?'

'Perfectly not, Bloss.' Jennifer turned quickly and ran out of the room, helter skelter towards the downstairs gents cloakroom, all polished mahogany, wooden trees for riding boots, and flower paintings done by Pember's grandmother. Also cool marble washstands, thank goodness, against which she could lean her face after she had been heartily sick.

Bloss stared after her. In his experience her ladyship only ran from the room to be sick for one particular reason. Of all the luck! Oh, the poor lady. It just wasn't possible. Except it was possible. It was just too awful

305

for her. It could only mean not that she had eaten too many strawberry shortcakes at supper the previous night but that there was another Melbury on the way. It must have happened just before his lordship went to *Real Man*. Although come to think of it, it didn't really matter when it had happened, only that it had. Bloss took a quick nip from the cooking sherry bottle while he had time, because he could see the temporary staff pouring through the back gates even as he drank. He was just so glad that his lordship had let him order the Starduster when he had. Had he waited a few more weeks he would have had as much chance of being given it as he had of becoming an officer in the Guards. No, if he knew who or what was on its way the Starduster would have remained just a twinkle in his lordship's eye.

'Where's her ladyship?' his lordship enquired, entering the kitchen, a most unusual sight among the larger mixing bowls and wooden spoons.

It caught at Bloss's heart to see how much brighter his lordship was looking. There had been a bit of sitting about in faded leather armchairs after he had flung himself over the top at *Real Man*, not to mention a great many stiffies. But now he was quite himself again, positively kittenish in fact, ringing up Lady Tizzy on the staff telephone from the snug, and giggling away the happy hour with her. Quite like old times it seemed. They were planning a reunion in the old summerhouse after the ball, which was how it should be. He had a spring in his step, his lordship did, a spring that Bloss was ever so reluctant to see removed. He only hoped that her ladyship's newest malaise would not manifest itself to his lordship until after the ball. It might spoil everything for him, and just when doubtless he was ripening up and looking forward to some frolics.

'Ah, there you are, Jennifer,' he called affably to her ladyship who looked across at Bloss with something more than just a look, something nearer to a warning. A 'One word from you and that Pewgot will be out on the motorway with a For Sale sign around its neck' type of look.

'Here I am, Pember,' she agreed, turning her attention back to her husband with a sweet but false brightness.

'Everything all right?'

'Couldn't be more perfect.'

'Are you sure? You look a trifle pale around the gills.'

'Just nerves before the ball, wanting everything to be perfect, that's all. You know how it is.'

Pemberton nodded. He was only too aware that a great social gathering from London would take it out of most girls, particularly Jennifer who was inordinately shy, usually only liking to sit about in her dog skirt doing her tatting. But there you are, it had been her idea to give the thing and now it was going ahead he was very grateful to her, especially since it was now the Countess who was paying for it, not himself. He eased himself back into the hall with a view to going across to Bloss's snug and having a bevvy. In his opinion it was the nicest part of having a party or helping to give a ball, all the bevvies under the stairs beforehand and one's friends arriving and chucking themselves under the stairs with you and everyone enjoying themselves no end.

'Good heavens, you're at it a bit early, aren't you, Gillott old boy?'

Andrew turned back from the silver cleaning basket

where Bloss always obligingly kept a half bottle of his favourite kind of whisky, and nodded.

'Not at it yet; just about to be, though. Like you I like to enjoy myself a bit before the tumbrils roll, and the orchestra arrives, and the hostess faints, and that sort of thing.'

'Something happen to China?'

'It had, but it's stopped now. Oh yes, I'm going to China all right, the Countess insists. Must go, nothing for it. Got to go now it's open again. But before I go I intend to make an honest woman of Lady Tisbury, I'll tell you that. That's why I'm here, you see. I'm stocking up in order to get together the courage to get down on one knee and demand her hand in holy deadlock.'

Pemberton stared at Andrew. Blasted cheek.

'You can't make an honest woman of Lady Tizzy, you jackanapes,' he protested. 'You ain't divorced yet, and she's married anyway!'

As he spoke he thought with fury of how much he himself had been looking forward to making a dishonest woman of her in the summerhouse once the ball was well under way.

'She's only officially married,' Andrew protested. 'Unofficially she can be anyone's. Want to see the ring I've bought her?'

Pemberton averted his eyes as from a traffic accident.

'No. Can't stand that sort of thing. Will you be. Take me for. Thou wilt and such like.'

'Pity. It's jolly fine. Used to belong to my mother. That's how much she means to me, Lady Tisbury. That's how much.'

'Shouldn't you be giving that to Mrs Andrew Gillott, on account or something?'

'No, don't think so, not now I'm divorcing her. That's the whole point of divorcing someone, so you don't have to give them anything.'

'What about the Countess? She's been very kind to you.'

'She's got rings enough of her own. No, this is for Lady Tisbury, God bless her. And with it will go my love for ever.'

'Supposing she won't accept?' asked Pemberton hopefully.

'Oh, she will, it's invaluable. One of the few emeralds to be cut on the cross bias, or something like that.'

'In that case, dear boy, don't give it to Lady Tizzy. She's so unreliable. You know how it is – she'll put it in a pocket and send it to the laundry. Or give it to Oxfam because she can't find change for a pound. No, you keep it, as a hedge against inflation. You know, instead of an overdraft. You know what life can be like, one minute hey nonny no, and the next you're scrabbling around for threepence three farthings, and all ends to the middle.'

'Well, never mind that. I want to give it to the object of my love,' Andrew said. 'And she can do what she likes with it, bless her cotton petticoats.'

'How do you know her petticoats are cotton?'

'Because I do. She told me.'

'When?'

'Years ago. When we were at some fearful fund-raising for the new portacabins for the Vicar's modelling classes.'

'Vicars modelling, whatever next?' Pemberton muttered as the impact of the rather too early drink hit him somewhere between his recent alteration and his collar and tie.

'Not vicars modelling, people modelling for vicars.'

'That's what I mean,' Pemberton persisted. 'Whatever next?'

'No, I mean modelling plasticine.'

'They will wear anything nowadays, you know,' said Pemberton, gloomily re-filling his glass. 'Personally I like cashmere and lace, but plasticine – it wouldn't surprise me in the least.'

'Nothing's going to stop me getting down on one knee to the divine Lady Tisbury,' Andrew went on. 'But nothing. I am hers whether she wants me or not.'

'Which she won't,' said Pemberton quite firmly. 'She's got better things to do with her time, mark my words.'

He picked up his drink and knocked it back, dreaming of summerhouses and the kinds of things people could do in them, if like him they were lucky enough to own one. As he did so he watched Andrew scribbling a note on an old page of his racing diary. Right across CHEPSTOW he was writing something that looked like 'Meet me in the summerhouse after the last dance?'

'Can you read that all right?'

Pemberton stared at him. 'Perfectly,' he said.

'In that case she'll be able to,' Andrew said happily.

'Tell you what?'

'Mmm?'

'How about if I gave it to her, not you?'

At that moment the door opened once more and Bloss

entered his own little kingdom, the kingdom of which he was the king.

'Ah, Bloss,' said Andrew. 'The very man I want. Give this to Lady Tisbury, would you, there's a good fellow? At the right moment, of course.'

Bloss nodded. 'Of course, sir.'

'You're a good man, Bloss,' Andrew told him. 'Now I'm going to toddle off and have a kip before the roll of the drums. The Countess needs me to be on hand to take charge of her reticule, and I know not what. The sort of thing that keeps a fellow on his toes.'

He disappeared back into the hall as Pemberton's hand fell upon his butler's shoulder.

'You can give me that, Bloss, if you will,' he said.

'A gentleman's word is meant to be as good as his life, milord.' Bloss looked his lordship calmly in the eye. 'I promised Mr Gillott I would give this to Lady Tisbury personally,' he told his employer, looking down at the message scrawled over the page of the racing diary. 'I must be seen to be as good as my word.'

'You know that Pewgot Starduster, Bloss?' Pemberton began.

'As I said,' Bloss continued smoothly, 'I promised I would give Lady Tisbury this note. What I did not promise was on whose behalf I would give it.'

Pemberton stared at his butler. Bloss. The devil. He was the brightest thing out. And moral with it. Of course.

'Meet me in the summerhouse . . .'

It was just what he himself wanted to convey to Lady Tisbury.

'You know something, Bloss, you should be running the country instead of the shower we've got in at the moment. Singlehandedly you would see us through.'

Bloss couldn't help smiling, nor, quite silently, could he help agreeing with his lordship. After all it must be simpler than running the Hall, he thought, but quite discreetly.

The Countess surveyed herself in the mirror. It was rather fun seeing herself once more decked out as a countess should be, tiara, rose taille (the dress was an old Molyneux but the cut was the newest around), long white gloves, everything as it should be, and nothing smelling of mothballs. She nodded to herself and to the man standing behind her.

'You'll do, you'll do very, very well,' he said.

She smiled at him before he faded from her sight. Freddie. Her own darling Freddie. He always had said that to her, and it had been so nice. 'You'll do.' It didn't need anything more; just that, and the look in his eyes. Miss him? She missed him all the time. One of these days she would be joining him in an eternal waltz. She would look forward to that, but meanwhile, thanks to the Empress's Box, she was giving a great ball in the old manner, and everyone was coming who could come. All Mary's friends re-routed, all Jennifer's friends, and even Georgiana.

'My dear, you look quite, quite wonderful.'

The Countess stared at Georgiana. The ability to look perfect in jewellery and evening dress belonged to patrician Englishwomen. It was like that. It would always be like that. It was a fact. The rest of the world could look good in everything else but there was nothing like

312

an Englishwoman in a beautiful evening dress, her family jewels gleaming, everything just so.

Georgiana's dress was pink where the Countess's was old rose. Georgiana's was beautifully wide, where the Countess's was figure clinging and cut on the bias. How perfectly they complemented each other they could both see. Georgiana brushed the Countess's cheek in the accepted manner. Georgiana's hair was folded into her neck, the Countess's brushed up. Georgiana's head shimmered, because the family tiara was made up of thousands of small stones, the centrepiece a rose for England which moved slightly as her head moved.

'What on earth is that?' asked the Countess as she peered at the decoration on Andrew's sash.

'It's made out of milk bottle tops. Rather good, don't you think?'

'I'm not sure. Depends what it's for.'

Andrew held out an arm to her. 'For surviving.'

'In that case you can leave it,' the Countess smiled. 'As a matter of fact we should all be wearing one.'

Georgiana looked round her. The great room was festooned with fresh flowers, and the people with jewels. Perhaps because the Countess was in charge there was a definite aura of another era, and she had long ago lost count of the number of tiaras that had entered the room, and were now drifting in and out of the silk-lined tents as the orchestra played a medley of tunes. The faces were not much changed since she was a debutante. The general mix was not too different either, only she was. So changed in only a few years that the sight of one face alone could make her feel that it was worth dancing life's insistent waltz. If he didn't arrive, if he had already left for Los Angeles, she didn't really care, she told herself as she laughed and talked to the whole world who jostled each other to be by her side, to pay her compliments, to stand near her. At the end of the famous day Kaminski was after all only Sasha. On the other hand if he arrived and headed straight for her he would be again the great Kaminski, whose genius and talent would shine as long as the stones in her tiara, perhaps longer, thanks to celluloid. And to be singled out by him, to be taken by the hand and led in to dinner would cause a scandal, but only of the kind that everyone liked and envied, in other words a scandal of the very best kind.

Nanny was waiting with George in a nearby hotel. Everything was set fair for them all to escape to the West Coast, to a warmer climate, away from the coming winter and the damp and the rain.

'May I take you in to dinner?'

Georgiana stared at the speaker, and her heart started to beat so loudly that for a second she imagined that it would be quite nice to forget about all the formalities, the dinner, the dancing, the breakfast served at midnight, and faint straight into his arms so that they could run away together that minute.

'I didn't think you were coming,' she whispered to him.

He smiled and held out his arm. Georgiana placed her kid glove on it, and as the orchestra played 'Violets for her Fur', a special request of the Countess's, it seemed to Georgiana that her fate was temporarily but gloriously sealed. They would run away together and it would be wonderful. No voice whispered in her ear 'What if?' or 'And after this?' but then with her it never did. To

Georgiana life was something to be danced, and dance it she would.

'It's so nice to see all the young people enjoying themselves,' someone said to the Countess.

'Do you think so, really?' the Countess replied. 'I always think it pretty ominous myself!'

THE END